THE
CLEVELAND
CREEP

The Milan Jacovich mysteries
by Les Roberts:

Pepper Pike

Full Cleveland

Deep Shaker

The Cleveland Connection

The Lake Effect

The Duke of Cleveland

Collision Bend

The Cleveland Local

A Shoot in Cleveland

The Best-Kept Secret

The Indian Sign

The Dutch

The Irish Sports Pages

King of the Holly Hop

The Cleveland Creep

THE CLEVELAND CREEP

A MILAN JACOVICH MYSTERY

LES ROBERTS

GRAY & COMPANY, PUBLISHERS
CLEVELAND

Gray & Company, Publishers
www.grayco.com

Library of Congress Cataloging-in-Publication Data
Roberts, Les.
The Cleveland creep : a Milan Jacovich mystery / Les Roberts.
p. cm.
ISBN 978-1-59851-071-3
1. Jacovich, Milan (Fictitious character)—Fiction. 2. Private investigators—Ohio—Cleveland—Fiction. 3. Slovenian Americans—Fiction. 4. Missing persons—Fiction. 5. Cleveland (Ohio)—Fiction. I. Title.
PS3568.O23894C575 2011
813'.54—dc22
2011004565

Printed in the United States of America

10 9 8 7 6 5 4 3 2 1

*To Parker G. Roberts, my love boy, who
will someday grow up to be a movie-star
heartthrob, to play third base and bat
cleanup for the Cleveland Indians—
and to eventually read my books.*

THE
CLEVELAND
CREEP

PROLOGUE

It was near the end of a long, hot Saturday afternoon in July, the kind of heat that makes Clevelanders quietly wish in their hearts for winter. When the overhead clouds refuse to move and the high temperature is locked in along with the high humidity, everybody is wet, annoyed, tired, and dragged out by day's end. I didn't bother checking the mirror in the small bathroom adjoining my office—I didn't have to. I knew how lousy I must have looked. Maybe it was spending the morning at a funeral.

The Monday-to-Friday work week is a given, but not for those making a living in retail or the restaurant business, or people like me—self-employed private investigators, whose only means of telling a weekend from a weekday is checking the daytime TV listings for sports. And for those of us who've grown older and wiser, watching sports has deteriorated from a must-see, don't-disturb-me, pass-the-beer addiction to a loud, often boring pastime that doesn't mean much anymore.

I'd written off this particular Saturday, office-wise; new clients hardly ever drop in unannounced on a weekend, nor does anybody else on a day like this one. The lung-burning July air makes breathing feel like gasping through a wet washcloth. Locals whine about Cleveland's winters, but summers always get to me.

So I finished everything I had to do in my office—bringing my records and notes up to date, checking my laptop and reading a comic e-mail that had me smiling, thinking over a case that had started out almost lighthearted and silly and had turned deadly serious. I was looking forward to going home, showering, and dressing a little more casually for a first-date dinner with an attractive woman I'd met the week before, to try forgetting about things in my professional life that were weighing me down—namely the missing persons case. It had begun as a second thought and turned into a nightmare. Now there were tears for the tragedy, pressure from the cops, self-disgust for cutting some corners to make it look easy, and my own conscience eating away at my liver.

It was then that I heard heavy footsteps on the stairs leading up to my office on the second floor of the building I own—deliberately noisy footsteps, loud and clunking. Whoever was coming up the steps was hoping I'd be intimidated before my door opened. Unfortunately for them, the last time I was scared was when Linda Blair rotated her head three hundred sixty degrees and vomited green pea soup in *The Exorcist*.

I was more saddened than annoyed, though, because whoever belonged to those footsteps sounded as if he was coming to make my life just a little more miserable. I have an instinct for those things—damn it.

The man made an abrupt appearance through the door marked MILAN SECURITIES like a lifetime marine, a guy who didn't know any other way to walk. His shoulders were back, braced, and his head high. His entrance was in-your-face challenging. He sported a short, light brown crew cut, and a shave so close that his five o'clock shadow wouldn't make an appearance until several hours later that evening. I could barely make out his eyes behind his expensive dark shades. Clevelanders admittedly wear sunglasses on very sunny days, especially if they're driving east in the morning or west at night—but *never* inside unless it's a prideful and silly affectation. His stylized Ray-Bans meant to me that he was not only a jag-off, but wanted everyone in the world to know it. Maybe it was the air of arrogant self-confidence that stuck to him like a skunk odor.

His dark blue suit showed subtle pinstripes; it hadn't been purchased at a ready-to-wear store. His brown shoes shimmered with freshly applied polish and were buffed to shine like the sun.

Not a wrinkle or a crease could I see anywhere, nor a drop of perspiration on his forehead. Even before he put his business card on my desk, I knew exactly where he was coming from, although I didn't know his name. Nobody dressed that formally in Cleveland on a ninety-degree scorcher like this one unless he was a corporate attorney arguing a megamillion-buck case in court, a funeral director, or the senior vice president of a bank. Or what he really was.

It was the necktie that gave him away. Few Clevelanders wear ties, and when they do, their neckwear is conservative and boring enough to put you to sleep—but agents of some federal organizations wear designer ties like this guy's that can knock your socks off.

"Jacovich?" he said—one word as he stared at me through the dark glasses and waited, breathing impatiently through his nose. He'd have a wait. Most people call me Milan, which I prefer. I despise being called by my last name unless one puts "mister" in front of it, because it's another maneuver with which the speaker hopes to diminish you. They always used last names when I was in the army, and I didn't like it any better then. But that was the army. That was then. It's not anymore, not for me, especially coming from smart-ass guys in their thirties wearing two grand's worth of clothing. I nodded back at him.

"Special Agent Jeffrey Kitzberger, Federal Bureau of Investigation," he announced at the same time he flipped open his leather badge folder and pushed it across the desk at me. No hello, no small talk, not even asking politely if I were the *real* Milan Jacovich, Security Specialist, or the guy who sweeps the office at night, or maybe a sweat-stained burglar. He reminded me of a court chamberlain announcing his own arrival to the reigning king and queen of France at the masked ball.

I was neither awed nor impressed. I get along fine with most local cops, and I've done okay with the Ohio state police. But the FBI special agents I've encountered were inculcated with the notion that they were better than everyone else. I suppose it had to do with attitude, having learned perceived superiority from J. Edgar Hoover, the first director of the FBI, who died before Kitzberger was born. Hoover's philosophy survived over the years. I suppose if he were still alive, he'd be in his Washington office—maybe wearing ladies' lingerie under his tailored suits—in a building named after him.

My spine stiffened, and I drew myself up to my full height, towering over Kitzberger. I was taller when I was thirty than I am now—shrinkage comes with age—but even at less than the six foot three I used to be, I could still look down on the special agent's pale scalp gleaming through the haircut. That was a proud moment, even though my irritation was, so far, only in my head. But it was *my* head.

"What do you need?" I said, showing him I could be as rude as he was.

He extracted an envelope from his inside jacket pocket, removed eight snapshot-sized photos, and laid them side by side on my desk as if he were playing solitaire. "Do these people mean anything to you?" he said, flicking a finger at the photographs.

They were mug shots—seven ugly, glowering white guys and one middle-aged woman with a sophisticated blond hairdo who looked like she played canasta at the country club every Friday, except for her defiant half snarl. I looked at all eight faces. "Number Two needs a haircut," I said, "maybe just a little around the ears. Number Four is showing his age; he should get a face-lift, or Botox. And Number Five ought to wear different glasses frames to make his face look thinner."

I watched Special Agent Jeffrey Kitzberger try to recall the last time he laughed, but the memory didn't come to him, nor did the whisper of a smile. "Are you trying to be amusing?"

"If I were," I said, "I'd tell you the one about the Catholic cardinal and the businessman with an Indian feather in his cowboy hat, walking into a bar—"

"Which of these people do you know?" he interrupted. "Identify them by name."

I recognized a few of them but knew none of them well, even though one had paid me a recent visit. But that didn't mean I'd paint their names on a wall in big red letters because some fatuous pissant like Kitzberger was throwing his weight around. "What's this about?"

"*I* ask the questions."

"Not in *my* office, you don't," I said.

That stunned him. People rarely say no to G-men—or G-women—who wave an FBI badge and expect you to sink to one knee with bowed head and treat them like they were Queen Elizabeth—the first one, the daughter of Henry the Eighth. He expected me to have my own personal O just because he had shown up in my office. "Damn it, Jacovich," he sputtered, "where do you get off—?"

"I get off the streetcar right here. This is my stop—not yours. If you'd bothered to look, you could have even seen my name on the door."

"Who do you think you're talking to?" He was trying to sound menacing; I suppose to most people he was. "Are you trying to get arrested?"

"For what?"

"I'll think of something."

"Oh, woe is me!" I said.

"Interfering with a federal investigation—how's that, then?"

"I don't even know what you're investigating. I haven't done a damn thing wrong—at least nothing the federal government would be mad about." I wanted to sit-lean against my desk, but if I did that, one or two of his photos might fall to the floor, and both of us were too proud to pick them up, so they'd stay there until after I died of old age and someone else moved into my office. "If you have an arrest warrant, I'll come quietly—and be out of your hands within an hour. You'll look pretty damn silly. Or if you share *why* I should accede to your demands—and that's what they are, rude and insolent demands and not a civil request—maybe we can have a meeting of the minds. But I can tell your mind won't ever meet mine except maybe in some dark alley. So it's late, I'm tired, and ready to head home. If you back-shoot me, make up an excuse for your superiors. In the meantime, take your baby shower pictures and clear your ass the hell out of my office."

My guess was that he was educated at some Ivy League school, his father was a high-level corporate attorney in the East, and he was assigned to the Cleveland office whether he'd wanted to be here or not. Either way, he shot me one more epithet—the two-word curse we've all heard at one time or another—picked up his photos, and left in an angry huff. Was it a 1997 Huff? A two-door or a four-door? That's the level of humor I could manage after meeting Jeffrey Kitzberger. Five minutes with him could make anyone forget how to chuckle.

I opened the windows again, took a Pepsi from my fridge, and stood near the window, hoping for a cool breeze. Cleveland doesn't often smell terrific, but there's something clean and invigorating about breathing summer air in the evening.

I didn't cool down about Kitzberger, though. He rubbed me the wrong way from the first second—besides, I *did* know some people in those pictures. How I got to know them, and why the FBI decided to push me around is a long story, which means you should sit back, kick off your shoes, and read all about it.

My case had started a few days earlier, right here in my office on another warm day, when I was minding my own business . . .

CHAPTER ONE

When a child goes missing, there is nothing more frightening, tragic, or terror-inducing for the distraught parent. Most never give up hoping. That's how it was for my new client, Savannah Dacey—even though her "child" was a grown man in his twenties.

Savannah is one of the most atmospheric cities in America, on the Atlantic coast in Georgia—full of beautiful old buildings, hanging moss, eccentric natives, and weeping willows. Its summertime humidity can knock you off your feet, and it's been the subject of a series of books, including one that wound up a Clint Eastwood movie. A river with the same name, Savannah, runs nearby. Additionally, Savannah is the name of a woman who does stand-up news at the White House for NBC television, Savannah Guthrie. Like her, most women named Savannah are attractive and as tropical-looking as their names—or at least they seem more that way than if they'd been christened Sadie or Gertrude.

But Savannah Dacey didn't fit the name in any way. She'd sounded like a sad sack when she made the phone appointment, and whiny to boot, and she looked like a sad sack, too. She was close to fifty, and looked ten years older. Her fingers were thick as bratwursts, fingernails polished the vivid crimson women stopped wearing in 1972. Her hair had been "done" and dyed an improbable red by someone in a low-rent beauty shop. Her eyeglasses, also of a long-gone era, were bright green, shaped like cat's eyes, with ungainly rhinestones twinkling in each corner. Her forehead and upper lip were shiny with perspiration, and half-moon sweat stains appeared at the underarms of her short-sleeved white blouse. Her wrinkled, inexpensive peasant skirt made her appear as if she'd walked in the heat and humidity from her West Park home all the way to my office on the west bank of the Flats.

How anyone named "Savannah" wound up in Cleveland is anyone's guess; it's not a Savannah kind of town. But I've met women with even more exotic names, as you'll learn.

"It's kind of you to see me on such short notice, Mr. Jacovich," she said. She'd phoned me the day before and had mispronounced my last name. If it gives you trouble, just sound it out properly with the *J* sounding like a *Y*—*Yock*-o-vitch. It's hard to say, I think, which is why I christened my private investigation business Milan Securities after my *first* name. Put the American slant on it—*My*-lan—and don't say it the way you'd pronounce the name of an Eastern European, or the Italian city noted for its fashion shows and its opera house. I'd gently corrected her on the phone, and now Savannah said my name carefully, as if she'd been practicing.

Her son, twenty-eight-year-old Earl Dacey, was missing. He had left the house six days earlier and hadn't been heard from since. Now his mother wanted to know what had become of him. "He never stayed out all night in his life," she moaned. "If he's ever half an hour late getting home, he always calls me. Always. He's a good boy."

"Does he have a car?"

"An old crappy car," she said. "A two-door blue Dodge from around 1985. He bought it himself last fall. I never axed him where he got the money."

Axed him: fingernails on a blackboard. I'd been on the edge of the Earl Dacey disappearance for less than five minutes, and he was already an albatross around my neck. I said, "Is he someplace with a—" I paused, not wanting to say "woman." I had no right to assume Earl's sexual preferences. "With a lover?"

"He don't date girls. He don't have men friends, either. The best friend he has in the whole world is me." Savannah said it proudly.

"Where does he work?"

"He don't have a job right now." She shifted her spreading backside in my visitor's chair. "He never had a *proper* job. He don't get along with people he don't know. He's shy." Her eyes twinkled behind the cat's-eye glasses. Maybe she was flirting with me; I hoped not.

"Does Earl have any hobbies?"

"No—he watches TV, an' plays on his computer for hours at a time. He likes watching baseball." Her round whey-face lit up as she glanced out my full-length windows across the Cuyahoga River to where the Indians play—Progressive Field is its official name now, although almost everyone in Cleveland still refers to it as what they called it when it opened in 1994, Jacobs Field, or more familiarly, "The Jake." The ballpark and my office are on opposite sides of a peculiar, sometimes dangerous kink in the river known as Collision Bend—I'm always amazed that few Clevelanders know what it's called.

"Does Earl *play* baseball?"

"Lord, no! He's not very athletic."

"Nothing else he likes?"

"Eating—spaghetti a couple times a week, or pizza or cheeseburgers. And he likes taking pitchers, too."

The start of a headache thrummed against my eyeballs. Pitchers! I couldn't correct my prospective client. Not only isn't it my job, but half the people in Cleveland call a photograph or a painting a "pitcher," not realizing a pitcher is a guy on the mound who accurately throws a ball ninety miles an hour at another guy with a big stick in his hand and dares him to hit it. "Pitcher" is also a vessel from which to pour milk, water, or Kool-Aid. But Savannah and lots of other people don't even know how to pronounce "picture."

I wasn't overjoyed about my headache, either. I was getting lots of them—more than I used to. They weren't blinding migraines that put me out of commission; they were more the *essence* of a headache. Maybe I was getting old. Sixty is the new forty, or so they say—and sixty was still almost a year ahead of me. I rubbed the back of my neck. "He likes taking pictures?"

"He never goes anywhere without his camera—or his video-cam."

"He has a videocam?"

She nodded. "I dunno what he films with it, but I guess he's having a good time so I don't even ask."

"Did you contact the police?"

"Fer sure," she said—another expression that quietly died in the late sixties. "I told them he was gone, but they didn't have much interest."

"He's an adult. They assumed he'd left of his own accord." I cleared my throat. "Maybe he has."

"No way!" There was real emotion behind her whine. "He wouldn't worry me like that unless he's got to."

I nodded. "It's a hot morning, Ms. Dacey," I said, more out of pity than anything else. "How about something cold to drink? A Pepsi, or a Mountain Dew?"

She was immediately interested. "Regular or diet?"

"Regular Mountain Dew, Diet Pepsi."

"Eew, no diet *anything*. But I wouldn't say no to a Mountain Dew," she simpered. I got a Dew from my office-size refrigerator, painted to look like an old-fashioned Wells Fargo safe, and she poured it into a plastic glass I gave her from my bottom desk drawer.

I said, "Does Earl belong to a photography group or a camera club?"

She shook her head.

"Who does he take pictures *of*, then?"

"I don't know. People? Maybe just buildings—or dogs or squirrels. He don't show me his pitchers very often."

"And he has no friends—even casual ones?"

"Earl isn't so at ease with strangers. They scare him." She examined me with an admiring frankness that weirded me out. "You're a big guy—I bet you'll scare him, too."

"I'll try not to," I said. "So he doesn't have a job or a girlfriend, he doesn't spend time with friends. Where do I start looking for him, Ms. Dacey?"

"If I knew, I'd look there myself. That's why I want to hire you."

"That brings us around to money." I told her how much I charged, half expecting her to turn pale and scurry from my office, because the whole country was struggling against a recession—

but when someone has an important reason to want a private investigator on the job, they somehow get the money they need. Savannah took my quoted prices in stride. Her late husband, Earl's father, had died eight years earlier, leaving her a handsome pension from his long career on the line at the Ford plant. Shortly thereafter she hired on as night manager of a family restaurant on Detroit Avenue, so it didn't bother her to whip out her checkbook and write me a retainer.

"I want to start by looking at your house first," I said.

"Earl's not *at* my house."

"No, but maybe I could find information that will help show me where I might look for him."

She looked dubious but said it was okay.

"Will you be home in about an hour and a half? At noon?"

"Yeah, but I have to work tonight—I'll leave at about four thirty," she said, sneaking another fond glance out the windows. "This is a lovely office—such a nice view of downtown."

It *is* a nice view of downtown. It makes me feel good just looking at it. The familiar downtown skyline is *my* town—or I've always thought so. Born and bred, and though I've traveled—two years in Vietnam being a military policeman was a large part of it—I've never wanted to move anywhere else. "Thank you, Ms. Dacey."

She fluttered her eyelashes at me. "You can call me Savannah— um—*Milan*."

Now we were on a first-name basis—in moments we would become lifelong buddies.

Her high heels clattered down the steps. I didn't move until I heard her car start up and pull out of the lot. Then I breathed more freely.

I'm never comfortable with my clients. People at the end of their rope wouldn't hire me if they weren't under great stress. Still, I had sympathy for a mother whose son vanished, even if he was nearly thirty.

I created a new Earl Dacey file on my computer and typed in all his mother had told me. It didn't even fill up one page. I feared this would be a long haul, because I had other active jobs on my calendar, the main one an assignment from a large warehouse on the East Side in which brand-new refrigerators, stoves, air conditioners, and giant TV sets were kept until the retail store called for them to be delivered. One of the warehouse employees was claiming workers' comp and had been staying home from his job for the past six weeks, nursing what he swore was a very badly injured back from wrestling those heavy appliances out to a delivery truck. His bosses wanted to know if he *really* was disabled—so my assignment was to follow him around and see whether those supposedly misaligned vertebrae were truly keeping him from going back to work. I'd already seen him lug his heavy trash cans from his back door to the curb on garbage days, heft two cases of beer from his shopping cart to the back of his pickup at a Dave's supermarket, and even struggle with a gigantic watermelon.

I had more written about him than I did about Earl Dacey— but with Earl I was just getting started. I wish I didn't have to take Savannah's case.

I guess I'm just a sucker for mothers who tremble on the edge of crying.

It was still early for lunch, but I found my way to Stone Mad, a little bar-restaurant on West 65th Street. It's in an ancient building with naked bricks inside, and elegant old wood—something to look at if you happened to be dining alone, like me. I've been eating by myself for far too long, but Stone Mad serves a fast lunch when there's no one to talk to. After twenty minutes I headed south and west to the Dacey house, about a hundred blocks from downtown Cleveland.

In the West Park neighborhood, most of the homes are neatly cared for but old and tired. If Savannah repainted her house something other than faded gray, the upgrade would make all the rest of the homes on her block look even worse. The wooden steps up to a small front porch were swaybacked, and the swing seat, covered in sickly apple-green and bilious pink plastic, sported a coat of dust.

I pushed the doorbell, but didn't hear it ring. I waited twenty seconds, then knocked firmly. When Savannah let me in, I noticed she wore a dark blue sundress with extra-large white polka dots, and she'd redone her makeup, apparently for my benefit. She wore too much orangey base and green eye shadow, and she'd rushed applying a new coat of lipstick, which crept out from the outline of her lips like something drawn by a first grader trying to crayon a picture in his coloring book.

In her living room the air conditioner didn't work hard enough. The house was a modest, not-nice and not-crappy place you'd forget about as soon as you left. The furniture was either from Value City a decade ago or bought used from one of a dozen gritty resale stores on Lorain Avenue calling themselves antique shops. At both ends of the sofa were matching lamps, their bases made out of small tin pails painted bright yellow and then adorned with drawings—a contented-looking cow on one and a hog on the other. My taste in furniture has never been high class, but someone would have to shoot me before I allowed them to put those two lamps in my living room.

There were no paintings or decorations on Savannah's walls save for a star-shaped 1960s-era clock, but every flat surface was dotted with framed photographs, mostly of her child Earl—and I use the word "*child*" advisedly, because every picture was of a kid under the age of ten.

The chairs, side tables, and sofa in the living room were all outdated. I lowered myself slowly onto the least-uncomfortable-looking chair, feeling a broken spring inside the cushion. The most expensive thing in the room was a fifty-two-inch plasma TV playing a daytime drama. Embarrassed, Savannah muted the sound. "I got hooked on soap operas," she said as if confessing to a string of serial murders. "I work nights, so I never get to look at good TV shows. That's when I started watching soaps in the daytime and—well, I'm hooked."

"That's okay," I said. I'd never watched more than five minutes of any soap opera in my life. On the screen two impossibly good-looking actors were lying in bed under a sheet, hoping their audience believed they'd just had a wild sex moment, though neither of them had messed up their stiffly gelled hair even a little bit. I decided to look at Savannah instead.

Bad idea.

"So, Milan—now that you're in my house, can I return the favor?" She batted her false eyelashes at me and crinkled up her nose. "Do *you* want a Mountain Dew?"

"Nothing, thanks. I just had lunch."

Her mouth took on one of those teasing, "your-loss" looks. "I wish I knew you were going to eat before you came. Maybe we could have had lunch together." She sat across from me on her flowered sofa, crossing her legs and hoping I'd notice them. "So," she said, "what should I tell you about Earl?"

"Everything you can. Let's start with a photograph, if you have one."

"Hmmm," she cooed, cocking her head at what she believed to be an adorable angle, "there's lots a pitchers right here in this room. Take your pick."

"I'd prefer one a little more current."

"Earl likes taking pitchers, but hates having *his* pitcher took. I'll go look for one."

She disappeared down the hall and into what I assumed was her bedroom. The two drop-dead-beautiful soap opera people in bed had been replaced with two different drop-dead beautiful people, this time having an intense conversation in somebody's living room. Neither was a good enough actor to indicate a scintilla of sexual tension between them. On those daytime dramas they usually shoot everyone in close-up, but the TV was still muted—and I didn't care enough about what they were saying to try reading lips.

Eventually Savannah returned with a snapshot of Earl and surrendered it to me. "I took this Christmas morning," she said, "and surprised him."

In the photo Earl sat cross-legged near a Christmas tree, opening a present, wearing the ugliest pair of blue-and-white-striped pajamas I'd ever seen. Either he'd kicked off his slippers, or he didn't own a pair to hide his large, bony, ghost-white feet. His lank black hair flopped over his forehead in unkempt chunks, and smiling unfortunately crinkled up his nose, making him look like he was smelling something foul. His snaggly teeth were yellow, his face bore an active case of acne, and he was a hundred pounds overweight. No wonder he didn't pose for pictures.

"That's my Earl," Savannah said.

I searched fruitlessly for an appropriate compliment. "May I hang on to this?"

"Long as you bring it back."

"I promise." I slipped it into the inside pocket of my jacket. "You last saw him six days ago—on Wednesday. What time was that?"

She seemed vague. "I'm not sure. Morning, I guess—eleven o'clock or so."

"He didn't mention where he was going?"

"No, he just said, 'See you later, Mom.'"

"What was he wearing?"

She seemed shocked at the question. "Gosh, I don't know. Umm—khaki pants, I guess. And a short-sleeved sports shirt." With her fingers she showed me that the shirt probably had buttons and was not a pullover.

I nodded. "Did he take anything with him, like a gym bag or a package? Was he taking clothes to the cleaners?"

Savannah tapped her forehead with one finger. "I—don't recall. Lotsa times when he goes out, he takes a shopping bag with him."

"Does he go shopping with that shopping bag?"

"I don't know *what* he does with it. But he don't shop. He don't have much money ever."

"Not many people leave to go shopping already carrying a shopping bag," I said—discounting those "green" shoppers who buy reusable canvas bags and carry them around everywhere. "Savannah, I hate to ask this, but—does Earl shoplift?"

Her back stiffened. "What?"

"I'm not suggesting—just asking questions."

"Well, ask a different one," she ordered. "I don't like that."

"Can I take a look in his room, then?"

She relaxed a little. "Earl don't like nobody poking around his private things."

"Earl isn't here," I reminded her.

Savannah couldn't argue with that logic, but she took nearly a minute thinking about it. Then she led me back through the house to the kitchen. She pointed toward a closed door to one side of the refrigerator. "That's Earl's room, there." The room was too damn small for two large people to be inside, looking under the mattress and feeling around inside dresser drawers. I couldn't imagine why a very large adult man slept in a single bed held over from childhood. The nubby white chenille bedspread was yellow with age, and a tattered Indians pennant on the wall curled at the tip.

I said, "I'd work better and quicker by myself. I promise I won't steal anything."

"You aren't the stealing type," she said, heading back toward the living room. "I'll be out here—I don't want to miss my soaps."

No federal prison cell was more depressing than Earl Dacey's bedroom. There were no books anywhere, and no artwork unless you count assorted color "pitchers" of Lindsay Lohan, Britney Spears, Jessica Simpson, and Khloe Kardashian, cut from celebrity magazines and thumbtacked to the wall and to a large corkboard propped up on his desk. Despite her printed signature across the bottom, I had no idea who Khloe Kardashian was—but that's just me.

An off-brand laptop sat atop the desk, open, with no dust on the monitor. On the floor was a photo printer. The desk drawers contained loose paper clips and rubber bands, eleven pennies and two nickels, and five Tic Tac containers, three of which were empty. His address book contained only six names and numbers scrawled in a childlike hand, none familiar to me. I took from my pocket a folded-up plastic bag from Giant Eagle and slipped the receipts and the address book inside.

On a low table was a TV set, half the size of the one in the living room, with a DVD player built in. Below it, on another shelf, was a short stack of DVDs. I squatted to examine them. The top one was *The Godfather*—the first one, the great one, with Brando— in a jewel case that bore signs of repeated viewings. I didn't have much in common with Earl, but we evidently shared a love for this particular movie. I can quote much of it by heart; the line that stays with me best is: "Leave the gun. Take the cannoli." Classic.

The other DVDs, in colored plastic envelopes, were unmarked except by Post-It notes with numbers scrawled on them, starting with Number 1 and ending with Number 9.

I went through an old dresser desperately in need of paint. Inside were T-shirts, washed and folded neatly, which made me imagine Savannah did all her son's laundry. About eight pairs of underwear were in the other corner of the drawer, all whitey-tighty briefs.

Cleveland gets hotter than hell in summer and doesn't cool off much in the evening. Everyone sweats and everyone smells. When I opened the door to the closet I was nearly overpowered by the stink of old sneakers and clothes recently worn and not washed. Earl's passion for plaid shirts emphasized his girth. There were no dress slacks—just jeans and khaki pants, hung on wire hangers.

On a high shelf Earl had folded a few sweaters and several more sweatshirts, including one hoodie with the Browns' orange helmet logo on it. I noticed three magazines nearly hidden beneath the sweaters. The tacky color photographs on the covers were thumbprint-smudged. I'd never noticed these publications on an ordinary magazine shelf in Barnes and Noble. They were usually for sale in one of those grubby Lorain Road establishments called "bookstores" that peddled such items as these to raincoat-wearing middle-aged men who'd sneak in the back door from the parking lot so no one would see them. Earl's small collection wasn't exactly pornographic, but the magazines featured photos of young women cheerfully baring their backsides to the camera.

Almost everyone has enjoyed looking at nude pictures of *someone*, depending on their taste. However, not everyone stashes their stroke-off magazines on a closet shelf hidden beneath a stack of clothing. Earl had gone out of his way so Savannah wouldn't discover his literary preferences. I stuffed the magazines into my plastic bag, too.

On the floor were three pair of sneakers with Velcro tabs, easier to open and close for someone one hundred pounds too heavy, and a pair of work boots that he must have worn instead of galoshes during winter snow. Next to them, squished into a corner, was a shopping bag bearing the name of a long-gone department store, Kaufmann's. The top was covered with white tissue paper. I slid it out into the middle of the closet and looked inside carefully to find several sheets of bubble wrap, two thick eighteen-inch-square patches of soft rubber used for packing, and, stacked neatly near the top so that its lens pointed upward, a camcorder that recorded live action as well as taking still photographs.

I couldn't help noticing that a thumbnail-sized piece of tape was affixed to the front of the camcorder. I lifted it to find some-one—probably Earl—had used the tape so no one could see the red light announcing the camcorder was recording.

I picked up the laptop, collected some other possessions of Earl's I wanted to examine more closely, hooked his shopping bag over my wrist along with my own from Giant Eagle, and went back into the living room, where Savannah was still watch-ing a soap opera, a different program, since the top of the hour had come and gone. Two more beautiful actors in another love scene—different faces and a different bedroom, but probably the same hair stylist, because their hair wasn't mussed up, either.

"I want to take some things with me," I said. "A stack of DVDs, his computer, his address book, and his shopping bag, okay? I'll write out a receipt for you."

"Don't bother with the receipt, Milan" she said, reluctantly hit-ting the mute button on her TV remote and tearing her attention away from the actors. "I trust you."

"Where did Earl get that camcorder?"

"I bought it for him two Christmases ago." She put her finger to her forehead to look like she was thinking about it and appearing adorable. "He'd been asking for it—hinting for it."

So Earl owned the camcorder he'd begged for. I wondered what he did with it, and why he kept it in that shopping bag. I wrote out a receipt for Savannah before I left, though—whether she trusted me or not.

I headed home to get comfortable and to play Earl's unmarked DVDs. For more than twenty years I've lived in an apartment at the crest of Cedar Hill in Cleveland Heights. I'd moved there when my marriage fell apart, figuring it would be a short-term stopover—no more than a year or two—but since then I'd thought of no valid reason to move again. My ex, Lila, got the house—my house—and she and her longtime live-in lover, Joe Bradac, enjoy it, and my bed, too. Even though I've never hit him, Joe is still scared to death of me. He'd slept with Lila for at least eighteen months before she announced she wanted a divorce from me, and I desperately wanted to eat his lunch, but I've kept my knotted fists in my pockets whenever I see him.

I've stared through my bay window by the hour—at the triangle where Cedar Road and Fairmount Boulevard come together, across the street from a Dave's supermarket and the Mad Greek restaurant, in which people frequently gather for happy hour, especially during the summer when the Mad Greek lifts its windows and I can see directly into their lounge. For years I used my living room as my office until I bought the old building on the riverfront in the Flats. So here I am, two decades later and now an old-timer in my rented digs. It's fine with me; I don't want the trouble of landscaping, grass cutting, repairs, and maintenance on a house. I'm apartment-bound and happy as a clam—a lonely clam, admittedly, but contented nonetheless.

I shuffled through the mail, threw it all away, and felt bad for the trees that died to produce it, grabbed a cold Stroh's, and repaired to the bedroom to change into shorts and a T-shirt with the Cleveland Indians logo on it. I'm as uneasy about wearing Chief Wahoo garb as anyone else—but that's our team and our mascot, so Clevelanders live with it. When the phone rang, I hadn't yet begun watching Earl Dacey's discs.

My home number isn't listed, and the only people who know it are people I like, so I didn't even check the Caller ID when I picked up and said hello.

"It's summertime! I thought you'd be out drinking a beer and enjoying the female scenery in their halter tops and miniskirts," Suzanne Davis said. She always makes me smile. She's a private investigator too, but plies her trade in Lake County, so we don't get together often enough. She's aided me on a few cases, and I've given her a helping hand when she needed it. She's a few years younger than I am, and one of my best friends.

"You're right about the beer part," I said. "How are you anyway?"

"Slowing down like everyone else in this recession, waiting for a miracle. What are you up to at eight o'clock tomorrow morning?"

"Ye Gods, do you percolate that early?"

"Usually not. But there's someone I want you to meet—someone kind of interesting."

"You want me to get up early just to meet your new boyfriend?"

She snorted. "He's practically a boy and he's a friend, but I wouldn't put those two words together about him."

"I thought you went for the young ones."

"Not *this* young—he's twenty-four. I refuse to write a note to some teacher for permission to sleep with him. He's had some bad times, so I care about him. Besides, there's a reason for getting the two of you together." She got serious. "You need assistance."

"Somebody to help me stand up or walk down the stairs?"

"Bingo!" Suzanne chuckled. "Besides, he needs a job. So—breakfast tomorrow, or not? I'm buying."

"Buying," I said, "is the magic word."

We picked a place—Jack's Deli, on Cedar Road just east of Green Road—and said goodbye so I could begin my serious inquiries into the whereabouts of Earl Dacey.

My second Stroh's was opened when DVD Number 1 began to play. At first, all I could see on the screen was what looked like a high ceiling, studded with wide glass panels letting in bright sunshine; the tape was made during the spring or summer. There was bouncing, as if the camera operator moved briskly along, not paying attention to what was being photographed. My mind drifted off to other things, such as my current stakeout on the guy cheating the insurance company out of worker's comp.

Then the cameraman made a sharp right turn and went through a wide public doorway, and the ceiling in the frame changed. Now it was lower, with fluorescent light fixtures, finished in rough-hewn blown plaster. The videographer was walking through a mall and now had turned into a retail venue, probably a department store. I glanced at the shopping bag. Probably what I was watching was Earl Dacey's camera work—but why was he shooting ceilings and keeping the video collection unmarked in his bedroom?

The movement slowed down, stopped—and I was looking directly up someone's dress.

She—whoever she was—wore a short dark blue skirt, and beneath it a tiny black thong. The camera angle distorted the view, but her legs were smooth and tan, her thighs slim and firm, her butt tight. She moved slightly while the camera ground away, probably clueless that someone was taping up her skirt. She was being assaulted.

After a few moments the cameraman moved a little, and I was treated to a shot of another pair of panties—flowered bikinis this time. This woman had slightly thicker legs than the previous victim, but wore the same type of dark blue skirt. Her bikini was pulled up tight, creating what's known in the pornography trade as a camel toe.

I watched for another ten minutes. During that time the voyeur found two more women wearing skirts or dresses with interesting underwear. One of them, also wearing a thong, bore an interesting butterfly tattoo on her left buttock. I was learning more from this DVD than I'd ever wanted to know.

I stopped watching and rewound it. Earl must have done this recently. Cleveland women don't wear short skirts and bare legs unless it's summertime.

I changed discs and began studying Number 2. Different setting—I think a different mall altogether—but more of the same subject. I skipped to Number 5—same old same old.

I took Earl's camcorder out of the shopping bag, removed the memory disc, and plugged it into my own laptop computer. Within moments I was witnessing his current artistic endeavors—more upskirt videos.

Earl Dacey, whose mother had paid me to find him, was an active pervert, and only God knew where he might be now and what he could be doing.

And me? I shook my head sadly. Unbidden, I'd suddenly turned into a dirty old man.

CHAPTER TWO

Several times that evening I'd let my hand hover over the telephone uncertainly—to tell Savannah Dacey I'd return her retainer check and Earl's property. I wanted nothing to do with her son or his fetish—I didn't need the money that badly, and I hated it when Savannah batted her eyelashes at me. I just wanted out.

Everyone with a computer has peeked at some sort of porn at least once, out of curiosity if nothing else. But if someone is actually *photographing* the porn without the victims realizing it, that's another story—and a crime.

I was too old for this. Tracking down missing persons was one thing—but getting involved with a voyeur and his dirty picture taking was quite another. This could get rough. It had taken me a while to recover from my last concussion, and I still got headaches the likes of which I'd never experienced before.

What the hell, I thought as I dressed for breakfast the next morning—I'll call Savannah from the office.

I eat breakfast often at Jack's Deli, and did so even before it relocated around the corner from its original location several years ago. I miss the Al Hirschfeld caricatures of celebrities on the wall, but I still love the food. For me, Jack's has Cleveland's best corned beef. I wound up in a booth, the one in which I'd carried on a fascinating conversation with a notorious bookie the year before after he'd sent two tough guys to my office to bounce money out of my pocket that I hadn't owed him in the first place.

I ordered a pot of green tea, checked out the other customers, and read the menu I practically knew by heart. They had instituted a new menu a while back, including lots of things that are good for you—but it's still a delicatessen, and the bosses there, Alvy and Gary, would never give up the great corned beef, pastrami, blintzes, and potato pancakes and replace them with broccoli and brussels sprouts.

Suzanne Davis arrived ten minutes late to breakfast—but she's late for everything. She's one of those over-fifty women who turns heads wherever she goes. Her skirts display terrific legs, especially when she wears three-inch heels. This morning her blond hair was pulled into a ponytail. Her dark-colored peasant blouse caressed her shoulders, and her general look caressed every man in the joint. She was too damn sexy to be a private eye. I often thought we probably would have made an interesting "couple." But I've never been good at doing the couples thing, so we were better off being good friends.

Her new friend was young enough to be my son, though there was no trace of my Slavic face in his. As they used to say, he looked as Irish as Paddy's pig—a good-looking kid, medium height and pugnacious, in a polo shirt whose cut exaggerated his biceps, pectorals, and six-pack. His blondish-reddish hair was short, his mouth thin and angry-looking. Wherever Suzanne found him, somebody had forgotten to teach him to smile.

His eyes were indigo blue, like the color of ink people used in fountain pens fifty years ago—and the secret behind those eyes was impenetrable, like the depths of a still, small pool in the midst of a forest. No one realizes the pond is there until they find it, and then wonder why they cannot see to the bottom of the water. Those eyes drew my interest; I wanted to know more about him, know him better, beyond this hastily arranged breakfast in Cleveland's best Jewish delicatessen.

When I rose to meet them, he obviously wasn't enchanted with how much bigger I was than him. That's why our handshake turned into a war game.

"Milan," Suzanne said, "this is Kevin O'Bannion."

"Nice to meet you, Kevin," I said, trying not to pretend a tank just ran over my fingers.

He cocked his head toward his left shoulder. "I prefer being called K.O."

K.O. wasn't much of a talker, so Suzanne and I chatted until the waitress arrived to take our order. I opted for my favorite breakfast at Jack's, matzo brei—pieces of matzos crumbled up and cooked with scrambled eggs—and Suzanne chose french toast, the thick kind made with challah. Though we were aware of our diets, we couldn't resist Jack's breakfasts. K.O. ordered coffee and nothing else.

"K.O. is looking for a job," Suzanne said.

"Doing what?"

"He works for me sometimes—the usual investigative stuff. I keep track of his hours to record his experience. When he racks up enough hours, he wants to be a P.I., too."

"How can I talk you out of it?" I said to him, smiling. He didn't smile back, so I switched from humor. "Ever do any investigative work before?"

He shook his head. "No. I was in the army six years. Twice in Iraq, once in Afghanistan."

"Glad you made it through okay. You joined the army right after high school?"

He frowned, throwing a look at Suzanne, who nodded at him. He slumped into the booth, crossing his arms defensively. "I got a GED. I didn't finish high school. I spent three years in juvie." He didn't blink. "That's juvenile custody."

"I know what it is," I said. "Why were you in juvie?"

"Assault."

"With a deadly weapon?"

He held up his hands. "With these."

Now I understood why he was called K.O.—"knockout." I wondered if he punched as hard as he shook hands. "I'm not looking for employees."

"You have more than one case?" Suzanne asked.

"Besides my regular corporate work, I have two active gigs: a workers' comp case—and looking for a missing guy."

"A guy?"

"He's twenty-eight—unemployed and lives with his mother. Kind of a geek. He disappeared a week ago."

"K.O.'s good at asking questions and not wasting time. He can write good reports, too. You should hire him to help you out."

"Why would I do that?"

"You're no kid anymore," Suzanne said. "You get hurt a lot. You've been shot, stabbed, beaten up—last winter you got a concussion and almost died in somebody's basement. You should take things easier. Hire a young, smart assistant to stick his neck out so you don't have to."

I wanted as little as possible to do with Earl Dacey and his peculiar hobby, and I wouldn't like hanging around department stores asking about voyeurs poking videocams up the skirts of young women. Plus I'd started getting those headaches. I'd cut down on coffee and quit cigarettes; I was damn near sixty and I couldn't treat my body like I was twenty anymore. Suzanne might be right about my not getting hit in the head again. But . . .

"I can't have K.O. laying everybody out with one punch," I protested. "I don't operate that way."

"Neither do I—and he's been working for me, off and on, for the last three months."

I turned to K.O. "Can you behave yourself?"

He didn't answer me, but those deep eyes smoldered from within. He looked as if he might bite my throat.

"No losing your temper," I went on. "You remember how to keep your hands in your pockets?"

"Sure." His dry voice was like the crinkling of a paper bag. "I tie my own shoelaces, too."

I didn't sigh, shake my head, or roll my eyes—I'm not that dramatic. I just curled my toes inside my shoes. I was about to hire an assistant with a temper, a cutting wit, an attitude, and fists that should be registered as deadly weapons. Maybe he would help me avoid one concussion too many.

We decided he'd accompany me back to my apartment, where he could watch some of Earl Dacey's handiwork and decide whether or not *he* was interested, and if so, how we would split up the work. Suzanne took her own car east to Beachwood Place to do some upscale shopping—there's nothing in Lake County like Nordstrom's, Saks Fifth Avenue, or the small, elegant clothing stores—and then collect K.O. and drive him home.

On the way down Cedar Road I asked him if he got to Cleveland Heights very often.

"To do what? Hang out with a bunch of liberals?"

"You're political, huh?"

"I don't vote."

"Everybody should vote."

"Everybody should pay their taxes, too—but the richer they are, the more they screw the IRS." He stared out the window as I passed Cleveland Heights High School.

"Is there anything you're *not* pissed off about?"

He considered it. "Suzanne. She's a pretty terrific person."

"We agree about something. Anybody else?"

"Nobody comes to mind at the moment."

I laughed even though I wasn't amused. "Mad at me, too?"

"I don't know you well enough, one way or the other. Are you a tight-ass?"

"Nobody ever called me that."

"Not yet," he said with assurance. "Browns or Steelers?"

"You gotta be kidding. I'm a Browns fan ever since I could walk."

A corner of his mouth struggled with an incipient smile and he nodded with reluctant satisfaction.

I parked at the curb in front of my apartment and we climbed a flight of outside stairs and another one inside the building. I was at that age when the climb made me a little short of breath, but K.O. was young and fit enough to climb another ten flights without breaking a sweat.

Inside he glanced around my place. He checked out the framed photographs of my two boys on the wall. "Your kids?"

"Yes," I said. "They were younger then. My older son, Milan Junior, lives in Chicago. He's close to your age. The other one is Stephen."

He looked around. "No dogs or cats—not even a turtle. Hate animals?"

"I like animals. My parents wouldn't let me have pets."

"No home is really a home without a dog or cat."

"My landlord doesn't accept pets, either. Does that get me off the hook?"

He shrugged off my question. "I'll let you know."

He said nothing else about my apartment. He turned down coffee, and when I suggested I'd take him and Suzanne to lunch, he neither agreed nor demurred, waiting to see how things proceeded before he locked himself into a decision. He went his own way whether other people approved or not. I understood that.

I gave him a notepad and sat him in front of the TV set, popping Earl's DVD Number 1 into the VCR. Then I made myself a cup of tea in the microwave, wondering what I'd do with the rest of the morning. By the time I came out of the kitchen, he'd already jotted something on his pad. He hit the pause button on the remote.

"Somebody has a sick mind," he said.

I had to agree, but I couldn't resist poking at him while I had the chance. "Seeing young women wearing sexy underwear doesn't get to you?"

"Sure—in person. Otherwise it's a bore. Why are you looking for this pervo anyway?"

"Because his mother's paying me to do it," I explained. "Private investigators can't always help wonderful people. Freaks need help, too."

"By the way, on this tape, that's the Great Lakes Mall." He stood up and rotated his head so the bones of his neck popped softly. "I live in Mentor. I've hung out in that mall, so I spotted the skylights right away. It's bright during the day. I think the store—where the cosmetics counter is—is Macy's. At least that's what it is now, it used to be Kaufmann's. It *could* be Dillard's, at the other end of the mall, but I'm guessing Macy's."

I thought about the shopping bag with the Kaufmann name on it. "Do they have security people at Macy's?"

"Sure, watching for shoplifters. Mostly the small-time thieves are women, wearing long raincoats or parkas so they can stash things underneath. But that's in the winter. Wearing a coat in the summer is hanging a big sign around their neck saying 'thief.'"

"So security doesn't watch for voyeurs and upskirt photographers?"

"They'll bust them if they catch them—but they don't spend that much time in cosmetics because there are so many sales associates. By the way—the girls wearing blue skirts are from St. Bonaventure. The other Catholic girls' schools wear black, maroon, or plaid skirts."

"And you know this because . . . ?"

"Because I'm Irish, ex-Catholic, and I know about Lake County Catholic schools."

"Good. I even remember a little about St. Bonaventure from when *I* went to church. He was a theologian and a philosopher."

"Weren't they all?"

"And the rumor is that he was poisoned to death."

"Maybe they ought to poison nutsos like this who film up schoolgirls' dresses."

"That's radical."

"Anyone who abuses or victimizes children—or animals—deserves the worst. That's my belief, anyway. By the way—I do have a cat." He said it almost defensively. "His name is Rodney."

"So are you interested in lending me a hand?"

"I need the money—and the experience. So I'm up for it. But I hope you find this Earl guy and not me. I won't have pleasant things to say to him."

"We don't have to like him—just locate him." I jerked my thumb at the stack of DVDs. "There are more videos to watch."

"Are they all the same subject?"

"I haven't looked at all of them, but I think they're all like the first one."

He clicked the remote from PAUSE to STOP. "I'm gonna skip the rest for now. Watching porn is like ordering a great restaurant meal and then just looking at it."

Point taken. He told me he had a car and a computer at home, and I suggested he drop by Great Lakes Mall and talk to the security people and the cosmetics counter saleswomen in Macy's and Dillard's in case they had seen someone lurking around their customers. I promised I'd pay him the same money Suzanne did—but it would be easier on everyone if I didn't have to take notes from him and then copy them every night. "Just e-mail me a report," I said, giving him my business card with my office location, phone number, and e-mail address on it. "If we need to communicate directly, there's always the phone."

"I have a phone," he said. Deadpan. I ran over every joke I'd ever heard, wondering if any of them would make him smile. Finally I gave up. "Remember our deal, K.O." I made a fist of my right hand and showed it to him. "No rough stuff."

He bristled. "You think I'll beat up on the girls who sell cosmetics?"

"I don't know who you beat up."

He almost mumbled. "It wasn't girls."

"You want to tell me about it?"

"About what?"

"About why you got thrown into juvie."

"Assault," he said. "I told you that."

"If I'm paying you, I'd like the details." I pointed him to his chair. "Talk to me."

He ignored that, shoving his hands into his pockets and pacing back and forth for almost a minute. Then he said, "I was fifteen years old. I beat up two kids—one was seventeen and one was eighteen."

"In self-defense?"

"No."

I waited. Apparently I'd get nothing more until I asked for it. "Did you get hurt, too?"

"I broke one of my fingers—punching." He held up the middle finger of his left hand to show me it was crooked. I didn't take the gesture as an insult. "I can't even remember which guy I broke it on."

"You want to tell me what the fight was about?"

"No."

"Tell me anyway," I said. "I can pay you, I can help you rack up experience hours for when you apply for a license, I can even be your friend. But I *would* like to know where you're coming from."

He stared at me for a long moment before deciding to answer.

"I come from Mentor," he said without emotion.

CHAPTER THREE

uzanne arrived at my apartment about twenty minutes later to find Kevin O'Bannion had refused lunch. He was deficient in the smile department, and his conversation was limited to occasional grunts and growls, so for me perhaps one meal per day with him was enough. I made a copy of Earl Dacey's photo for him, and then Suzanne took him away. I sat quietly, considering what I'd just done to myself—hired an assistant, a sidekick I'd never wanted. Batman and Robin? The Lone Ranger and Tonto? The Green Hornet and Kato? Milan and K.O.? It sounded strange inside my head.

Excepting occasional assistance from Suzanne Davis and advice from my late, great pal Marko Meglich, who'd been head of the Homicide Squad for the Cleveland Police, I'd always worked alone. It wasn't paying him money that bothered me . . . Stand-up guy believes in justice? Check. Takes care of himself when things get tough? Check. Bright, intuitive, with a quick mind? Check.

But then there was that personality. No check there—nor one for his temper. Where had that thinly disguised fury come from? What roiled him with rage? I worried that hair trigger in his brain would eventually get *me* in trouble.

I had no time to worry myself about K.O. I had other things on my mind, specifically Earl Dacey and his particular kink.

I headed out toward Lake County.

During winter Lake County is frequently buried under several feet of snow, but in the spring and summer it's pretty out there—

trees, big skies, farms, and orchards. Except for Painesville and Mentor, Lake County is small-town. In places like Kirtland and Chardon and Concord, there are quaint town squares, gazebos, wineries, roadside country stores selling homemade candy and decorative but useless craft items, and pleasant houses spread far apart. I'd worked a political case in Lake Erie Shores years ago— which ended in storm-battered violence—but had hardly visited since, so I enjoyed the ride.

St. Bonaventure High School looks much like every other high school in America, not counting the statues of saints and martyrs on the front lawn and the ponderously religious stained-glass windows in the chapel. Quite a few summer school students walked through the halls—all wearing white blouses and blue skirts that appeared to be at least three inches longer than the ones on Earl Dacey's videos. Maybe they turned their waistbands under a few times to make the skirts shorter when they weren't under the supervision of priests and nuns. I asked one of the girls to direct me to the principal's office.

Sister Maria Augusta didn't look like the sisters in old movies with Loretta Young or Ingrid Bergman in full nun drag. The principal of St. Bonaventure was about forty-five, pleasant-looking, with shoulder-length dark brown hair randomly sprinkled with silver. She wore a gray blouse and a dark blue skirt—not the kind her students wore—and a golden cross. Her eyes were alive and downright merry. Her smile was warm and sincere.

"Are you the father of one of our girls here?"

"No, Sister." I gave her one of my business cards. "I'm a private investigator."

She studied the card before putting it on the desk. "I hope none of my students have done anything wrong."

"Not at all. But some of them may have been victims, not wrongdoers."

Her hand moved to her throat, touching the cross for reassurance. "Victims?"

"Yes, ma'am." I hadn't been inside a Catholic church or school for almost forty years, not counting other people's weddings and a few sad funerals, but the fear and awe grafted onto me when I was a small child always returned when I talked to a nun or a priest. Even fallen-away Catholics get ruffled whenever they're anywhere near Catholic clergy. Now I'd have to explain the videos to Sister Maria Augusta. As I carefully chose my words, a blush suffused my cheeks. Even as a kid dragged weekly by my parents to St. Vitus Church in the St. Clair Avenue neighborhood, I'd never been chatty with nuns—especially when it came to describing thongs and bikinis and flowery underwear. The word *panties* stuck in my throat.

When I finished, the principal breathed deeply and released the air between her lips. "Wow," she said. I didn't know nuns used words like *Wow*.

"The man who took these videos has disappeared," I said, "and his mother wants me to find him."

"I hope when you do, they'll throw him away," she said sternly. "Why would I know him, or where he is?"

"I just wondered if any St. Bonaventure girls complained—or if they knew about him."

"Middle school girls don't tell nuns about men taking pictures up their skirts, Mr. Jacovich, so I wouldn't have any idea." She raised her head slightly to expose her neck when the fan blew some cool air her way. "I'm not about to line up everyone in school and ask them." She pointed at me. "You're not going to, either."

I recognized that stern finger point; Sister Maria Augusta wasn't the first nun to level an accusing finger at me. "Which of your students hang out at the Great Lakes Mall?"

She laughed. "You're kidding. Everybody in Lake County winds up at the Great Lakes Mall. I've been there many times, and as far as I know, no perverts ever videotaped up *my* skirt." She didn't even blush. "Voyeurs don't restrict their activities to one particular mall."

"I have an assistant from Mentor, and he identified the mall from watching the discs. He connected the blue skirts with St. Bonaventure."

"Yes, all our students wear them to school." She fought another smile.

"He also said some recordings were made at a cosmetics counter in a department store there—so the girls were probably in high school, not middle school."

"None of them are permitted to wear makeup here," she said. "But I'm sure the older ones slap some on the minute they walk off campus. Every woman wears *some* makeup. Even me." She tapped her fingers on the desktop. "A few girls are more—sophisticated than the rest. They also come from wealthier families, so they can afford cosmetics." She rolled her eyes toward the ceiling. "I'm too busy teaching and administering and filling out paperwork to ride herd on teenagers dipping their toes into the water too early. But—I can ask a few discreet questions. We have to make a deal, though."

"A deal? Does that mean I have to come to confession?"

She laughed louder. "Not my job. And I wouldn't want to hear it anyway."

"Don't be too sure."

"But when you find this young man—and if he *is* the one cruising around with a camera—I want him prosecuted."

"That isn't *my* job," I said. "The only way to get him off the streets—or out of the malls—is to convince a student victim and her parents to file criminal charges."

"That's a piece of cake. I'll see what I can find out. If I uncover anything," she held up my business card, "I'll call you, okay?"

"I'd appreciate it," I said. "Are there other schools out here I should check out?"

"Probably. But only if your assistant recognizes the school skirts."

"There were nine different DVDs," I said. "Neither K.O. or I watched all of them."

"K.O.?"

I shrugged. "That's his nickname."

"Some nickname, Mr. Jacovich," she said. "Watch out for a left hook."

"A left hook? Are you a boxing fan, Sister?"

"My dad boxed—amateur—and I've always loved it. I even went to Youngstown to see Kelly Pavlik fight. Great seats, too, when I told them who I was. Fourth row." She winked broadly. "Nobody," Sister Maria Augusta said, "sloughs off lousy prizefight seats on a nun."

*   *   *

My next trip was to St. Katherine's, about a mile and a half away. I didn't recognize the red and gray plaid skirts. But it wouldn't hurt to talk to the principal, too—there weren't that many Catholic girls' schools in Lake County.

As I walked up the steps to the front door, a woman in her thirties was coming out. Her long hair was dark blond, and she'd seized it up in an attractive bun. I could have happily looked at her very blue eyes for hours. Her smile made me smile, too. "Good morning," she said. "Can I help you find something?"

"Oh—are you cutting class?"

"Do I look like a teen-aged student here?"

"I thought you might be."

"That's because the sun's in your eyes."

I sighed melodramatically. "I've spent my life getting the sun in my eyes."

"You poor thing," she cooed. "Well, I'm a teacher, not a student. Advanced English. I have this period off, so I thought I'd go walking in the sunshine." She raised her head; the rays of the sun made her face golden. "I'm Cisne Kelly."

I told her my name and watched as she tried to spell it out in her head. Finally she gave up and shook my hand. "Clearly we both have unusual names."

"Everyone struggles with mine." I said. "It's Slovenian—the Cleveland version. But Cisne? That's a new one."

"It rhymes with Disney—like in Walt. *Cisne* means *swan* in Spanish." And she made a graceful, swanlike sweep of her hand in the air.

"What an unusual, beautiful name."

"I'm not exactly the swan type," she said. "But my mother is Panamanian—and she loves swans and geese and any other elegant big bird."

"Like the bird of paradise."

"I don't think I'd pass the physical."

"You underestimate yourself. What other kind of big bird?"

She giggled. "The one on *Sesame Street.*"

"You're more elegant than that, Cisne Kelly." I liked the way it felt when I said her name aloud.

"My father was Irish, in case you wondered why the two names go together." A dimple nestled in her left cheek when she smiled. "I know all the girls here at school. Are you somebody's dad?"

"Two somebodies. But they don't call me 'Dad' anymore. They're men now—all grown up."

"One day I'll grow up, too. So, can I direct you somewhere?"

"I'm looking for the principal's office."

"Are you expected?"

"No."

"Oh my," she said, her smile changing to a mild frown. "The principal hates to be surprised. Are you a surprise kind of guy?"

"You might say that." I gave her one of my cards. "I'm a private investigator."

She raised her eyebrows. "This is a new one on St. Kat's. We've never welcomed a private eye to our campus. Has there been trouble?"

"It's a long story."

"I wish I had time to hear it." She looked up at the gentle blue sky. "The principal hates long stories. I don't wish I were you."

"A pretty English teacher *shouldn't* wish she were me," I said.

"That's very kind. You know where you're going once you get inside?"

"Hopelessly lost."

She told me where the office was and how to get there. Then she wished me good luck before strolling off down the walkway for her midmorning constitutional, taking deep breaths of the summer day. Before she turned a corner and disappeared from my sight, she smiled over her shoulder. I watched her longer than I should have—watched the empty place she'd just vacated. She was about five foot five—too short for me. Too young for me, too, and as I thought those thoughts I wanted to smack myself on the side of the head.

I went inside and looked for the office.

The principal at St. Katherine's wasn't a nun. Father Arthur Laughlin was a squat, gruff sixtyish man, his clerical collar rubbing an angry rash on his neck from the heat. Habitually he'd stretch, wriggle his shoulders, and move his head around looking for comfort.

When he found out why I was visiting, his expression darkened; I was as welcome as a Seventh-day Adventist, and let he me know it. He had a perspiring upper lip like Nixon's, and his face was sunburned pink except for a white band across his forehead, which indicated he played a lot of summer golf. I imagined him hitting a bad slice, losing his temper altogether, going postal, swearing, and hurling his golf clubs into the water hazard. Then he'd seek forgiveness in the confession booth.

Father Laughlin read my business card, handling it with his fingertips as if it were an illegal betting slip. "We don't have police here very often," he said heavily.

"I'm not the police," I reminded him. "See on the card where it says 'Security'?"

"That doesn't mean much. There are young girls here—*children!* I can't allow someone like you to wander around the school, approaching adolescent girls and asking them embarrassing personal questions."

"I didn't plan on 'wandering around,' Father," I said. "I was hoping you, or some of the teachers, can help me." I briefly explained Earl Dacey's hobby.

He shook his head. "You'll find no help here. We don't know anything about movies being shot up children's dresses, and we don't *want* to know."

"If I were a principal, I'd want to know."

"That's why you're *not* a principal. We have no time for people like you."

"People like me?" I said, my cheeks warming. "You've referred to me that way twice in thirty seconds."

"Deal with it! I'm here to educate young women—and do God's work. I'm *not* doing your work, too."

"To help find this pervert?"

"That's not the work of priests—or nuns, either. I'm not interested."

"So you don't want *people like me* bothering your students, and you don't give a damn about this pervert."

"Don't curse at me," Father Laughlin scolded. "This is a house of God."

"The house of God is next door, in the church. This is just a school."

He sniffed. "For all I know, *you're* the one with the camera."

It felt like a sharp, shocking slap. Laughlin's turned-around collar kept me from returning the insult—but I steamed anyway. "Jumping to conclusions, Father?"

He shrugged. "If it walks like a duck and quacks like a duck . . ."

"Is that from the New Testament? Well, *you* don't quack like a duck," I said. "But you remind me of an ostrich—who buries his head in the sand, unaware his ass is exposed."

The priest almost jumped from his seat and drew himself up to his full height, about five foot six. His face reddened—especially his nose. Anyone could take one look and know *why* his nose turned that shade. "How dare you speak to me like that? How *dare* you?"

"Neither your job nor your collar makes you immune." I stood up too, yet another moment in my life I found myself delighted to be bigger and taller than the other guy. "I came here with goodwill, for help on a problem that might victimize girls from your school. So you're in a lousy mood, or maybe that lousy mood is actually one of your better days. But if I can't get the smallest bit of assistance from you, I'll have to call the bishop and see whether he's more amenable than you are."

His eyes narrowed to slits. "The bishop?"

"We're—well acquainted," I lied. I'd met the bishop of the Cleveland archdiocese *once*, we shook hands, and he'd forgotten me within seconds.

"Is that a threat? You have the nerve to threaten me?"

"No—but it's not a good idea to threaten *me*, either. I haven't been scared of priests since I was ten years old."

"Ah-ha!" he said, making a pistol out of his thumb and forefinger and pointing it at me. One doesn't hear "Ah-ha!" anymore. "A fallen-away Catholic. I thought as much."

"That's because I stopped being scared of priests," I said.

On my way out I didn't speak with any of the girls attending St. Katherine's, or Father Laughlin would have had me locked up before I could explain I wasn't a pedophile. I didn't know many

Lake County cops, either. How in hell did Father Laughlin keep his job as principal of a girls' school? He should have been focusing all that anger as an armed guard in a high-security prison. The day had been a total loss for me except that I spent a few minutes talking to Cisne Kelly. They were pleasant minutes, although it was unlikely there would be more. I headed westward on I-90, my stomach growling because I'd passed up lunch.

At home, I put on a pair of shorts and a T-shirt, slipped into a pair of flip-flops, and fixed a salad—a big bowl overflowing with green leaf lettuce, black olives, mushrooms, and green pepper strips, splashed with extra virgin olive oil and enhanced with shredded Asiago cheese—and ate in front of the TV, watching Channel 12 News. Vivian Truscott, the longtime anchorwoman, grew better looking with every passing year—and her delivery, especially on national stories, had grown more serious since I first watched her about twenty-five years earlier. I knew her personally from more than one case. Before she was a tall, blond, beautiful Cleveland news anchorperson, she'd been a tall, blond, beautiful Las Vegas call girl. Few local people know that about her—and they'll never hear a whisper of it from me.

My gaze strayed from the screen to the stack of DVDs, reminding me how frowzy the search for Earl Dacey had become. I didn't want to slug my way through the rest of the videos I hadn't watched yet; bikinis and thongs without faces to go with them bored me. But how could I tell Savannah about her precious boy without turning her ballistic with rage? She wouldn't believe Earl was a secret pervert—and she'd fire me on the spot.

That meant I'd have to fire K.O. Part of me wanted to get rid of him. But maybe I'd grown old and had worked too hard. Maybe it was time for me to train a bright young man to do what I've been doing for close to thirty years.

I dug his phone number out of my wallet and called him. He answered halfway through the second ring. "K.O. here. Hello, Mr. Jacovich."

"You knew it was me. You have caller ID?"

"Don't take it personally—I *did* answer when I knew it was you." He sounded defensive as hell.

"I don't take anything personally," I fibbed. "Anything to report?"

His sigh of impatience sounded like the beginning of a very sad Tchaikovsky symphony. "I thought you told me to write up my report and send it to you."

"I did."

"Bully for you," he said. "So read your fucking e-mail." It didn't exactly sound as if he slammed down the receiver—but it *was* an emphatic click.

CHAPTER FOUR

I called up Kevin O'Bannion's e-mail, a report that was long but interesting. I was pleasantly surprised at how well he wrote. The kid was far from predictable. I made myself comfortable with my laptop on the coffee table in front of me, and opened a beer. Back in the day I could drink six beers without batting an eye—but time catches up with one's drinking habits the way it catches up with everything else. I slipped on my reading glasses— I can hardly see the page without them—and began.

> Mr. Jacovich,
> I visited the Great Lakes Mall at about two this afternoon. (I'd have gone earlier but I stopped for lunch—the one you were supposed to buy Suzanne and me.) I brought my own camera—the one in my cell phone that I can use without anyone's noticing. I also brought a mini-tape recorder and a notebook. Hope that's okay—you didn't cover this stuff with me because it all happened pretty fast.
> When I got there the lunch crowd had split. The mall was crowded for a weekday, though—lots of teen agers. Some of the girls wore their school uniforms. I guess they're stuck in summer school and wear those outfits because they had to. What a bore! Summer is for fun, not homework. Some wore skirts or dresses of their own, usually even shorter than the school skirts. Some grown women wore short skirts, too.
> Here are a few pix of women of all ages wearing skirts

to the mall. Nobody noticed me taking pictures. I checked
the background people in the pix, too, but I didn't see any
pervert with a shopping bag.

K.O. had emailed me several photos. I recognized red plaid
skirts from St. Katherine and dark blue ones from St. Bonaventure. A few young women wore casual miniskirts, and one around
fifty years old sported a denim skirt with ragged fringe at the hem.
All the other females in the photos wore slacks, shorts, or jeans.

I was hoping to spot a guy with a shopping bag standing
too close to the girls, but didn't see any likely suspects.
I bought a root beer and sat in the food court looking for
anyone suspicious, but no sale. By the way, you said you'll
pick up all my expenses while I'm in the field; does the two
bucks for the root beer count, or do I pay for it out of my
own pocket?

Anyway, I checked out the stores. I went into Dillard's
to see the head of security there. He was more interested in
shoplifting than photographers of panties, so he didn't know
what I was talking about. Learning there were creeps roaming
around with camcorders shocked the crap out of him—maybe
now he'll pay better attention. I talked to two salesclerks
manning the cosmetics counters—can I say "manning" even
though they're both women? I showed them Earl Dacey's
photograph, but they didn't remember him. I didn't go into
Sears. I'm not that sharp about where young women shop,
but I don't think many of them check out make-up in Sears—
refrigerators or lawnmowers, maybe, but not lipsticks.

In Great Lakes Mall the head of security is Carol
Shepard—a few years older than me, with a nice rack and a
pixie haircut. Here's HER pic.

Carol Shepard wore a skirt, too—slim, black, and ending just
above the knee—proper but elegant looking. Her makeup could
have been carefully applied by a movie makeup artist. She apparently knew K.O. was snapping her picture, so she copped a
pose, one foot slightly in front of the other and a three-quarter

profile stance with breasts pushed forward, but she looked more annoyed about it than sexy.

She told me she's a Kent State grad—business entrepreneurship—with a three-point-nine grade average, and she acts like she owns most of Lake County—very stuck-up. But when I told her who I was looking for, she got serious. I think the whole subject made her nervous because she started biting her nails—strange habit for a grown woman, no? She didn't recognize Earl, but she said men hanging around leering at young girls was an almost daily occurrence—not always the same men, and not always young, either. She hasn't got much patience with older guys, so it's a good thing I talked with her instead of you.

I chose to ignore the dig in the ribs. I don't look like a nonagenarian quite yet, but I didn't look anywhere near as young as K.O. So let him make remarks; it's my money he spends on root beers. Yeah, I'm picking up that particular expense, too.

Shepard said three weeks ago a customer complained that some young guy was following her around standing too close, but when one of her employees, who looks like a sumo wrestler—his name is Leon—came to investigate, the suspected perv disappeared.

K.O. had actually taken a snapshot of Leon and e-mailed it to me. The guy was built like a Patton tanker—overweight, but mostly muscle. One look at him would discourage anyone from causing trouble in the mall.

She said she'd heard that some guys snapped pictures from their shopping bags—but she never caught anybody doing it. She's been head of security for less than a year. There aren't that many women, of any age, wearing short skirts or dresses in the wintertime because it's too damn cold. (That last is my opinion, not hers.)
Here are the two women working at the Macy's make-up

counter—Michelle Burton on the left, and Tamara Windfield.
I don't think either of them are too crazy about Shepard
because it grew icy when the three of them were together—
but what do I know? I'm too young to figure women
out. Burton said she might have seen Earl Dacey in the
department, but wasn't sure. She also said if it was him, she
never actually saw him do anything wrong.

Both clerks were women over forty. Michelle was African
American, tall and stunning. Tamara was short, slim, and blond.
I think K.O. went crazy with that camera phone, taking pictures
of everyone who'd stand still and pose, and a few who wouldn't.

I laid an idea on Carol Shepard, suggesting she set a trap
by sending a woman in a short skirt to spend some time at
the make-up counter. Her plant could spot the picture-taker
right away and have him arrested. Then word would spread,
so perverts would have to find some other place to take their
pictures. She didn't say yes or no. She's about as warm and
cuddly as a ball of ice cream that fell off the end of your cone
onto your lap. I think she's got lots of unresolved issues,
which makes her a 24/7 bitch. Wish I had time to figure her
out, but I don't—at least not as long as I work for you.
Making suggestions isn't my job, but it just popped into
my head—and sometimes things like that come out of my
mouth right away. Maybe it pissed her off. I hope you aren't
pissed off at me, too. Oh well, if you are, you are—there's
not much I can do about it.

K.O. had been my assistant for about an hour at that point and
had come up with an impressive idea that had never crossed my
mind. I jotted a note to mention it to him when next we talked.
Not praise, mind you—K.O. is not the kind of guy who takes well
to praise.

The nice thing for me about being a lowly intern is that
I'm not the one having to tell your client her son is a sicko
fuck. Glad that's your job, not mine.

Was it only a day ago that Savannah appeared in my office whining about a missing son? Was it only last night I'd watched his dirty videos for the first time, shocked I'd been hired to find a degenerate? Was it only this morning that K.O. shouldered his way into my business and my case, and already he was sending me long e-mails—with suggestions?

> Let me know what you want me to do tomorrow. I thought I'd check some other malls around town, not just Lake County. Earl Dacey lives on the near west side, so he must have visited lots of other malls and stores and places where young women hang out. Maybe he started where he didn't have to drive that far—or maybe the fancy ritzy one in Beachwood. We'll see,
> Respectfully submitted,
> K. O'Bannion ☺

I couldn't remember anyone else ever sending me a business e-mail and embellishing it with a smiley face—his form of sarcasm, fitting in perfectly with some of the other smart-ass remarks couched in his report, including "respectfully submitted." Where the hell did he think he was? In the U.S. Senate?

I read his report again, then clicked "Reply" to send an e-mail back to him.

> K.O.—You're good—people open up to you. Checking more high-end department stores in Cuyahoga County sounds right. Start with Beachwood Mall and then move west.
> By the way, most people call me by my first name. I assume Suzanne told you how to pronounce it correctly. If she didn't, ask her.
> Yes, I WILL reimburse your expenses. If you stop for a beer or a margarita, though, that's out of your pocket. Also, keep track of your miles driven. I'll pay you for eight hours work yesterday, including breakfast time at Jack's (and I paid for the breakfast, too) and the time you spent watching the videotapes.

I'm glad you got Carol Shepard thinking about things.
I liked your sarcasm—and don't think it all sailed over my
head. Just be sarcastic between the two of us and don't
aggravate other people who don't owe you a damn thing.

You have my cell number and my home and office
numbers; I have yours, too. But let's try not to bother each
other unless we absolutely have to.

Milan

It was after nine o'clock. Savannah Dacey worked as night
manager at the so-called family restaurant for another hour, so I
called her there. From the flirtatious sound of her voice when she
heard me, it was as if Gregory Peck had rung her up instead. That
made me think once again of how damn old I am. Gregory Peck
was the first sexy movie star I thought of—and he worked in films
before I was born.

"Savannah," I said, "I need to talk with you—tonight, if possible. Can we meet?"

She sucked in a fast breath as if I'd proposed something
naughty to her over the phone. "Of course, Milan—anything you
say—if you want to *talk* with me."

"How about your place at ten o'clock?"

"Why, Milan!" she giggled.

Big mistake—I knew it as soon as the words left my mouth.
I didn't want to be alone with Savannah in her own house in
the evening, especially now that she was giggling. Her flirting
didn't help; it got in my way. I corrected course—quickly. "Better
still, can we meet someplace for a drink, maybe near where you
work?"

That only slowed her down for a second. She picked a little bar
on Lorain Avenue, not far from the restaurant she managed, in
an area known as "West Cleveland." It's not a city of its own—just
a neighborhood, with a personality mostly working class. Beer
and cigarette smoke hung in the air all day and evening like a
fog in London, and for most male residents, getting all dressed
up consisted of putting on a clean shirt. There are lots of these
neighborhoods—Collinwood and Hough and Little Italy on the

East Side, and Tremont, Ohio City, and West Park on the West Side. But they're varied, with their own personalities, quirks, peculiarities and virtues—and they're all Cleveland.

I showered, ran a razor over my stubble, and put on khaki slacks and a dark purple polo shirt. I wasn't feeling the beer yet, but I brewed myself a cup of Lapsang souchong tea, extra strong, and drank it as hot as I could stand it, letting the caffeine help clear my mind.

I got to the saloon before Savannah. The place was tiny—a retail store in an earlier incarnation. Now it seated fewer than thirty customers at the bar or in booths under a barrage of psychedelic black lights and tinted spotlights. There were only eight drinkers there—all twentyish males. The music blasted Barry Manilow from the seventies. The waiter, wearing a tie-dyed undershirt, a gold earring, and curly permed hair that made him look like a Hollywood movie pirate, disdainfully told me they didn't carry Stroh's. I couldn't imagine why Savannah chose this place. I told him to bring me whatever was on tap, and when it arrived I took one sip and didn't have a clue as to what it was. I pushed the glass off to one side and waited for her.

She arrived late, almost exploding into the room, out of breath and ragged as if she'd kept me waiting an hour. When she saw me, her face lit up from within.

"I'm so glad you wanted to get together, Milan." Savannah leaned on the word *glad* as she installed herself across from me. She wore her work clothes—another peasant skirt, a nicer one, and a white button-up blouse, but she'd not utilized the top two buttons. "I enjoy being with you," she fluttered. "You look so good in that purple shirt—it's your color!"

She made me wish I'd worn a neutral color instead. She was a client, not a date—and not my type, anyway. I made my tone professional. "What would you like to drink?"

She cocked her head sideways, bending her wrist to put the tip of her index finger into her cheek, like Shirley Temple. "Um—how 'bout a rum and Coke?"

I called the waiter over; he contemplated us like exotic animals at a zoo, and flounced away.

"This is a cute place," Savannah said, her gaze pausing on every young man, all of whom were looking at us and wondering what we were doing in a bar they probably considered their nighttime living room. "I've never been in here before."

"I wouldn't imagine you had."

Her eyes opened very wide. "Why?"

"I think it's a gay bar."

She acted as if she'd never heard the expression. "A gay bar?"

"Yes. The young men in here are gay. Homosexual."

Her gasp was audible. "Oh, no! Oh, my goodness!"

"It's fine," I said.

"I don't think so." Her cuteness went into hiding, and her whisper was a rasp. "I don't trust them—those homos. They're child molesters, you know."

"They're nothing of the sort, and what they do in bed is none of your business. Besides, we won't be here that long."

The muscles in her face failed and she looked shattered. Her rum and Coke arrived and when the waiter scooted back behind the bar, I was relieved he didn't look to see the way Savannah glared at him.

"Well," she said, forcing a smile and clinking our drinks, "cheers, anyway."

I waited until she swallowed her first gulp. "We need to talk about Earl."

Now she was frightened she might hear something she didn't want to. "You found my son?"

"No. But I watched several of those videos I took from his room."

She licked her lips as though her mouth were dry. She sounded annoyed. "I'd think you'd be out looking for him instead of sitting around watching DVDs."

"Do you know what's on them?"

"How would I know? They're his DVDs, so I don't bother with them."

I described them, keeping it as brief as possible, not going into details.

"Oh, dear," she said. "Where on earth did he get those?"

"I think he took them himself—with the camcorder he keeps in that shopping bag."

"That's not true—couldn't be. Earl's not like that. He's always been a good boy."

"Maybe he's a good boy with a problem," I said. "He owns that camcorder and has the DVDs to prove it—numbered. He probably spent lots of time watching them."

"Oh, no—he didn't watch TV all that much. He spent his spare time playing around on his computer."

All at once I felt dumb. I'd been so busy watching tapes and interviewing the principals of Lake County Catholic schools, I hadn't even checked Earl's computer. "I can just imagine what he might store on his computer."

Savannah began pulling on the loose skin of her cheek. "Oh my God," she said. "Oh my *God!*" Her voice rose to a wail as tears welled out of her eyes and down her cheek, leaving a mascara trail behind them. Everyone looked at us again. I tried not glaring back, but I'm not nearly as cool as I'd like to be.

"I'm sorry," I said, squinting against the black lights, waiting for her to finish crying.

When she did—after snuffling and blowing her nose into a bar napkin that had been set under her drink—her first words were: "You goddamn traitor!"

"Me?"

"Digging up all this—this crap—about my son!"

"It'd be immoral to keep from you what I found out."

"Well, it's not your job anymore! You're fired—as of right now!" Savannah had gone from flirtatious to emotionally battered to mad as hell within the course of five minutes.

"I'll return all Earl's possessions and prorate my advance, if that's what you want. But anyone will discover the same thing I have—and Earl might be in more trouble than you'd imagine. It'd be best to let me find him as quickly as possible."

That took the anger right out of her. "Oh, God," she said again, only this time it was a whisper. "What kind of trouble?"

"I don't want to worry you unnecessarily. If Earl is taking pictures up women's dresses, it's a misdemeanor—but . . ."

"What are you saying to me, Milan?"

"There's more to be looked into, whether Earl stays missing or not. Give me three days. If I don't come up with anything I'll just back away—and return your money. It'll take you that long, or even longer, to find another private investigator and get him or her up to speed. What do you say?"

It took her almost three minutes before she answered me—she spent it chewing all the dead skin away from her left thumb until it was seeping blood. When we finally left the bar, she'd hardly touched her rum and coke. But we'd come to an understanding.

I'd come to an understanding too, all by myself—and I was going home to check into it further. It was going to be another long night.

Earl Dacey's laptop wasn't hard to get into, although it gave me more trouble than it might the average fourth grader. I don't like computers. By the time they took over the world, I was too old to figure out how to use them properly. But before my son, Milan Junior, went off to Chicago, he taught me some tricks. That was a few years ago and the tricks don't always work anymore because computers have gone even more high tech—but Earl's HP was several years old, too, so I was on relatively safe ground.

It took me ten minutes to figure out his password. I tried all the variations of his given name, such as "Early" or "earlytobed" or "brightandearly," and his last name, like "daceydoze." If you don't remember that song from your childhood—the one about Mairzy Does and Dozey Doze—I can't help you. I even attempted several versions of "upskirt" or "skirtup" or "sexythongs" but to no avail. Then I thought about Earl's home life, and how his mother adored him, and I started using her name. I tried "savannahmom" and "savannahmama" in all its variable spellings. Then I started getting creative, and after several attempts typed in "savannah-rama," then dropped the final "h," and added, as I was supposed to, a number to go with it. "Savannarama2" did the job, and I suddenly found myself staring at Earl Dacey's desktop page. Not many icons of interest there, but just one more click got me onto his Internet Explorer.

There were no sports scores, TV listings, local movie sched-ules, not even lottery results on his home page. Even people over-dosing on pornography occasionally look at a baseball game, go to a film, or blow a buck on lottery tickets, but apparently Earl didn't care about anything except women's underwear—while they were wearing it, of course.

It took me only a few seconds to find his bookmarks and check them out.

His "My Favorite Places" bookmark was a festival of soft-core porn. In the thumbnailed photos and videos there was no sexual activity per se, because all the women were alone; I got the feeling Earl Dacey preferred it that way. I'm sure many of the raunchier sites on the Net showed actual sex in action, and that must have bothered Earl, mainly because he wasn't *them*. Several sites were entitled with a play on the words *upskirt* or *panties*, a few more used *freaky* or *horny*, and almost all had the word *teens* somewhere. Most sites were similar to what I'd found on Earl's tapes. A few of his bookmarks featured women who knew their underwear was being photographed and smiled down enticingly at the camera. Some were not wearing underwear at all.

There were more sites featuring blogs and panels, mostly dealing with spanking, voyeuristic peeking, or the deliberate stripping and showing off of somebody's wife or girlfriend to other men. I had to shake my head to clear it. Mindless stuff like this keeps me reading books, watching TV, and staying off the Internet.

Then I found something on Earl's computer that shocked me more than anything else I'd seen. I looked at just enough of it to figure out what it was all about, and then closed the lid of the laptop.

It made me think of some of Earl's shots I'd already seen.

I made a phone call and set up a date for lunch the next day.

CHAPTER FIVE

Cleveland is always erecting something or other, but despite everyone's efforts, the landscape doesn't change much. They built the city's tallest building, the Key Tower, more than twenty years ago, and erected the baseball and basketball stadiums right next to each other in 1994, and since then there have been no downtown surprises. Cleveland State University erected huge letters, csu, near the top of its tallest building, and a few of the other mini-skyscrapers around Public Square changed their names along with their owners, but for the most part, Cleveland is comfortable and familiar, especially for a hometown native like me. It's why I feel a little catch in my throat whenever I look out at my city.

I was downtown at John Q's, a venerable restaurant on Public Square. Not only are the steaks terrific, but the place has a classic, mid-twentieth-century feel to it. The windows look across the square to the Terminal Tower and the Renaissance Hotel. No passersby who are really boring walk around on Public Square. They all either look busy and involved, or else homeless and wandering—or just having lunch, as I was, with an old acquaintance who might be the least boring person I've ever met.

He's not really *that* old—nearly the same age I am. I call him "acquaintance" because we don't hang out watching sports, we've never played cards, and it has never occurred to us to go on a double date, so we aren't exactly friends. We began as enemies—violent ones. The story is long and involved, but I wound up punching and breaking his nose, and he sent two of his employees to beat me senseless. Since then, our paths have crossed more times than I can remember, and our enmity has changed into something else. So I suppose we are more friends than we are anything else.

He is Victor Gaimari. I think of him as third runner-up in a Cesar Romero look-alike contest, for anyone who is old enough to recall Cesar Romero as the Latin Lover in 1940s movies. His hair had turned silver at the temples, but he still had all of his, damn him, while we Slovenian men fight a hopeless battle to keep ours.

When I first met Victor, his venerable uncle, Giancarlo D'Allessandro, was the Cleveland godfather, the *capo di tutti capi* of the Italian mob. While Victor spent much time in his stockbroker office juggling legitimate investments and the kind of mortgage brokering that helped drive our country into a recession toward the end of the Bush 43 years, he was The Outfit's second-in-command. The "second" part came from respect for the don; for all intents and purposes Victor made most of the decisions.

The Cleveland mafia was a criminal organization, but Don Giancarlo ran it with style, class, and wit, and would never touch anything like drugs, prostitution, or pornography. Even the violence originating from the local mob was so many steps down from the Capone or Lucky Luciano days in Chicago and New York that Cleveland hardly considered them cruel and uncaring bad men. Criminality is defined only by your own state of mind, and to me the don was decent and kind. I cared about him, and he was fond of me, too. In the "guy" sense of the term, I think we loved each other.

Last year, Mr. D'Allessandro died, and Victor quietly and efficiently took over. His methods and practices are more modern than the don's, but he never forgot his upbringing or all the things Giancarlo taught him.

When I arrived at John Q's, I saw that Victor was there already. He wore a lightweight summer suit in an unusual shade of medium blue that might have seemed bizarre on anyone else.

On him, it looked elegant. He always looked elegant—cool as ice, or perhaps a popsicle, because there was taste to his coolness. Cary Grant, Humphrey Bogart, Steve McQueen are always considered "cool," but they could never compete with a man like Victor Gaimari.

When I came in, he stood and embraced me, kissing me on the cheek. Very Italian—but truly cool, too, like a kiss from your maiden aunt who doesn't visit very often.

"You look well, Milan," he said as we took our seats. "Losing weight?"

"Not much," I said. "Maybe ten pounds or so—it fluctuates."

"Does that mean you're having a salad for lunch?"

I laughed. "That would be an insult to an Italian like you, Victor."

"As a matter of fact, I eat lots of salads—at home. When I'm in a restaurant, I have to maintain my gourmet standing with lasagna, gnocchi with meatballs, all those heart attacks on a plate." He flagged down the waitress and ordered a stinger, a cool cocktail for a summer day. I chose an iced tea.

"Stopped drinking?" he said when the drinks arrived.

"No—just rethinking it."

"We both have calendars and we pay attention to them, don't we?" He lifted his glass in a mock salute. "Those headaches you were getting last year—have they gone away?"

"Not away—just on vacation."

"Concussions can be dangerous if you're not careful."

"I'm being careful. That's why I wanted to tell you about my new case. It looked pretty simple, to start with, but it's gotten more complicated."

"You asked me to lunch because I might know something that'll help you."

I leaned back in my chair. "You know something about everything, Victor. But my story is a bit weird."

"Haunted houses? Things that go bump in the night?"

"No. Just—peculiar." And I told him all about Earl Dacey.

When I finished, Victor said, "So you're looking for a panty freak with a camcorder." He shook his head sadly. "You're usually more particular with whom you do business."

"I had no idea he was a pervert. His mother didn't know, either."

"Uh-huh. So you think all my friends are porn perverts?"

"Victor, I know your—people never messed with pornography."

"My uncle was firm about that. So am I."

"Who *is* into it, though?"

"At one time—thirty or forty years ago—almost all the pornography in the United States was controlled either in the San Fernando Valley in Los Angeles, or in Cleveland—and not by Italians, either. You remember the big man's name, right? Most Americans past forty know that name—because he grossed about four million dollars a *week*. But he's gone—and on the Internet you can find whatever obscenities you'd want." He shook his head sadly. "There's even a guy on the West Side who recruits young, good-looking men for gay porn and photographs them while they're taking a dump." He looked as if he'd taken a bite out of a stale egg. "I haven't seen those films, just heard about them."

I glanced around to ensure no one heard him. People were eating.

"That's the wonderful world of computers for you," Victor observed. "Porn was big business when they made movies like *Deep Throat*. Compared to today, that was no worse than Mary Poppins naked. I've seen dirty pictures before, but I didn't think there were that many exhibitionists in the world. Germany, Japan, Russia, the UK, and God knows where else, they're filming every possible kind of sex and exhibiting it for big money—but no one really knows who's doing what and with whom."

"There are a million pimps on the street—but I'm concerned about people who *take* dirty voyeur pictures and sell them on the Internet."

Victor frowned at me. "Is that your missing person?"

"He's actively making movies, so he might be selling to the big players, but I doubt it. Earl Dacey is a simple-minded letch without a clue."

Victor was pretending to peruse his menu. "I still don't know what you're asking of me."

I looked at the other diners in John Q and lowered my voice to

a near whisper. "Some of the pictures and videos on Earl's computer—and some of those he shot himself—are of minors."

Victor put down the menu. For all his womanizing and high-
profile lifestyle, he's at heart a conservative, almost priggish man.
"That's beyond dirty movies."

"All Earl's tapes are what they call upskirt—nothing hardcore,"
I said. "And you rarely see the faces of the people being taped, so
I can't be sure. But when I checked out sites on his laptop, I realized some of them involve adolescent—or even preadolescent—
girls."

"How can I help you?" he said carefully.

I took out my notebook and pushed it across the table. "Write
down the names of everyone in Northeast Ohio distributing porn.
I'm certain you know who they are."

"I know of people who might be involved in this sort of thing,
but they aren't buddies; I don't keep up with what they're doing at the moment." He sighed, pulling the notebook closer. "This
isn't my area."

He held the pen over the paper, hesitating, moving the point
back and forth, thinking about it. I remember my father doing
that; he wasn't much of a reader or writer, but always wiggled
his pen or pencil over the paper before he wrote anything. "The
names I give you," Victor said, "you never heard from me. Don't
mention me in the same breath as these—twisted people. I trea-
sure my reputation." He gritted his teeth and began writing.

As for me, I read my menu and decided what I wanted for
lunch.

I didn't give Victor's list a second glance until I got back to my
office. But while I was driving—it's not far at all, about five minutes in midday traffic—my cell phone chirped in my pocket. I
hadn't bothered programming it to announce an incoming call
with something like Beethoven's Fifth or "Yankee Doodle Dandy"
or some country-pop song by Miley Cyrus or Jessica Simpson. It
just rings.

I hate cell phones. Everybody in the civilized world seems to
carry a phone constantly, and to use it at the most discommodi-

ous times, almost always in public where everyone else can hear what they say. When someone breaks off talking to me face to face so they can answer their phone, I consider it the pinnacle of rudeness, and so I walk away and leave them there. These individuals seem to feel they must be connected to the whole world every moment of their lives—but I'm not one of them. My cell phone even takes photographs—but the only one I've ever snapped with it was by accident, making a portrait of my own left knee.

Once in my office, I listened to K.O.'s message. It was five words long: "I've got something. Call me."

His cell rang four times before he answered.

"I took your advice," he said. I could hear noise around him, as if he were in the middle of a crowd. "I've worked Beachwood Place all morning, showing Dacey's picture to employees here— and I found someone who recognizes him."

"Who's that?"

"Her name's Carli Wysocki. She's employed at one of the shops in the mall—where women come to buy makeup. I think you ought to talk to her." He put his hand over the mouthpiece and mumbled something, then said, "She's here working until six o'clock."

My watch said two forty. "I'm on my way."

The upscale Beachwood Place was the closest mall to my apartment, but I hadn't been there in a long time. I feel funny rubbing shoulders with well-dressed men and women, and even more sumptuously dressed teenagers, all running from store to store with a BlackBerry clutched in one hand and a platinum American Express card in the other. My roots are in the St. Clair-Superior corridor, with its neighborhood candy stores and coffee shops and an amazing bakery on St. Clair Avenue—now gone— just down the street from the Slovenian National Home, where they have fish suppers every Friday night. Back then I'd never heard of Nordstrom's—and Saks Fifth Avenue existed in faraway New York.

Kevin O'Bannion said Carli worked in a sprawling cosmetics store on the main floor. The two high-end chain restaurants— Maggiano's of Little Italy and McCormick & Schmick, a seafood house—framed the entrance to the mall, and the large cosmetics emporium was there on the left, almost in one's face. It seemed, like all of Beachwood Place, to target the young and wealthy.

I didn't need to look far for Carli Wysocki, because K.O. was near the cash register talking to her. He seemed unable to tear his eyes away from her. I couldn't blame him. Carli was around K.O.'s age, about five foot eight, with a willowy, sexy body and big, expressive, brown eyes. She wore a pretty pink blouse with a scoop neck and a just-above-the-knee denim skirt. It was apparent that K.O. was hopelessly enchanted, hanging on her every word and move, as if he'd be quizzed on a test later. I enjoyed looking at her too, but I couldn't fight a growing annoyance that my brand-new employee was easily distracted by beautiful women.

However, after I introduced myself to Carli, K.O. was all business.

"Carli recognized Earl's picture right away," K.O. said. "She says he was at Beachwood Place a lot."

I took out my notebook and looked at her. "Carli, when did you first see him?"

Her voice was young and melodic. "During the late spring, I noticed him on weekends—wandering around in the mall with a sort of pained look, carrying his beat-up shopping bag. He'd always slow down and peek through the window in here. When he finally came in, he said he was just looking."

"A man by himself in a cosmetics store—and 'just looking'? How long did he stay?"

"It varied. Sometimes he'd come in, look around, and leave right away. Other times he'd wander the aisles." Her eyebrows lifted. "I didn't really think about it at the time, but he seemed to stay when there were a lot of younger women wearing skirts or dresses. I didn't pay much attention. Then one Saturday, maybe after about three or four weekends—our eyes kind of met, and I smiled at him."

"She wasn't flirting," K.O. said defensively, "just being friendly with a customer."

Carli nodded. "The next day—a Sunday—he stopped and said hi. We talked a while."

"About anything in particular?"

She shook her head. "Not much. We exchanged first names, silly nothing-stuff."

"He had his shopping bag with him," K.O. put in. "Carli never saw him without it."

"Carli, I'm not trying to embarrass you, but—do you wear skirts all the time, the way you are now?"

Her blush turned her cheeks pink. It made her look adorable—and I could tell K.O. thought so, too. "I always wear skirts to work. It's more professional. Mostly in winter I wear tights, but when it gets warm . . ." Her blush deepened.

"So when Earl was standing here talking with you . . . ?"

"I think he always set his shopping bag on the floor when he was near any woman—including me." The smile had drifted from her eyes, leaving her looking royally pissed off. "That's when I caught him. I heard a noise from his bag, looked down and saw the camcorder, and told him to get the hell out of here and never come back."

"He left?"

"Scooted out of here like a scared rabbit," Carli answered. "I called mall security about him. I warned the girls at the makeup counters at Saks and Nordstrom's, too."

"But nobody caught him."

She shook her head. "They posted extra security guards up by the food court. But in the afternoon it's too crowded, with people waiting for Chick-fil-A or Chinese fast food—and in the morning nobody goes there except elderly people hanging out for three hours over a cup of coffee." She smiled sadly. "Most come by themselves to meet with others their age. I guess they've lost their spouses and are just lonesome for someone to talk to."

"So," I said, glancing out the store's doorway toward the up escalator that headed to the food court, "Earl never cruised up there."

"Not that I noticed," Carli said, cheeks pink again, "until I caught him poking his camera up *my* skirt."

"Don't worry," K.O. said—*very* sincerely—"we'll catch the little deviate."

"Not so little," Carli observed. "He was a big guy—tall and fat, with a bad complexion and lousy teeth."

"And he never came back?"

"He might have come back to the mall—maybe used a different entrance. But I never saw him after that." She sighed. "It's a damn good thing."

"Why?"

"Because I was ready to deck the son of a bitch where he stood," she said, meaning it. The profanity coming from that angel face made me grin.

"Carli," I said, "you've helped a lot."

"I just want to do what's right."

I turned to K.O. "Talk to the makeup counter women at Saks and Nordstrom's—and to the head of mall security. I'll e-mail you a few names to track down on the Internet. You can work from home."

"Yeah, okay," he said, but I sensed he was losing interest—in me, anyway. If Carli was quietly battling me for his attention, she was winning handily. And who was I to get in the way of young love, or at least lust? K.O. was doing good work on my case. The least I could do was help him out here.

"And K.O.—Carli has been so forthcoming with us, we should take her to dinner sometime, to show our appreciation. Uh—set it up between the two of you," I said. "I have to go somewhere else this afternoon."

The kid's face lit up like a pinball machine. I think it was the best gift of his lifetime.

Carli was a pretty young woman, and whatever conversation, flirtation, or heated looks passed between them before I got there had snared him inescapably in silken webs of fantasy.

Good for K.O. I wished them the best—that first rush of passion, the wonderment, the ups and downs of one another's foibles and eccentricities, the fights followed by passionate makeups, the comfort when they ratify what they have built together. All this romance and adventure and a life history, I thought, as I constructed in my head a future couple who had yet to do more than shake hands.

I did have somewhere else to go—to speak to the people Victor Gaimari had suggested, one of them not too far from where I was now, a five-minute drive to Chagrin Boulevard.

WACO Distributing was several blocks west of the Eton Collection, a sprawling shopping complex with several restaurants, high-priced shops, and the only Trader Joe's market on Greater Cleveland's East Side, where much of what they sold was healthy. I go to Trader Joe's more often than I used to—and I read food labels.

WACO was in a different sort of building, with none of the charm of its down-the-street neighbors. I elevatored to the third floor and walked into the small office—a front room with two doors, one to what I assumed was a larger office and one, slightly open, to a supply room with an IBM copy machine and desktop computers inside. The receptionist was not quite chunky but close to it, in her fifties, with a pencil stuck into her hair behind one ear. She was rummaging in the file cabinet when I entered, and she closed it quickly—let's be honest, she slammed it. Maybe I frightened her by not knocking first. But it *was* an office in a public building, and it had a sign on the door, so I had no problems marching in unannounced.

"Yes?" She was as welcoming as a hyena who'd stolen a fresh carcass from a pride of lions.

"I'm looking for Wade Applegate," I said.

She stood up straight. "You have an appointment? He doesn't see people without appointments. You'd have to call ahead of time."

"Is he in?"

For one millisecond her eyes flicked to the closed door, then back to me. "No."

I nodded and smiled. "You're fibbing."

"I am not."

"Are too," I said.

"Am *not*!"

I gave her a business card. "Please tell Mr. Applegate Victor Gaimari sent me."

The mere mention of Victor elicited a gasp. His name has that effect in Northeast Ohio. She turned, opened the inner door just wide enough for her to slide inside, and disappeared. I heard her voice, low and stressed, without understanding her words, nor those of the male who answered her. After some back and forth, she came out, flushed, and stepped aside so I could go in. She marched right in after me.

Wade Applegate, standing behind his secondhand desk with his fingertips tentatively touching his wide blotter—who in hell ever uses blotters anymore?—wore a short-sleeved rayon shirt, blue dress pants, and horn-rimmed spectacles woefully out of style. He looked more shaky than she did.

"What can I do for you?" he said, his high voice nervous.

I introduced myself. "I got your name from Victor Gaimari."

"Uh-huh," he said, trying to sound wise. "I see."

"You're a film distributor?"

He felt around behind him for the chair and then sank into it as if he feared he'd never get up again. "What's this about? I hardly know Mr. Gaimari."

"I'm looking for people who deal in the kinds of films you do."

"The kinds of films? I don't know what you mean."

"Don't yank my crank, Mr. Applegate. Porn—we're talking porn." I didn't give him the chance to deny it. "I'm not a cop and I'm not here to shut down your operation."

Applegate looked puzzled. "You mean you want to buy films?"

I didn't reply, but looked toward the woman. He said, "This is Mrs. Applegate. Anything you say to me, you can say in front of her."

There must be truth to the saying that people who stay married for many years begin resembling each other. The Applegates were close to the same age, height, and weight, and both displayed their tenseness in the same fashion. I said, "I *don't* want to buy films; I'm looking for information. Have you ever done business with a man named Earl Dacey?"

"Earl? I don't even *know* anyone named Earl. Rose, do we know an Earl?"

Rose shook her head. "I never met anybody named Earl in my whole life."

I showed them the photo of Earl in his pajamas, opening a Christmas present.

"Doesn't ring a bell," Applegate said, shaking his head. He

didn't have much spare hair, but the shake loosened a strand of comb-over that fell across his forehead. It was long and too wispy, rendering him ludicrous.

"He looks faggy," Rose said, disapproving. "Doesn't he look faggy, Wade?"

"Maybe." Then, to me: "Who is this guy, anyway?"

"He might be taking voyeuristic pictures and trying to peddle them to—uh—distributors."

"I don't *take* those kinds of pictures. Look around this office—does it look like an X-rated movie studio to you?"

"Nobody made dirty movies in Louie B. Mayer's office, either."

Rose looked puzzled. "*Whose* office?"

"Okay—you don't make movies," I said. "Whose do you distribute?"

Wade Applegate cleared his throat whether he had to or not, and flapped his elbows as if his pits were sweating. "What kinda pictures we talkin' about?"

"Upskirt shots." I waved Earl's photo in their direction. "Dacey wanders around malls taking pictures of women from a camera hidden in a shopping bag."

Rose wrinkled her nose. "Eeew! That's disgusting."

"I think he might be selling them," I said, "to people like you."

Her husband spread his hands in front of him, lips pursed. "That's not our thing—our business. We distribute straight porno—just two people having sex." He shrugged. "Sometimes three people."

"Three people?"

He nodded reassuringly. "Nothing really kinky."

"Just good clean fun?"

"Exactly," Rose said.

It would've taken me several days to respond. "Who in town makes kinky stuff?"

Applegate leaned back in his chair and made a steeple with his fingers, pretending to be a wise man. "This isn't that kind of town, Mister, uh . . ." He checked my business card again, then mispronounced my name with a hard *J.* "People are conservative here."

"This is Cleveland, not Vatican City. Who produces dirty movies locally?"

Applegate studied the wall behind me. "I get most of my shows from Southern California—Reseda, part of L.A., in the San Fernando Valley."

"That doesn't answer my question."

"I don't think there's anybody here in town—"

"Reuben Sturman made three hundred million bucks a year in the porn business, operating out of Cleveland," I snapped, "and it was an invitation for everyone else, like you, to stake a claim. I'm not trying to take you down—I just want to locate Earl Dacey."

"Like I said, we don't know him. What do you want with him anyway?"

"That's my business."

"You don't tell me your business but you want to hear mine. Is that how it goes?"

"That's how it goes."

"I don't have to tell you a damn thing."

"No, you don't. But you'll have a lot to tell the police after I talk to them—and the FBI and the IRS, too."

Applegate paled, thinking about the repercussions. He waved a hand at his surroundings. "Look at this craphole office. I'm no goddamn millionaire, I got nothing to say to the IRS—"

"Not about that new Mercedes parked downstairs—with the personalized license plate saying WACO?" I tried not to laugh. "I thought you were from Texas—but WACO stands for Wade Applegate Company, right?"

Rose took a few steps forward. "What do you want from us?"

"Names," I said.

"We won't put our necks on the line for you. Somebody could get hurt that way."

"I'm not out to hassle anyone, like I don't want to hassle you."

"It sounds like you are," Applegate said.

"I wanted your attention. You distribute porn films—to adult bookstores and to the Internet. You know where that stuff is produced right here in town."

"Nobody could nail me about that."

"Maybe not—but one phone call from me, and you'll spend six months ducking out of the way of all the spitballs thrown at you. So be smart. Come up with the legitimate names I need. If I get annoyed with you—well, you won't like me much."

"I don't like you now." He hesitated, his fingers crawling toward a ballpoint pen like a confused tarantula.

Rose finally screamed, "Give him what he wants, for crysakes! You want the Feds all over us?"

It made him start; for a millisecond his ass actually lost contact with his chair. I wondered if Rose made him jump like that often. My guess was yes.

"You never heard this from me," Wade said, almost stroking the notepad the way one might smooth out a pillowcase before making the bed. "Earl Dacey," he breathed. "That's some guy, Earl. Huh, Rose?"

Rose Applegate shook her head sadly, her shoulders slumped as if she were finally worn out by a tough day. "Some Earl," she sighed.

CHAPTER SIX

t six o'clock, most legitimate Cleveland businesses say goodnight and close their doors, but Diamond Photography was
open, lights cheerily burning, despite the still-bright July
sunshine, on the third floor of a sooty, sagging warehouse on Superior Avenue in the East Twenties. Then again, from what Rose
and Wade Applegate had told me, Diamond Photography was
hardly a legitimate business.

If you've never climbed stairs in one of those century-old ware-
houses, you have no idea how difficult it is to make your way to
the third floor. There was no carpeting on the staircase—beneath
my feet was cement. Each step was approximately three quarters
of an inch higher than most steps. So when I finally wound up
in a cavernous hallway with walls last painted when Eisenhower
was president, with a floor that dipped in the middle and might
collapse under my weight, I wheezed quietly, searching for a full
breath.

A venerable door bore a fake-brass nameplate announcing
DIAMOND PHOTOGRAPHY. I walked into a bare-looking room with
windows staring at the brick wall of the building next door. Despite the day's heat, it was chilly in there—the sun couldn't shine
through the grimy glass. On the walls were blown-up photographs of models, some displaying their underwear. There were
wedding portraits, too, and one of a bat mitzvah.

Two men lounged on a sofa that was older than I am. One,

balding and muscle-bound, was in his forties, and every inch of
his bare arms was tattooed, from his knuckles all the way up to
where his biceps disappeared beneath the sleeves of his Indians
T-shirt, images so close together that I couldn't identify any of
them. The color on his face was almost yellow, perhaps because
he smoked a suspicious-looking roll-your-own cigarette. He
drank Bud Light from the can, thumbing through a worn copy of
Cosmopolitan, the only magazine in the room.

The other man was wiry, in his mid-twenties and wearing
jeans and a bright red Hawaiian shirt with white plumeria flowers; one doesn't often see colorful Hawaiian shirts in Cleveland,
even in July. The half-inch-wide sideburns of his butch haircut
connected to a strange-looking goatee. If it were 1949, he'd be
cast as the villain in an Errol Flynn swordfight movie. In his lap,
he cradled a large movie camera while he diligently polished the
lens.

He didn't meet my eyes, almost didn't acknowledge I was
there except that his backbone straightened out. Not bothering
to cover his annoyance, he growled, "Yeah?"

"I'm here for Helene Diamond," I said.

"Uh-huh."

Pregnant pause.

"Is she in?"

He nodded. The guy with the tattooed arms nodded as well.

"I'd like to see her for a few minutes."

That seemed to cheese him off more. "About what?"

"That's my special secret," I said.

"Well, what *is* your special secret, grandpa? That you only had
to get up and piss twice last night? Whoop-de-doo! Standing O
for you."

I tried to keep looking pleasant, even though I itched to twist
his head like the lid on a jar of Smucker's strawberry jam. I'm
not a grandfather—even though I'm old enough to be one—and I
don't like the word being used instead of my name. Or sir.

Instead I said, "Does that excite you, sonny boy? Talking about
pissing?"

He moved the camera from his lap to the sofa between the two
of them, and laid the lens gently on the floor. He didn't stand,

though. Despite our age difference, I was eight inches taller than him, and could still render him unconscious without mussing my hair—and he knew it.

"I don't get excited talking to guys like you at all," he said.

"Maybe Helene Diamond might like it better."

"She's busy."

"I'll wait."

"She'll be busy all evening."

"I'll wait all evening, then."

"Does this look like the fucking waiting room at the train station?" the tattoo guy said.

"You hang around train stations a lot?" I said. "You must be older than you look."

He didn't seem anxious to stand up to me either. Tough-talking guys talk tough—it's a deliberate choice, like whether or not they put cream in their coffee. Call their bluff, and they invariably back down.

Unless they're packing heat, in which case they'll shoot you dead.

Tattoo Guy apparently wasn't carrying. He tried to outstare me—it didn't work—and then dropped his eyes and lowered his chin to carefully study whatever fascinated him about his feet.

"I changed my mind." I handed the bearded one my calling card. "I don't want to wait all evening. One of you hard-asses tell her she has a visitor."

He examined my card. "Security? That makes you a private eye, huh?"

"You catch on fast."

"I can't bother her when she's busy."

"Why not? Is she getting laid in there?"

That seemed to break the tension because Tattoo Guy actually laughed—one short little burst, but a laugh nonetheless. "She's the only one who doesn't," he said.

I said, "Everybody else gets laid in there?"

He crossed his arms in front of him and I found a large colorful bird living on his left bicep in a swirl of yellow-green palm trees. "I dunno. *I* do—when I get paid for it."

"You get paid to screw? You're a male whore?"

He tried not to let that bother him. "I'm an actor. In adult films."

"Ah," I said. "The leading man type."

The Beard Guy said, "His type is hung as big as an elephant—that's what type he is."

I raised a hand as if stopping an oncoming bus. "Too much information."

The Beard Guy rose reluctantly and sidled toward the inner door, then opened it and slipped inside. Tattoo Guy and I looked at each other.

"Full time, I'm a bartender," he said. "In Tremont."

"So this is your hobby—fucking on camera."

"Not a hobby—just a job. I don't mean it's not fun, making these films, because it is. But it's hard work. It's usually somebody I don't know until five minutes before we start—and a film crew is standing there watching, too. It creeps me out." He sighed. "I'm married; thank God I don't get into trouble at home because my wife knows all about it."

"Open-minded wife," I said.

"She's got an open pocket, too. I get anywhere from seven hundred to a grand for one of these sessions, and that goes right into her piggy bank."

"Good money."

"Not like it used to be," he said almost wistfully. "Back in the sixties and seventies there were guys in the adult film community, like John Holmes—y' know, Johnny Wadd—and Ron Jeremy, they made humongo bucks back then. That was before the Internet."

"Everything changes."

"Ain't *that* the truth? Are you here to bust everybody?"

"I just want to ask Ms. Diamond a few questions. Maybe I should ask you some, too."

"Knock yourself out."

I showed him Earl's photo. "Do you know this man?"

He shook his head. "No, he doesn't come in my bar in his jammies. Friend of yours?"

"Sure," I said. "We have pajama parties all the time."

The Beard Guy reentered and beckoned me. "She'll see you for a minute."

"You're too kind," I said.

Helene Diamond was in her fifties, tall and thin with blond hair, wearing slacks and a black blouse. Later, FBI Agent Kitzberger would show me her photograph, and I'd think back to this moment. Behind her a younger woman, in jeans and a billowing top, with thick glasses and brown hair pulled back in a messy ponytail, didn't even look at me when I came in. She was making up a couch set against some painted scenery flats made to look like a bedroom, and fluffing gigantic decorator pillows.

"Ms. Diamond," I said, "I'm Milan Jacovich."

Half her mouth smiled at the business card she held. "I was trying to decide how to pronounce that. I suppose you aren't here to arrest anyone."

"I would if I could," I said easily.

"What I do is legal. Adult movies. I have a business license around here somewhere."

"I don't care," I said. "Setting up for filming this evening?"

"You can watch if you want. Free entertainment."

"And miss Jay Leno? No, thanks. I hope you'll look at a photo for me. Then I'll be out of your way."

"Why not?" She extended her hand for Earl's picture. She looked at it for a while. "Yeah. His name is Earl, I think. Is that it? Earl? I don't remember his last name."

"Dacey."

"Earl Dacey. Okay." She returned the photo to me. "He was in here maybe three weeks ago, trying to peddle his panty shots. I told him no. I shoot porn, Mr. Jacovich, of people actually having sex and not faking it. This isn't MGM, but my shows are professional looking, and the women are all attractive—men, too, depending on your taste."

"I've met tonight's leading man—with the tattoos."

"Larry," she said. "I use him often. He's no George Clooney, but he's inventive and always interesting to watch. The other guy, he's my cinematographer."

I glanced at the girl with the ponytail. "Is this your leading lady?"

"Jesus Christ, no! That's my daughter, Ruth. She sets things up, and does the lighting. It's a creative artistic job."

Ruth looked up at me and nodded as she worked, proud of her creativity.

"This is like any other business," Helene said. "If you worked at WalMart or the airport or some insurance company, you'd do what you hate—and get paid a fraction of what you can make in the adult film world. All people screw—at least I hope they do, for their sakes—so why not profit from it?"

"Is Earl Dacey trying to go into business too?"

"I think he just wanted to sell upskirt shots and make a few bucks."

"And you weren't interested?"

"He showed me a DVD—said he had eight more. But what would I need them for?"

"You tell me," I said.

"Well, if you're an underwear freak, go stand under a balcony in one of the malls, or watch a woman in a short skirt going up the stairs—it's the same thing. Call it soft-core or call it dishwater-dull—but people surfing the Internet with one hand inside their pants want something raunchier than a girl whose face you can't see wearing bikinis or thongs." She shook her head sadly. "My guess is Earl Whatsisname gets a thrill out of shooting pictures, but that's it as far as I'm concerned."

"You just make the films, then. You don't distribute them."

"Distribution is *big* money, and the distributors are heavyweights. A lot is international. I just run a small business and let the rich guys throw me a dollar or two."

"Like WACO?"

"Waco, Texas?"

"Wade Applegate—and his lovely wife, Rose."

Ruth Diamond snorted back a laugh. Her mother said, "Applegate is hanging on by his fingernails. He's on the bottom rung—like me. I've done business with him, but most distributors aren't interested in old-fashioned fuck shows like I shoot. Interracial, gay, lesbian—that hardly raises an eyebrow. They want stuff off the beaten track. Now they like what looks like incest, even if it's not. Phony forced sex, granny sex—"

"Granny sex?"

Helene winked at me. "You hear about cougars these days, but perverts, when they say 'granny,' they mean *really* old ladies. In their seventies or eighties, women who really do look like your grandmother."

"God," I said.

"Piss and poop movies are old and tired because everybody's seen them," she continued, leaving me feeling obtuse because I'm not just *everybody*, "but fat sex, with women or men who are actually morbidly obese, still sells like crazy. And sex with midgets."

"They don't like being called midgets," I said, "they prefer 'little people.'"

"If they get paid three large for a shoot, you can call them the Munchkins if you want. But that's fairly mild. There's also films of girls giving up their virginity on camera, or fucking when they're on their period. Then there's animal sex—what they call zoo sex."

"Animals having sex?"

"Animals having sex with *people*. Amazingly popular on the Internet. I've heard of weirder stuff or stone cold illegal stuff, but frankly I've never seen any—and don't want to."

I knew better than that, sadly—I'd broken open a case involving snuff films several years ago and I still got nightmares about it—but I didn't mention it to Helene Diamond.

"Some girls on Earl Dacey's DVDs might be underage."

She glowered. "I don't mess with anybody younger than eighteen—and I wouldn't allow a virgin into this place even if she *paid* to get in. I'm a moviemaker, not crazy."

Ruth brought a vacuum cleaner from behind one of the flats, plugged it into the wall, and started sucking up dirt and dust from the floor so her mother had to raise her voice for her next question. "Why are you asking about Earl? Does he owe you money?"

"He's disappeared—and his mother hired me to find him."

That got her frowning. She waved at Ruth to turn off the machine so we could hear each other. "Like I said, I only met him one time, we talked for ten minutes, and I turned him down—politely. He's a half-baked kid trying to push his way into a gazillion-dollar business, and maybe some people didn't like the idea."

"What people?"

Ms. Diamond raised her eyebrows and offered a little moue.

"Probably no one I know—but then I don't know a hell of a lot of people."

The evening summer sun hovered low and bright, glaring right into my westbound eyes as I drove back to my office. I had notes to make and thoughts to think, and I couldn't do that at home watching a Tribe game on TV to cap off a long day running all over the Cleveland area talking to people who, for the most part, didn't want to talk to me.

Before I'd left Helene Diamond's studio a young and sort-of-pretty woman with russet hair hanging down past her waist came in, greeted Helene and Ruth—even giving Helene a friendly hug—and then introduced herself to her tattooed soon-to-be co-star, the camera operator with the beard, and me. I guess she thought I was part of the film crew. She wore dark blue shorts and a Kent State University T-shirt, and carried a garment bag. I didn't catch her name, but she looked more like a biology major than a porn star.

In my office, I booted up my computer and checked my e-mail. Does anyone bother with e-mail anymore? Most of what I get is junk, and I delete it automatically. How in hell anyone gets the idea that I want to angrily write my senators twice a week, hook up with a romantic stranger on SpankMe.dot.com, enlarge my penis, enhance my breasts (maybe they think "Milan" is a woman's name), or lower my car insurance premiums, I don't know.

There were a few personal notes in my in-box, one from my son, Milan Junior, in Chicago. He'd been to a Cubs game the day before and observed that Wrigley Field has tremendous personality to it.

"I'm not going to change my spots and become a Cub fan at this stage of my life," he wrote. "But I can't remember enjoying a ball game so much as I did at Wrigley, in spite of the terrible-tasting hot dogs and undrinkable beer. The Cubbies have much in common with the Tribe, including an even longer failure at winning a World Series. Maybe I should have moved to the Bronx and cheered for the Yankees. (Just kidding.)"

I smiled at his message. Milan Junior had always been moody and dark like his mother, while my younger son, Stephen, was more like me, blond, blue-eyed, and easygoing—but both loved the Indians and the Browns, no matter where they lived. I'd raised them right after all.

Then I clicked onto K.O.'s message of the day.

> Glad you got to Beachwood Place so fast to find out Earl hung around there. Carli said lots of teenage girls who came into her shop didn't know he was taking sneaky videos up their skirts but they all felt he was weird. One of these days you have to tell me more about him and why his mother's looking for him in the first place.
>
> I didn't hang around Beachwood Mall after you left. I dropped into that small shopping center right next to it—La Place, is it?—but most of the customers were middle-aged, so there weren't many right 'subjects' for Earl.
>
> Then I went into Target, on top of that University Place Center. It's a big store. Half the merchandise is upstairs on another level—there's a long, steep escalator, but Earl wouldn't be standing at the bottom with his camera because not many young girls go up there; it's the men's department along with home decor and electronics. Women who go to Target don't wear miniskirts too often—it's super-casual, like a grocery store. The women's clothes are downstairs, along with jewelry, make-up, greeting cards, and things like soap and detergent and vitamins and cleaning stuff.
>
> There's so many people working here, I didn't know where to start. They all wear red shirts. I talked to one assistant manager, Jamal Pinkard. When he saw the photograph he said Earl had been in several times with his shopping bag, but he hadn't been caught taking upskirt shots—or buying a damn thing at Target, either.

Jamal's photo, snapped on K.O.'s cell phone and included in his e-mail, was of a young man, somewhere in his mid-twenties. The expression on his face was slightly amused.

Hey, BTW, thanks for setting up a dinner date with Carli. I can't remember the last time I saw any girl that pretty. Don't know where it's going—she'll probably think I'm a pain in the ass—and I might think she's one, too. But you gotta try, if you catch my drift.

So what should I do tomorrow? Hang around more malls and interview more clerks? I hope you think of something that'll keep my interest—besides Carli, I mean. Don't worry, she won't distract me. Nothing distracted me in Afghanistan, so nothing will in Cleveland.

Waiting to hear from you.

K.O.

This time he didn't add "respectfully submitted"—*or* a smiley face. Good choice.

I hit "Reply" and e-mailed him the names Victor Gaimari had supplied for me—people in Greater Cleveland that were in one way or another connected to the pornography industry.

"Get in and talk to them if you can," I typed. "If any of them react positively, follow it up and find out if they've seen Earl recently or might know where he is. Don't act judgmental even if you feel that way; we're not trying to shut down porno, just to find a missing guy."

Then I told him to have a good day and clicked "Send." I moved his e-mail, as I had the last one, to the K.O. file I'd already created.

Maybe taking on an assistant was as good an idea as Suzanne thought. Kevin O'Bannion was bright, efficient, and prompt. Not the cheeriest guy in the world—but he wouldn't be in the office with me that much, anyway. I pondered that as I watched the departing sun turn orange.

I was within seconds of locking up and heading home—it was almost eight o'clock—when the phone rang. I was tempted to let the voice mail get it, but I'm too curious for my own good. I lifted the receiver and told the caller they'd reached Milan Securities.

"Gosh, it's actually you," a female voice said.

"My vast staff of secretaries and assistants has momentarily stepped out," I said, "so I have to answer my own phone."

"I thought you'd gone home already."

"I am home," I said. "This is on tape. May I politely ask who the hell this is?"

The laugh was hearty, sincere, real. "Of course you wouldn't know. It's Cisne Kelly—from St. Katherine's, remember?"

Cisne, which rhymes with Disney. Cisne, the swan. Cisne, the lovely blue-eyed English teacher who was too short and too young for me. *That* Cisne.

"I guess you and Father Laughlin got off to a bad start."

"Did he confide that in you, Cisne?"

"No, he hardly speaks to me at all except to bawl me out. But he complained about you to other people—mostly nuns—and word gets around."

"So if I come back to St. Katherine's I'll be shot on sight?"

"No," she giggled, "but he'll assign you contrition that'll knock your socks off." Then she got serious. "I asked around—just on the Q.T., so Father wouldn't find out—and I did some blogging. Finally I chatted with a St. Kat girl who can tell you all about the guy you're looking for. You should talk with her yourself to make sure."

"I'd be happy to—but probably not where Father Laughlin can see me."

"God, *no*! Can we meet someplace after school lets out tomorrow? I hate your having to drag all the way back out here to Lake County, but . . ."

That was no problem. We decided to meet for coffee or something at Barnes and Noble on Mentor Avenue. Their café serves excellent, full-bodied Seattle's Best coffee, which I enjoyed before I kicked the coffee habit. Now I'm on green tea. It's good for my heart, my doctor tells me, but it blows the hell out of my tough-guy image.

We talked for as long as possible before we said goodbye. Then, checking my watch one last time, I rang up Savannah Dacey at work.

I guess she stayed up front near the cash register because she answered the phone herself. When she heard my voice, hers grew cold; our one-sided flirtation was over.

"Why haven't you found Earl yet?" she demanded.

"Did you think I'd find him in twenty-four hours?"

She sounded forlorn. "I hoped so."

"I'm pretty good—but I can't work miracles."

"Yeah," she said, "but now you think he's a sicko you don't want nothing to do with."

"It's my job to find him. When I do, his . . . problems . . . are *your* job—your decision."

She sighed mournfully. "Why is it my job?"

"You're the mom. Your children are always your job, even when they get to be forty or fifty years old."

"Then keep looking—and when he comes home, I'll do whatever I have to."

Whatever she had to. I kept my hand on the receiver after I'd hung up, thinking about whatever she'd have to do. My guess would be: nothing. In Savannah's mind, Earl was "a good boy"—and he hadn't hurt anyone. Apparently he'd tried to score a few bucks peddling his videography—but that made me wonder if he really wore the deviate label I'd tagged him with, or if he was just an aggressive entrepreneur.

I thought it over as I drove back to my apartment. At one intersection I stopped for the red light—I'm a law-abiding citizen, naturally. The car next to me, in the left lane, was very slowly creeping out, over the crosswalk, into the intersection, as if the driver was in too much of a hurry to wait for the light to change. Finally the light turned green and we moved ahead—yet the driver next to me didn't zoom off. He actually paused for a beat or two before stepping on the gas pedal and continuing slowly down the street—to the next red light, five blocks away. And damned if he didn't do the exact same thing again, inching slowly into the intersection and then taking his own sweet time. It was a textbook example of that strange local driving habit I've heard people refer to as "the Cleveland Creep."

Which reminded me of Earl Dacey—a creep himself with an unfortunate yen for young girls' underwear.

But was he truly a creep—or a tortured soul? There are as many sexual kinks and perversions as there are people, but this is rarely admitted out loud. Earl was no rapist, no Peeping Tom, no fondler, no pedophile, and he didn't grope women or children without permission. Compared to many, his voyeuristic predilection for videotaping girls' panties was relatively mild. Most would want to stop him as much as I did, but I could think of no one that would cause him to vanish because of it.

Then why had a silly, slightly backward fetishist disappeared without a trace?

I hadn't given much thought to the address book that I'd taken from Earl's bedroom on my search of Savannah's home. There were only six names and numbers in it; most people with only six friends don't even *have* address books. At home, I cracked open a Stroh's, sat down, and checked out the entries.

Only one page, the one marked *M*, had two names. The first, naturally, was "Mom," followed by the phone number of the restaurant where she worked. The other I had trouble sounding out phonetically, even with my Slavic roots; the surname contained eight letters, and six of them were consonants: "Stanley Majkrzak," with his phone number and an address in Lakewood. I'd get in touch with him the next day, assuming the pronunciation would sound something like "*Mak*-ra-zak."

Helene Diamond was listed, but I'd already talked to her; she had little or nothing to do with Earl beyond the "business" that never happened. Anna Barna was on the *B* page, with an address near the Daceys in West Park. Penned in as a *T* was John Tyler. I wondered if he were distantly related to one of our more obscure U.S. presidents—the only president ever to die outside the United States, because he did so in Virginia during the Confederacy, which made Virginia not a part of our country at the time. This one lived in Shaker Heights, definitely within our national boundaries and about ten minutes from Cleveland Heights.

The only other name inscribed in Earl's address book was Stuart Eisen. No address, just a phone number with a 330 prefix, putting him in Summit County, to the south.

My investigation of Earl's address book was already pared down by a third; I'd interviewed Helene Diamond, and of course "Mom" was already my client. That left me with only four names to contact—but they'd just have to wait until tomorrow.

CHAPTER SEVEN

I f so inclined, one can almost throw a small stone from Lakewood, Cleveland's closest western suburb, to the heart of Public Square. Its border begins on West 117th Street, but unless you looked for the dividing line, you wouldn't know the difference.

Stanley Majkrzak lived south of Detroit Road and north of Madison on the third floor of a rough-hewn gray stone apartment building with a view of a similar building right across the street. He was pleasant when I'd called—he'd just said a curious "Oh?" and didn't even ask what I wanted. When I showed up around noon, I was surprised he was more than a decade older than me— and forty years older than Earl Dacey. He had a nearly full head of white hair, though—and as a Slovenian with a follicle problem, I was jealous of that.

"Welcome to my house, sir. You're the first honest-to-God private eye I ever shook hands with."

His welcoming grip was firm and vigorous. We settled into the floral-upholstered furniture that made his living room look too busy and crowded, and he screwed up his mouth when I mentioned Earl's name—less from dislike than from discomfort. "I haven't heard from Earl for two weeks," he said. "But we've never been everyday friends. Just every-so-often friends."

"His mother hasn't heard from him either. She hired me to find him."

"Savannah?" He clucked his tongue. "That's gotta be hard on her."

There was only one bedroom in his apartment, and he'd closed that door before I arrived so I couldn't see whether he'd made his bed that morning. Single men rarely do until they get older, and then their own conscience shames them into it. I started making mine about five years ago.

In one corner was a wall-mounted crucifix. The kitchen, open at one end of the living room, looked as if he'd wiped down the counters, but his unwashed cereal bowl, a plate with toast crumbs, and his coffee mug were in the sink. Stale tobacco odor hung in the air, a rancid smell you never get rid of. I had noticed cigarette smoke more since I quit smoking myself—and hated it because I'd puffed away more than forty years.

"What kind of every-so-often friends are you and Earl, Mr. Majkrzak?"

His wide grin exposed several empty spaces where his teeth used to be. "Pretty good job with the pronunciation," he said. "But let's make it easy—call me Stan." He licked his lips, ready to talk. "I struck up a flirtation with his mom a while back—in Heinen's supermarket, by the produce department. I lost my good lady almost twenty years ago, so I'm always lookin' around—but I'm too old for her, for Savannah." The thought made him wince. "I'm too old for everybody. Still, I got to know her and her son. Now he calls me every few weeks, an' he comes over and sits—it's nice to have the company since I retired. We talk, mostly about sports, but he's a major Tribe fan and I'm more into football. We have a coffee, some pound cake or cookies." He chuckled. "He loves sweets too much—sneaks a spoonful of sugar when nobody's watchin'. He should lose weight, take care of his complexion, an' brush his teeth regular. Otherwise he's a nice young fella."

"What did you retire from, Stan?"

"Plumbing—but that was later in my life. I started out with the old *Cleveland Press* until it shut down."

"Maintenance?"

"No, a real live newspaperman, 'cuz I had a little bit of talent. I was a news photographer."

"That must have been exciting."

"Sometimes. I got about a million pictures I took, even ones they never used in the paper." He thought for a moment. "Earl calls himself an out-of-work photographer, too."

I tiptoed, hoping Stan would tell me something I'd want to hear. "Has he shared his photography with you?"

"He did. He'd bring his pics over and I'd point out what was good and what wasn't."

"What kind of pictures?"

Stan flapped his hands aimlessly. "Mostly of strangers on the street—some okay looking, and some others not. I tell you one thing, though—they were unposed, like people didn't know he was taking their picture."

"Voyeur pictures?"

He paused, grimaced, cleared his throat one too many times— maneuvers designed to give him time not to answer. Finally he said, "Some."

"Did you see his videos—the ones of women's underwear he took when they didn't know it?"

Majkrzak wriggled uneasily in his chair. "I don't wanna get into that right now."

"Stan," I said as gently as I could, "I've seen them already."

He rubbed a leathery hand over his face. "Aw, jeez . . ."

"Does he bring over those tapes to show you, Stan? The up-skirt stuff?"

"He brought some still pictures like that—and once he came over with one of his tapes—but I wasn't interested."

"You weren't?"

He raised his voice. "I'm seventy-four years old, f'crysakes, a *course* I'm not interested. Damn it, I was embarrassed looking at that."

"Was Earl trying to sell it somewhere?"

He shrugged. "Don't know to who. He didn' name names." The corners of his mouth drooped. "They oughta keep old farts like me from knowing about those things—young kids photograph-ing young girls' underpants. Sickening—like all the crap about that golfer, whatsisname, the colored guy. Best golfer ever. Why should I give a damn how many ladies he tapped while his pretty wife waited at home for him? Got sick a that couple who crashed a dinner party at the White House, got sick a the people with the eight kids who got divorced on their own reality show, got sick a that actress into booze and drugs and dykes who gets tossed in the slammer alla time. I even got sick a hearing about LeBron James!

"Well, that's how I felt about Earl an' his pictures—sick! A man my age don't wanna hear all that crap." He shook his finger at me like a scolding grandma. "Wait'll you start noticing all this crap in your life—it'll make you sick to your stomach." Then he laid upon me the worst prophecy of all. "Whether you like it or not," he said.

I couldn't remember a time in my life when things happened to me "whether I liked it or not." Even when I was military police in Vietnam, I handled myself and my surroundings. My marriage to Lila spun out of control because I was dumb enough not to know she was leaving my bed to visit Joe Bradac's. Later, after I quit being married, decided against being a cop, and chose the profession that's brought me close to disaster more times than I can count, I was still able to take charge.

Now Stanley Majkrzak's warning made me think about my future. I tried believing I had another thirty-five years, until I was in my nineties, but I'd been doing that for a while, making myself happy—ever since I escaped my own personal end-of-days after getting involved in a murder at my fortieth high school reunion.

So I'm getting old—and there's not a damn thing to do about that. Everyone is.

I walked into Barnes and Noble in Mentor just after three. It's not in the mall proper, but built on the same large parcel of land in a stand-alone store. Bookshops aren't that crowded in summer; people find little time for pleasure reading. I go through about fifty books a year—but that's just me.

As good as the coffee smelled in the café, I ordered an innocuous green tea and sat at a table to wait. Everyone around me either talked on their cell phones, texted, or worked on their computers, which made me wonder what they were doing in a bookstore in the first place. Then again, I hadn't come in there to read, either.

I was halfway through the tea when Cisne Kelly came in, escorting a St. Katherine senior wearing her typical school outfit. The girl hadn't yet turned down the waistband to raise her skirt a few inches as she probably did every day after school, and she seemed awkward covering up her shapely legs instead of proudly showing them off. She was pretty, but there was an arrogant, snotty protective bubble around her—one of the clique leaders at school, the one all the boys letched after in their hearts. I'd bet she was the biggest, meanest bully to girls who were less good-looking, or from families less rich than hers. Before she even opened her mouth, she made me glad I'd fathered two sons.

I only looked at her for a moment, because Cisne Kelly got most of my attention. I stood up clumsily and shook her hand.

"Nice to see you again," she said. "Mr. Jacovich, this is Carolyn Alexander."

"Hey," Carolyn mumbled. Our eyes met for a millisecond before she turned her face away. I was too old for her to acknowledge, ancient enough to be her grandfather, and nowhere near where she set her standard for "cute." I was neither important nor a millionaire, and thus a time waster. She stretched her neck, looking all around Barnes and Noble in case anyone there was more interesting.

"Can I get either of you some coffee?" I asked, hoping to put her at ease.

"Iced tea for me, please," Cisne said. Carolyn didn't respond. She had no interest in coffee because Daddy could buy the whole store if she wanted him to.

Ordering at the counter, out of the corner of my eye I saw Cisne raising hell with Carolyn about her manners, and when I returned to the table the young girl at least tried to be civil.

"After we spoke," Cisne began, "I started questioning some St. Kat girls I know pretty well—the seniors. When I talked to Carolyn here—well, let her tell you."

The put-upon Carolyn sighed. "Bummer in the summer. Okay, so I was in Macy's after school with some girlfriends, trying on blush in the cosmetics department. God forbid Father Laughlin or the nuns find out, but that's what I was doing."

I took out my notebook. "Who are your girlfriends, Carolyn?"

"Um." She had to think about it. "Lourdes D'Anjou and Kristen Mallory. We hang out all the time."

I jotted down the names.

"So anyways—"

"Anyway," Cisne corrected her.

Carolyn's annoyed eyes rolled heavenward. "Any *way*," she emphasized, "this geeky guy with terminal acne was standing right next to me—too close—with an old shopping bag on the floor between us. I mean, nobody's supposed to invade your personal space like that. So I go, 'What's your problem, pal?' and he goes, 'Just looking,' and kind of turns away from me like he was shopping for some blush. That's when I glance down and see this camcorder sticking its nose out of the shopping bag with the red light on, which means he was taping right up my skirt, which really pi—, um, ticked me off! I mean, it's not like I wasn't wearing panties or anything, because I was, but it got me mad. So I give the shopping bag a big kick and knock it over, and I go, 'You better get out of here before I get the cops after you, you fu—, um, you dirty pervo.'" She flushed pink, having nearly used two vulgar words in front of grown-ups.

"Did he videotape your friends, too?"

"I don't think so—I caught him too quick." She glanced at her English teacher. " . . . -*ly*. Quick-*ly*. And he grabbed his shopping bag and split, fast."

"You told Lourdes and Kristen about it?"

Carolyn nodded. "Yeah. It was kinda embarrassing, but we laughed anyway—at him."

"Did you tell anyone else?"

"Not until Miss Kelly asked me yesterday. And oh yeah—my boyfriend was there too."

"Who's your boyfriend?"

"Shane," she said, irritated; *everybody*, she thought, knew Shane. The only Shane *I'd* ever heard of was a titular Alan Ladd role in a cowboy movie. Pretty good western, too.

I wrote *Shane* in my notebook. "What's his last name?"

"Ward. Shane Ward." She'd probably scribbled "Carolyn Ward," or "Carolyn Alexander Ward" or "Mrs. Shane Ward" a thousand times in her notebook. "He goes to Mac."

"Mac?" I thought that was a computer.

Cisne said quickly, "Immaculate Conception High School for boys. He's the quarterback—and plays third base and bats cleanup for the baseball team. Athletic and talented. His widowed father is the biggest contractor in Lake County—and *very* politically connected."

"Shane'll be a big man some day," Carolyn said, her eyes alive for the first time. "He was so furious at the guy videotaping my panties, he chased him clear out into the parking lot." She flapped her eyelids dreamily. "Shane gets so jealous. Of course he didn't know what was going on until I told him, so he got there too late. That weirdo was just driving away."

"But you didn't know his name?"

"The camera guy? Nuh-uh. He probably doesn't even live in Lake County."

"How would you know that?"

"I just *know*." She rested her chin in her hand, which was propped up on the table. She was running out of answers and it made her cranky. "You don't do stuff like that in your own neighborhood."

I slipped Earl Dacey's photograph from my pocket and pushed it across the table at her. "Is this the one with the camera, Carolyn?"

She looked at him, her face screwed up in disgust. "Yes! That's him! In his bare feet and his *pajamas*, too. Eeeewww!"

There are many words and phrases in the dictionary that have no roots in foreign languages and are made up, usually by kids— like "bling," and "hooking up." But when I was a kid, I never made a sound remotely like "Eeeewww." Still, I've been hearing it for almost four decades.

I gave Carolyn my business card, suggesting she contact me if she thought of anything else. She mumbled "whatever" and stuck it in her tiny purse. I was certain she'd throw it away before the sun went down. I watched as she sashayed out the door. I said to Cisne, "Didn't she come here in your car?"

"Yes, but Shane is picking her up. He's probably lurking out in the parking lot."

"Is he a rich kid, too?"

"His father's a big shot, and Shane drives a bright yellow Hummer, so . . ."

"Do people still call kids like Shane and Carolyn 'spoiled brats?'"

She looked almost embarrassed. "They're 'entitled' brats. They think they can have anything they want, without having to work for it—because they're entitled to it. Look, I'm sorry I dragged you all the way out here for nothing, just to talk to that little snip."

"It wasn't just nothing. Besides, you talk to her all the time."

"I get paid for it."

"You deserve every cent," I said. "You've taught her the difference between *quick* and *quickly*."

She smiled. "Teens are all jerks—but even rich ones like Carolyn grow up into halfway decent human beings."

"Sometimes," I said.

She shook her head at the injustice of it, but she smiled, too. Her dimple was getting to me. I said, "Well, *you've* turned into more than a halfway decent human being."

"How can you tell?"

"By looking."

"Is it that easy?"

"No, but I'm a private investigator. I look at things different than anyone else."

"-*ly*," she corrected me. "Different-*ly*."

"-*ly*. Thanks, teacher."

"Sorry," she said, putting a cool hand on mine. "It's a habit."

I swallowed the last splash of green tea from the cardboard cup. When you're about to stick your neck out, you can use something to gulp. "You can correct my grammar anytime you want to. Will you have dinner with me soon—so we can practice?"

There it was, out of my mouth—a question I hadn't asked for more than a year. The older I got, the less often I found myself "going out" with women. It seemed like too much trouble. The question troubled her, too, because she looked away, smoothing her crumpled napkin neatly on the tabletop. "Are you asking for a date?"

"I *think* I did. Didn't I do it right?"

"I don't date much," she said quietly.

"We don't have to pick out a silver pattern," I said. "It's just dinner."

Once more Cisne rewarded me with a broad smile, the almost undetectable tiny crow's-feet at the corners of her eyes making her even cuter. "No silver pattern?" she said. "Will we have to eat with our fingers?"

"Unless we order soup."

It was decided we'd dine together Saturday evening, as neither of us worked that day or had to get up early the next morning. There was something very special in Cisne Kelly, and it had only a little to do with the way she looked.

I was scared to death. I've never worried about age before. Then I realized I was nearly sixty and Cisne was probably twenty years or more younger. That didn't make her a kid, but she seemed like it to me. With that came all sorts of fears, insecurities—and perils.

I'm not what anyone considers a handsome man. I'm big, six foot three, or I used to be, and I wasn't bald—yet. My teeth are my own, but I have a space between the two front ones, which makes it easier to smile and spit in somebody's eye at the same time, but I knew it wasn't one of the sexy allures many men strived for. My body had aged. I didn't like looking in the mirror at the wrinkles in my neck or arms. My skin was thinner than it used to be, and tore or bruised more easily. Why Cisne Kelly agreed to our date escapes me. Maybe she saw something beneath the roughened and wrinkled skin, something she liked.

With the exception of my former wife, Lila, I've never enjoyed long-term relationships with women—and I've never been the breaker-upper. They always seem to leave me, either angry or just quietly drifting away. I worried the same thing might happen with Cisne—and I'd done no more than shake her hand. My energy isn't what it once was.

Should I have asked Cisne for a date in the first place? Should I have just let it go and spent Saturday evening watching a Bogart movie at home? Should I have—*dared*?

Well, I thought, it's too late to change my mind now. I headed toward Shaker Heights where John Tyler—*not* the tenth president of the United States—lived. I'd tried calling him earlier that day, before I'd seen Stanley Majkrzak, but no one answered, and he evidently didn't have voice mail—or if he did, it wasn't turned on.

Thirty years ago Shaker Heights had a reputation for elegance all over America, but in the twenty-first century the address for John Tyler wasn't all that glamorous. It was an old but cared-for sandstone apartment building that resembled Stan Majkrzak's in Lakewood. Tyler, who lived on the third floor, answered my ring and unlocked the downstairs door with a loud buzz. As I climbed the steps I realized there was no air-conditioning in the hall or stairwell. My shirt stuck to the small of my back by the time I knocked on his door.

Tyler opened it almost at once. "Yeah?" he said, suspicion surrounding him like porcupine quills. He was African American, in his mid-twenties, about five foot ten, and only slightly overweight. Like me, he was losing his hair in the front. He wore khakis slung so low that five inches of his underpants showed—dark blue boxers with big white polka dots. He also had on expensive but run-down basketball shoes and a LeBron Cavaliers T-shirt. Inside Tyler's apartment the TV blared, but the air conditioner was even louder—it was twenty degrees cooler in there than out in the hallway. He held a Budweiser in one hand, and over his shoulder I saw two more Bud empties on the table beside his easy chair. At one end of the room was a kitchenette.

The expression on John Tyler's face—narrow eyes, downturned mouth, and aggressively defiant chin—indicated contempt. He rolled his eyes. "Another fucking cop."

"Not quite," I said. I introduced myself and gave him one of my cards, which he studied resentfully, as if he'd been cited for driving three miles over the limit.

"So what?"

"I'm looking for Earl Dacey."

He made no effort to move out of the doorway. "Who?"

"I found you in his personal phone book, so I thought we could talk. I phoned earlier but there was no answer."

"I was at work," he said. "People work for a living, y' know."

"Do you have any idea where Earl might be?"

A shrug, noncommittal.

"As my card says, I'm a private investigator. I've been hired to locate him."

"By who?"

Cisne Kelly wasn't there to remind him that the proper word to employ in such a case was *whom*. I told him my client's name.

"His ol' lady don't even know where he's at? I dunno. I talked to him a week ago—that was the last time."

"You and he are homeboys?"

His brown eyes nearly disappeared. "I hate honkies sayin' shit like 'homeboy.'"

"Sorry—I didn't know it was a bad word. So you and Earl aren't friends?"

Another shrug. "We do some business."

"Would you mind inviting me in? It's hotter than hell out here in the hallway."

"I got nothin' to say to you," Tyler said.

"If you and Earl do business, you've got plenty to say to me."

"It's none a *your* business, though."

"I think it is."

His snicker was bereft of amusement. "You wanna come in, smart-ass motherfucker? Got a warrant?"

"I asked to be invited in. That's not a warrant."

"You wave a warrant at me, I'll cut your fuckin' eyes out. Don' walk up on me, grandpa! Go home an' let your old momma suck your dick."

He started to slam the door—a mistake, because that was one *grandpa* too many for the week. I threw all my weight against it. The door bounced off my shoulder, snapped back on him and smashed him in the nose. He dropped his beer and raised his hand to catch the blood running freely from his left nostril, stumbled backwards over his own feet, and landed hard on his ass. By the time he shook his head clear of the cobwebs and reached in his pocket for a knife or razor, I'd closed the door behind me, crossed to him in three long strides, and stepped down hard on his elbow, pinning his arm to the floor.

"Gah*damn!*" John Tyler said.

I didn't let him up until I'd relieved him of a switchblade. Tyler was evidently old-fashioned, because I hadn't seen a switchblade since attending a Cain Park summer production of *West Side Story*.

He finally sat up straight, both hands trying to stanch the nosebleed. "I coulda killed you," he said, bloody fingers muffling his mouth.

"Doubtful. Stop picking on your elders, Tyler. Us old guys have been around long enough to spot your bullshit a mile away."

His glare would have roasted me to medium-well.

"Let me tell you a true story about the mother of a friend of mine. She was in a wheelchair at the airport when someone grabbed her purse and tried to run off with it," I said. "She threw her walking cane at him and nailed him right in the head. When the cops arrived, that was the end of *his* purse-snatching career for a while. Don't underestimate seniors, homey. You're lucky I just busted your nose."

He sniffed magnificently. "Whaddya want from me?"

"Get off the floor, run cold water into a towel, and stop the bleeding. I'll wait."

He gave me that look again, like on a poster for a Godzilla movie. He disappeared into the bathroom and I made a visual inspection. The place wasn't a complete mess, though no one would perform brain surgery in the living room any time soon. A well-thumbed *Penthouse* was on the floor next to his chair. There were a few framed photographs scattered about. On the wall of the kitchenette was a calendar with a Varga-like illustration of a sexy young girl in a bikini.

Tyler came out with two wet bath towels, his head thrown back. One was blood-spattered from cleaning up his face, and the other was wadded up at the nape of his neck.

"Can we talk civilized? Or are we still name-calling?"

He plopped into his chair and clicked the MUTE button on the remote. The TV fell mercifully silent. "Get it over with," he growled.

"You said you did 'business' with Earl Dacey. Was this about his upskirt pictures?"

His eyes widened. "How you know about that shit?"

"Were you buying his pictures and videos to distribute them?"

"I work regular at the Clinic," he said. "When anybody needs to get wheelchaired from one place to another, they call me to push them through the halls. You think I make a fortune doing that? I was lookin' to make some money offa Earl."

"It didn't work out?"

"Dunno. Haven't heard from him for too long—like I said."

I nodded. "How'd you know about Earl in the first place?"

"I heard around."

"From . . . ?"

"Around. Some guys . . ."

"Some guys?" I moved closer to him. "Are you looking for another nosebleed, John?"

"Don't be a jag-off. I'm talkin' mob guys here." He shut his eyes and kept them that way. For a moment I thought he'd dozed off. Then he said, "What do I care, anyway? I heard about Earl from Jimmy Santocroce."

The name kicked in. Jimmy Santocroce—from Victor Gaimari's list. One of the local big-shot porn guys in Ohio—and I'd given his name to K.O. to check out.

"How do you know Santocroce?" I said.

Tyler's eyes opened and he looked right at me. "I'm tryin' to score some bucks. I went to Santocroce for a job, but he shot me down."

"Why?"

"You fuckin' blind? He's a wop, Santocroce. Wops don' like black folks—never have."

It wasn't that long ago that African Americans didn't dare hang around in Little Italy after dark—and probably thought twice about it before they showed up there during daylight. Maybe back then they carried knives, the way Tyler still did—but the Murray Hill guys preferred guns.

"Why did Santocroce tell you about Earl Dacey?"

"Probably outa pity. Look, man, the wop was into porn bigtime—kinky stuff. When Dacey come around, Santocroce thought those pics and vids was small potatoes, for cowards and wussies and needle-dicks. So he tossed me a bone—like I was a goddamn dog or somethin'—an' he tol' *me* to call Dacey."

"And you did?"

Tyler closed his eyes again. "I need cash so, yeah, I called him up. I met him for a coffee—an' I come to the same conclusion as the wop. Dacey was small-time."

"And you never talked to him again?"

"I put him off whenever he called." He dabbed at his nose with the towel he'd pressed to the back of his neck, relieved the blood had stopped. "That's all I can say to you."

"That's enough."

"Gimme my blade back, then."

"No, it'll join my collection. By the way," I said, "I don't think your nose is broken. I just wish you hadn't made things so hard."

I got the fierce glare again. "Aw, you know," he growled, anger roiling in his gut, blossoming in his throat like the rumble of far-off thunder, "us niggas all are stupid." Our eyes met. Eventually I had to look away. "Ain't we?" he said. "Ain't we just too-fuckin'-stupid niggas—Mister Phony Cop?"

CHAPTER EIGHT

I t had been a long, tough day: Lakewood on the West Side to visit Stan Majkrzak, then out to Mentor to interview stuck-up young Carolyn Alexander—and, delightfully, to make a dinner date with Cisne Kelly. Then to Shaker Heights, where I celebrated by smashing John Tyler in the nose with his own door and was called a bigot.

Not much information gleaned. I hoped I'd find a grain of truth on the Internet, wrap everything up, and gently deliver Earl, wherever he'd been, to his mother. I didn't look forward to a conversation with Savannah Dacey, and was reluctant to meet her again face to face.

When I let myself into my apartment, the voice-mail message light blinked—Suzanne Davis calling from her cell phone. Her words were clipped, her voice strained and worried, asking me to return her call ASAP. I took a Stroh's from the refrigerator, sat in my easy chair in the bay window so I could look across at the happy hour crowd at the Mad Greek, and made the call.

"Milan," Suzanne said, "I left you messages all over town. Where are you?"

I heard people talking in the background, and a TV playing a commercial for some ghastly prescription drug warning of worse side effects than what the medicine was supposed to cure. "I'm home, Suzanne. Where are you?"

"We're in Nighttown."

"We?"

"K.O. We need to talk. In person."

"You drove all the way from Mentor? I just walked in the door and got comfortable."

Her breathing pattern told me she was annoyed. "We'll come by in ten minutes."

When I opened the door, Suzanne looked grim and upset, and K.O.'s defiant attitude was wrapped around him like Bela Lugosi's flowing cape. They both refused refreshments. Maybe they'd already had enough to drink at Nighttown, or weren't in the mood.

When we were all seated, Suzanne said, "K.O. got himself in trouble."

K.O., sitting at stiff attention, his hands nearly tucked beneath his thighs, said, "I was working when it happened. On your behalf."

"Find anything out?"

"That's not the point," Suzanne reminded me.

"Then somebody tell me what *is* the point."

It took K.O. about thirty seconds to get wound up enough. Then: "You know that list you gave me? People to check out?"

Victor Gaimari's list.

"Well, I talked to one guy at eleven o'clock this morning. I guess those porn people don't start working at nine A.M. like the rest of us."

"Which guy was that?"

"Stuart Eisen—his office is in Cuyahoga Falls down in Summit County. He said he just distributes porn flicks—and not much of that anymore. He says anybody with a computer can dial up any kind they want for free, so it doesn't pay enough for him. And he swears he never heard of Earl Dacey."

"Those bastards cross their fingers when they swear," Suzanne said.

"So I went to the next guy on the list—in Bedford Heights. Angelo Nicolino."

I'd heard his name before, and not just from Victor's list. I couldn't place him, though. "Did you tell him you work for Milan Security?"

"I told him I'd just started and I didn't have business cards made up yet."

"He needs business cards, Milan," Suzanne scolded.

"Nicolino's got a nice office," K.O. said, "and a small studio three doors down on the same side of the street."

"Okay, he produces dirty movies. So?"

"Not just dirty movies. He said he'd talked to Earl Dacey on the phone three weeks ago but never met him, because Earl didn't have the kind of special material he looks for."

"What are we talking about here, K.O.?"

"Nicolino asked me if I knew what a crush film was."

"A crush film?"

"I told him I didn't know about it."

"Me, neither," Suzanne said. "I thought I'd heard of everything."

"Well, he offered to show me one," K.O. said. "I told him I wasn't there to look at porn, but he said this was different—*really* kinky, he said—and if I liked it, he'd give it to me at a discount, because he sells these movies for big bucks—sometimes on the Internet but mostly to private parties. He said it'd be easier for him to show me than explain it. So . . ."

"Milan," Suzanne said sadly, "you're going to hate this."

K.O.'s voice got low and shaky, and his eyes were sunken, hooded. His cheeks looked devoid of blood, as if he'd died several days before.

"There's this woman in a more or less empty room, with a curtain or drape hanging on one wall, a tile floor with no rug, and a sofa you could lie down on. The woman wears a garter belt and fishnet stockings, and nothing else but these really high stiletto heels."

"So far, so sexy," I said.

"There were three little puppies in that room, too." K.O. shook his head. "I don't know what kind of dogs, but they were tiny and very young, about six or seven weeks."

"Puppies?"

Suzanne said, "You don't want K.O. to go on with this. Let's make it simple. This girl, whoever she was, tortured and abused these animals for more than half an hour."

My living room grew as silent as a graveyard mausoleum at midnight.

"Nicolino told me," K.O. said, "if I wanted kittens or guinea pigs or something more exotic—like crickets, even, or lizards—he'd set it up and shoot it for me. He said sick, fucked-up men and women buy that evil shit because it turns them on and gets them off—supposedly at the moment of death."

I went into the kitchen and leaned against the sink, turning on the faucet and fighting down my gag reflex. Finally I caught some cold water in my palm, and drank it down. Another handful I used to cool off my face. Then I wiped my chin and returned to the living room, where K.O. and Suzanne sat side by side as if they'd both been arrested for a heinous crime and were waiting for arraignment.

I looked hard at K.O. "You could've put this all in an e-mail like you've been doing. Why didn't you?"

Each apparently expected the other one to begin. Finally Suzanne said, "K.O. lost it—lost his temper and his cool—and beat up Nicolino so bad he had to go to the hospital."

K.O. boasted, "I broke his jaw, closed one eye, knocked out some teeth, and busted ribs—and his elbow." His eyes glowed red—a vampire in a teen horror movie. "I'm an animal lover."

"Jesus," I said.

"Milan, what if Nicolino sics the law on K.O.?" Suzanne was logical—she always was when running her own business. "Will that affect you, too?"

"Guys like Angelo Nicolino don't run to the police."

"Maybe not," K.O. said, "but they'll get even. They'll come after me—and you, too. Hey, don't worry, I got your back. I'll stay with you—sleep on the couch here, so nobody comes busting in, and I'll spend my days in your office."

The headache was starting to return. "Even a tough guy like you can't take down four or five leg breakers with guns. Besides, there are other ways to settle this." I hoped I sounded braver than I felt. "I don't need a bodyguard or babysitter—or a roommate."

"Yeah, but it's my fault."

"You're damn right it is. What made you halfway kill him? You weren't supposed to hit anybody. What the hell got into you?"

K.O.'s chin jutted out like granite.

"I tried to get you to open up to me before I hired you," I said. "But you don't talk much, and because you're Suzanne's friend, I let it go. I can't let it go anymore." I sat back down. "You spent three years in a juvenile facility—for assault. I have to assume there's a connection between that assault and what you did today. What happened?"

"Milan," Suzanne protested, "he's spent seven years in the army, too."

"Learning how to kill in five easy lessons," I said. "I threw some work his way, Suzanne—and now the mob's after me. I want the whole story."

It grew church quiet. Finally Suzanne said, "You might as well tell him, K.O." She rose, straightening her skirt. "Sorry, I've heard this before. It was depressing enough the first time. I'm going back to Nighttown for another drink. Maybe I'll get lucky, maybe not." She rumpled K.O.'s hair. "Come get me when you're done, kiddo; I'll drive you home."

Neither of us spoke until my apartment door clicked shut. I said, "You want anything to drink?"

"No."

"Are you half shitfaced already?"

"One Nighttown beer—and I didn't want that one. Are you firing me?"

"I'm waiting."

He was sullen. "For the story of my life?"

"The good parts."

He took a few deep breaths, then leaned forward, his forearms on his thighs. "Should I start with when I was fifteen?"

"Wherever you want to."

"Okay." K.O. swallowed loudly. "Okay," he said again. "I lived with my old man—in Mentor. I grew up in that house. My mother walked out on us when I was nine, so him and I batched it— when he was home, which wasn't often. Otherwise I was on my own. I didn't go to Catholic school, though—by the time Dad was twenty-five, he forgot what Catholics *are*."

"We don't forget," I said, "but some of us don't practice."

"Yeah," he said with annoyance. "My father didn't practice the violin, either." He ran a hand over his chin, checking whether he'd shaved close enough that morning. "The rear of our house backed up on the neighbors' backyard—they lived on the next street over. The Philbrooks, their names were. They gave lots of parties and picnics from Memorial Day through the end of football season. Their buddies, mostly guys but a few chicks, too, hung around on weekends drinking too much and talking too loud. They had one of those humongo Weber kettles for cooking hot dogs and ham-burgers and chickens—it was so fucking big, they could of cooked a whole sheep in there."

"Did they invite you to those parties?"

"Hell, no. We didn't know 'em well—or want to. Anyways, this Philbrook kid—Donny was his name—had one of his good buddies over one Sunday. It was just the two of 'em, because his parents were away for the day." He studied the wall for a while, the muscles where his upper and lower jaw met jumping with nerves.

"I was in the basement most of the day," he finally went on. "I listened to music loud down there. Metallic stuff, y' know? So it was a long time till I heard the noise."

"What noise?"

"I didn't know what it was at first. But it went on for a while—a godawful sound—so I went upstairs and into my backyard to see what was going on."

It took him a while before he continued. I didn't know why he paused until I heard the rest, spoken softly and intensely. "They'd fired up that Weber kettle," K.O. said. "And they'd put a dog in there—a live dog, a mutt. The noise was him, screaming." He looked as if he might cry, but then clenched his teeth. He shook his head. "It was the most horrible fucking sound I ever heard."

He put his palms over his ears, but apparently it didn't help, because he dropped them at his side. "There are worse ways to die—but I can't think of any." Reliving this moment was K.O.'s own little personal piece of hell. "As soon as I figured out what was going on, I jumped the fence, but I got to the Weber kettle too late. The dog was dead—what was left of him besides char and ash." A long, loud sigh. "That's when I beat the crap out of them. Both of them. I wanted to ruin everything on their bodies—their eyes, mouths, hands, feet, and every fucking bone. I didn't stop until the cops showed up and pulled me off them—some neighbor called 911. I'd tell you all the things on 'em I broke, tore off, or busted up, but it'd take hours."

"And the court put you away until you were eighteen?"

He nodded, not turning around. "They made me go to a lot of shrink sessions inside—to help me 'manage my anger.'" His eyes were slits of rage, and the pupils had turned obsidian. "Torture a dog to death—just for laughs—and I showed the fuckers how I manage anger. But I had to go through that bullshit or they'd never let me out."

"What happened to them? The boys, I mean."

"Nothing," he said, his voice low, deep, and angry. "The old fart judge thought their injuries were punishment enough. Them getting hurt was more important to him than them cooking a dog alive for kicks. My old man had to pay their medical stuff, too. He's barely talked to me since." He coughed a few times. "He sold the house and moved away after I went into the joint. He lives down in Richfield County someplace. I've never been there." He sucked most of the air out of the room through his nose, then expelled it through his mouth.

I stayed quiet for a while. Finally I stood up. "I'm so damn sorry. For what it's worth, if it'd been my dog, I wouldn't have stopped with a beating. I would've killed them."

"I would've, too," he said, turning around to look at me. The color of his eyes had faded to subtle watercolor, looking cold as melting ice cubes. "But it was a stray. It wasn't *my* dog."

CHAPTER NINE

From my bay window I watched K.O. walk down Cedar toward Nighttown, where Suzanne Davis waited for him. Even after he was out of sight, I shivered inside, staring intently at something that wasn't there. Two punk teenage kids cooking a dog alive; a naked woman torturing puppies before she killed them for the sexual gratification of diseased minds—Jesus Christ! When you've been an army MP in Vietnam, a street cop in Cleveland, and a private investigator picking up concussions like teenagers pick up their socks, there were too many things you try like hell to forget. But you never manage to.

I do know this much: if I'd been the judge looming over that trial, Kevin O'Bannion wouldn't have been sent to juvenile jail for beating the crap out of both those sadistic kids, and he wouldn't have been forced to wade through the psychiatric system either, gritting his teeth and giving the shrink the answers he knew Dr. Mindfucker wanted to hear so they wouldn't keep him on ice any longer than they had to. If it were up to me, K.O. would have been given a standing ovation and awarded a silver star with clusters, and I would have handed it to him personally.

I'd award him another for what he did to Angelo Nicolino. Hurting innocent animals, inflicting incredible torture and violent death on them just for the fun of it—the *fun* of it, for Christ's sake—riles my guts like few other things do.

K.O. had broken the law, though, and had probably gotten me

in a hell of a lot of trouble as well. If word got back to the authorities, I'd lose my P.I. license—and K.O. might wind up in jail again. Grownup jail, this time. I spent a restless night worrying about it.

The next morning I called Victor Gaimari. It was better if he heard from me what happened between Kevin O'Bannion and Angelo Nicolino. When I told him I had to discuss something confidential, he wisely decided a public restaurant was not the place to do it, and invited me to his office in Terminal Tower.

The Terminal Tower was in Cleveland before I was. For half a century it was the tallest downtown building—until Key Tower was erected a few blocks away to cast a shadow on it. At ground level it connects with two elegant hotels, fine restaurants, a sprawling shopping center with a sometimes questionable food court, a central terminal for the RTA light rail trains, and a movie theater complex at which the annual Cleveland International Film Festival is held. Upstairs, classy offices overlooked the city, the Cuyahoga River, and Lake Erie.

Victor's office was on the eleventh floor. I've been there often. My first visit was decades earlier when I marched in and broke Victor's nose. Victor's receptionist refused to forgive me, glared daggers at me whenever I visited, and never answered my good mornings with so much as a brusque nod.

When I showed up at eleven, I noticed a different receptionist—a pleasant woman who greeted me warmly and ushered me into Victor's inner sanctum as if I were someone important. I guess her predecessor didn't mention that someone named Milan Jacovich was an archenemy, capable of violence.

Victor's coat jacket was hung carefully on a hook behind the door and there was nary a wrinkle in his white shirt, or the gold tie that complemented his suit pants. Victor kept his air conditioner cold enough to hang meat in the office. He told the receptionist to hold his calls and then shut the door. I started telling him about Nicolino, but he stopped me.

"I'll save you the trouble; I've heard about it. Angelo Nicolino's wife phoned me this morning in hysterics. She told me one of your people roughed him up yesterday, and that Angelo will be in pain—well, forever. It'll take a month to get some decent dentures to replace the teeth knocked out. Let's just say the family is hopping mad at you and your—what the hell is he, anyway? An intern?"

"Call him whatever you want. He's not my partner, my drinking buddy, or my best friend. He's been working for me part time the last few days."

"To hear Mary Nicolino tell it, he has anger problems."

"Don't we all?" I said. "His name is Kevin O'Bannion."

Victor nodded. "He did identify himself to Angelo before he beat him half to death. I'd like to meet him when he's having one of his good days."

"He's a bright kid—trying to straighten himself out. He wants to be a P.I., too."

"Just what the world needs," Victor said, "another private investigator. Watch out, or he'll steal your own business out from under your nose."

"He's also an animal lover."

"And you sent him after Angelo anyway?"

"I had no idea what Angelo did for a living."

"Frankly, I didn't, either. If I had, Milan, I probably would have shut him down like a roving crap game—because I like animals, too." He dug into his hip pocket for a wallet to show me a photograph. "I have dogs now. Did you know? Great Pyrenees."

I looked. Most people carry snapshots of their kids in their wallets; Victor kept pictures of his pets. If you don't know what a Great Pyrenees looks like, they're similar to St. Bernards, only with prettier faces—huge dogs, usually all white. Victor never married and, as far as I knew, had no children—so these were his "babies."

"You should drop by and meet them. You can hear them coming a mile away." Victor's smile was a 5 percent effort, but better than a scowl. "Look—Nicolino is an asshole. He's a third cousin twice removed to people who were close to the top of our family before my uncle . . ." He searched for the right phrase; he didn't have to because I knew what he was talking about. Finally he said, " . . . before my uncle stepped forward."

"Does that mean Nicolino will heal quietly, keep his yap shut, and not come after O'Bannion or me?"

"Nicolino won't do a damn thing, because he's all bullshit and no guts. Other people might, though."

"Who?"

"You mean 'whom,' don't you?"

"Victor, you sound like a pretty lady I just invited to dinner. She's an English teacher."

"I wish you were going out with a karate instructor instead, who could teach you how to duck. The 'whom' in question is probably Jimmy Santocroce. He's from the same crowd as Nicolino—his father was one of the old-timers. Jimmy's into many things, most I wouldn't like if I knew about them."

"There's little you don't know about."

"Not anymore," he said. "The don was old-fashioned—conservative. Now that he's gone and I've—inherited his status and position in the community, my interests are different. So all I know about Jimmy is he's involved in pornography, and from what little I've heard, it's probably underage porno. Not little children—mostly young middle school and high school girls. Maybe boys, too—I don't know."

"Jesus."

"I do know he's pals with Angelo Nicolino, which makes him twice as disgusting." He swiveled his leather chair around so he could look out on Public Square and beyond to Lake Erie, shimmering in the midmorning sunshine like a tub full of diamonds. "I can't do much with Santocroce. If I see him once a year at a Christmas party, it's a big deal." He shrugged. "If the don were still alive, one phone call is all it'd take."

"Aren't *you* the don now, Victor?"

"Ha ha," he said. Victor always laughed like that, as if reading the "ha-ha" from a script. A smart, highly educated man, Victor had no sense of humor whatever. To him, laughter was an afterthought. "Nobody calls me that anymore. The honorary title was buried along with my uncle. Besides, the *Godfather* movie is almost forty years old." He clasped his hands together as if he were praying. "I'll talk to Santocroce. But watch yourself—and your part-time shamus, too."

It took me longer to ride the elevator down to the main floor, cross Superior Avenue in Public Square, and maneuver my car out of its parking space without sideswiping or backing into someone else than it did to cross the river to my own office building on Collision Bend.

I immediately noticed the black Ford Fairlane waiting in my parking lot. Two people emerged. The driver didn't run around and assist the woman getting out of the passenger seat, but I hadn't expected him to. Cops don't treat each other like ladies and gentlemen.

Detective Sergeant Bob Matusen wore a loud seersucker jacket over light blue slacks and a short-sleeved dress shirt with a sky blue necktie that had been dry-cleaned too often. A step behind him was Lieutenant Florence McHargue—always in a business pants suit, summer or winter. This one was buttery gray, her blouse subtle magenta. Gray streaks now sprinkled her dark hair, setting off her coffee-with-cream complexion. She was quite handsome—and intimidating.

Victor had warned me to watch myself—and that clanged between my ears as McHargue approached. We have a stormy history; when I see her, I *always* watch myself.

"Where've you been?" she demanded. Anyone else would have said hello first.

McHargue became head of the Homicide Division after Marko Meglich was killed across the river in the Flats, before the east bank was closed and/or torn down—shot dead trying to protect my ass. We'd known each other since we were ten years old. Marko was the best friend I'd had in the world, and McHargue couldn't forget I caused his untimely death—just as she never forgave me being male and Caucasian—nor has she ever let me off her own personal hook for once being a Cleveland cop and then ankling my way off the force and hanging out a private-eye shingle.

But after a decade, I'd finally broken through—after nearly dying. Hoping to upgrade our relationship from enmity to civility, I invited her to lunch, and she surprised me by accepting. It was a cold day, a year and a half ago, and we'd sat upstairs at the Inn of the Barristers, across the street from the Justice Center, both aware of being the only ones there who were neither attorneys nor judges, and hammered out some of our differences. Not all of them, though. We'll never be friends but now at least we're on the same side—even if we approach problems from different angles.

"Good morning, Lieutenant. Hi, Bob."

"Milan." Matusen nodded a greeting. He spoke few words.

McHargue said, "Do we stand here roasting in ninety-degree heat?" She jerked her head in the direction of my front door.

The ironworks on the first floor clanked merrily away making decorative wrought-iron gates, fences, and window bars. From upstairs in my office, though, they could barely be heard. The building is nearly a hundred years old—when builders constructed something back then, they *meant* it.

"I haven't seen you in a while, Lieutenant," I said as we sat down. "How've you been?"

"I'm swell." She held her hand out to Matusen, palm up, and he slapped a large notebook into it the way an OR nurse passes a scalpel to a surgeon. She read: "Earl William Dacey—twenty-eight." She looked at me over her glasses. "You know him, I gather."

"You gather correctly, or you wouldn't be here."

"His mother—Savannah, is that her name?—hired you."

"She's worried about her boy. He's disappeared, I'm looking for him."

Her mouth was a tight, straight line across her face. "Looks like you're out of a job." She removed from her notebook five photographs, pushing them at me without comment. After my first glance, I didn't want to see the rest, but I had to.

They were vivid police crime-scene photographs. A severely beaten corpse, looking tall and overweight, wearing jeans and a short-sleeved rayon shirt, was lying face down in the wet underbrush near what appeared to be a riverbank. The fourth picture was taken after an investigating officer turned him over, and while the face was so bloodied and disfigured I couldn't recognize him, I added up the pieces.

I let trouble sigh out through my mouth. "Earl."

Until McHargue showed me the murder photos, my only glimpse of him was the Christmas morning picture of him in his pajamas—a pathetic weirdo with a camcorder who took advantage of unsuspecting young women and girls wearing skirts or dresses to go shopping. My hope was that when I corralled him and brought him home to Mommy, someone with a degree in psychology would begin taking care of him. Not now—he had been brutally murdered, and rage churned around inside me where it wasn't supposed to be.

McHargue explained, "The medical examiner's opinion—until they do an autopsy—is that he's been dead for several days."

"His wallet was still in his pocket," Matusen added, "with seventeen bucks in it, his Social Security card, and his driver's license."

"Who found him, and where?"

McHargue scooped the photographs back to her side of the desk. "Just before dark last night. Three kids were hanging around Tinker's Creek—God knows why they were there—and actually stumbled over him."

"Tinker's Creek," I said. "That's near Twinsburg."

She nodded. "In northern Summit County."

"Earl Dacey lived on the West Side, and I know he hung around at Beachwood Place, out east, and in Lake County up north. It surprises me he wound up in Twinsburg."

"Why is that?"

"Long story."

"Oh, goodie," she said without a single scrap of humor. She leaned back in her chair. "I've got all day."

It took about forty-five minutes to fill them in on what I'd been hired to do. I shared Earl Dacey's kinky sexual peculiarity and his forays into department stores and shops with his hidden camera. I also told them about my assistant, K.O.—except not *all* about him—and our conversations with cosmetics clerks, security officials, nuns, and priests. I didn't mention people in the pornography business—and wouldn't, unless I had to. I got those names, after all, from Victor Gaimari.

When I finished, McHargue drummed her fingers atop her thigh. "Has he been selling that voyeur crap around?"

"I guess he tried to—without success."

"I want those DVDs, Jacovich."

"I'll give you all of them. You'd better have a great big bowl of popcorn."

"You know any porn guys in Twinsburg?"

"I never pal around with porn guys," I said, "and I don't know any twins in Twinsburg, either."

"Earl's mother probably has questions for you."

"Is the Twinsburg P.D. running this investigation, or are they passing it on to you?"

"They called early this morning," McHargue said. "Dacey lived in Cleveland, and they figure he was dumped in Twinsburg after he was dead, so it's not their problem. We'll be doing the invest. I want everything you have. I hope you'll be cooperative as hell with us."

"Just like always, Lieutenant."

"Are you bullshitting me—*again*? Time doesn't change you?" She leveled a finger at me, her nail polish the same purple-red as her lipstick. "Don't lose my phone number."

"I've memorized it."

"Memorize this, too. Dacey's not your job anymore. The missing persons case is now a murder, and you're not invited."

"I know the rules," I said. "No involvement in capital murder cases."

Her tone got testy—for her that wasn't unusual. "Another thing. Your—whatever you call him—assistant? I want to meet him."

"Why?"

"You know how I feel about guys in your profession. If I get my hooks into this kid, maybe I can talk him out of being a P.I. before it's too late."

I couldn't help chuckle. "That's honorable of you, Lieutenant."

"Yeah, well," she said. "That's just the way I am."

CHAPTER TEN

The few times I'd met Savannah Dacey, she'd dressed in her idea of casually sexy—blouses with one button too many open, swinging peasant skirts, and too much makeup on her face—and despite her concern over her son's disappearance, she'd been twinkly and flirty with me, batting her lashes like a terrible actress in a corny movie about the pre-bellum South. When I'd told her about Earl's fetish photography, her face had hardened and she became angry and defensive. But now, in her living room, there was no light behind Savannah's eyes, as if someone had crept inside her head and turned off the power. She didn't give a damn what she looked like. Her spirit was shattered, never to be repaired, and her hopes were nonexistent. Her son was dead—and dead doesn't come back.

She'd now suffer the unbearable and always unexpected pain of a mother whose life lasts longer than her child's. There's no dealing with it, no "getting over" it. There's just sadness that won't ever go away.

"Why would anybody hurt him?" she whined. She didn't cry or sob anymore. She'd sobbed herself dry since McHargue knocked on her door with the dreadful news. Her soul was a small gully in the desert at the height of summer—dried up and leaving ugly irregular cracks in the dried mud. When she spoke, it was almost as if she were dead, too.

"He had no enemies you know of?"

"Earl hardly knew anybody at all. Until he got his camera, he pretty much stuck close to home."

"He had a few names in his address book, Savannah."

She studied the wall behind me. "I don't know those people. I never looked in his book. That would be—snooping. He's—he *was* a grown man. What he did, what he kept in his book, was—private."

"He didn't have a girlfriend? How about Anna Barna? She lives near here."

She had trouble swallowing before she spoke, so she took her time and I let her. "She's not his girlfriend. They went to kindergarten right through high school together—grade school, middle school, high school. They're—" She shut her eyes tight, appalled she'd used the present tense again and not the past one she'd have to get used to. "They *were* neighbors. They did everything together—what little they did."

"What do you mean?"

"Anna's like Earl. She's shy—not social. She hardly ever goes anywhere for fun. They just hung out—like going for coffee or maybe watching a movie at home." She shook her head sadly. "I should call her. I should tell her. She'd want to be told . . ." As I watched, those muscles in her neck holding her head erect stopped functioning, and her jaw dropped down to her chest. She put one hand over her eyes.

"Do you want *me* to tell her, Savannah?"

She stayed hidden behind her hand for almost a minute, finally emerging for a breath of air. "She works," she said. "She won't get home until five thirty or so. She's a file clerk for Progressive Insurance—a huge company with about a hundred people working in one room. She'll—dissolve in front of everybody."

"I'll see her at home, then. Does she live alone?"

"With her father. He's retired."

I nodded. "Savannah, I'm so sorry."

"Me too," she said, her voice so tiny I barely heard her.

"I want to return the money you've paid me."

She actually shied away with the top part of her body as if I'd said something obscene. "I don't want the money! I couldn't look at it! Give it to charity." She needed fifteen seconds to catch her breath. "Besides, I want you to stay on the job for me."

"I can't," I said. "Private investigators can't involve themselves in—uh—capital cases like this one. In fact, the police lieutenant warned me of that this morning."

"Is that the colored woman who came over here?"

People stopped referring to African Americans as "colored" about fifty years ago—but this was no time to remind Savannah. "Yes," I admitted, "Lieutenant McHargue."

She forced words through clenched teeth. "Cops don't give a goddamn. That bitch doesn't care about Earl. When she told me he was dead, it was like giving a weather report."

"Police can't get emotional about things they investigate—it'd make them ineffective."

"They *are*—ineffective! And now they know about Earl's—hobby—they'll go through the motions but they won't lift a finger, because they really won't care about a . . ." She couldn't bring herself to use any of the pejorative expressions that define perverts. "That's why you have to keep working for me—to find out why Earl got hurt, and who did it."

"Savannah, I'd lose my license."

"Do it on the sly. Nobody'll know—just you and me." Tears threatened behind her eyes. "If you don't help me, no one will, and then I'll never know." Her sniff was loud as she pushed her hair out of her eyes. "You're all I got left, Milan." She stood, heading for the rear of the house. "I'll give you more money. Whatever you want. I'll spend my last nickel to find out."

I stood up, too. "Don't get any more money. Sit down, now—relax."

She threw the remark over her shoulder. "I have to get money for you—"

"Not now," I said. Everything in me wanted to run and not look back—but I felt like that female character in the musical *Oklahoma* singing "I Can't Say No."

She stopped, framed in the hallway, looking at me—challenging me.

"Not now," I said again, and sighed. "Later."

*   *   *

Anna Barna's dusty-looking, dreary house was a few blocks from Savannah's. The patch of grass no one would have referred to as "a front lawn" had long ago died, leaving bare dirt and mud whenever it rained, and a few weeds. It was half past seven, the sun low in the west, its warm light not finding the Barna house. The front door was open to allow fresh air in, but the screen door was shut and hooked from the inside. When I pushed the buzzer, I heard no sound. After a few more seconds I knocked.

The man who came to the door was scrawny-hard, in his late sixties and wearing an undershirt, shoulder straps yellow with age. His narrow, bony shoulders and skinny arms were an unhealthy white. His fingernails probably hadn't been cleaned since his childhood, his hands were stained with tobacco smoke and grease. A cigarette dangled from his mouth as if he'd been born with it there, like a birthmark, and the smoke rising into his eye had inflicted him with a permanent one-eyed squint. On his right bicep was a tattoo of an American eagle in a crooked slump, a reminder that if you get tattooed when you're young, the tattoos will change as your skin ages.

"Yeah?" Accusing. Confrontational.

"Hi," I said. "I'm looking for Anna Barna."

"Yeah?" Sullen. Mean.

"Is she here?"

"Who're you?"

I showed him my business card through the screen door. He studied it hard, his lips moving. Finally he said, "Cop."

"Not exactly. Is Ms. Barna home?"

He took his time deciding. Then he called out: "Anna! Guy here to see you."

From somewhere inside, a faint voice answered, "Who is it?"

"How the hell would I know?" he snarled, then shuffled away, too much trouble for him to explain my presence.

How can I describe Anna Barna? Neither pretty nor homely; neither overweight nor slim. Her hair was not quite brunette and not quite anything else. She had on little makeup, and her outfit was probably what she'd worn to work—a short-sleeved white blouse buttoned to the neck that a certain class of woman has

worn since the 1940s and a black skirt, with scuffed black flats
that had seen better days. The only memorable thing about her
was her eyes—large, slightly Asian in shape, and the rich color of
Lindt dark chocolate.

"Hello," she said, offering the beginnings of a smile. I'd bet she
didn't smile a lot.

I introduced myself, told her I was a private investigator—
which shook her up—and said I had some news for her. "Can I
come in?"

Her eyes crept sideways as if her father lurked behind a corner listening to every word. "Let's stay outside." She opened the
screen and turned sideways to sidle out. "My father doesn't like
flies getting in the house." I got the idea her father didn't like *anything* getting in the house.

Anna descended the porch steps and sat on the second one
from the bottom. I sat next to her and informed her as gently as I
could that Earl Dacey was dead.

All her color fled, her eyes grew large as saucers. Her silent
tears came instantly; quiet tears are always more heartbreaking
than those accompanied by sobbing. They bubbled and coursed
down her cheeks leaving wet streaks. Beyond childhood friendship, I think she loved Earl Dacey very much.

I had nothing with which to console her, so I simply put my
hand over hers, which was doubled into a fist atop her thigh. She
left it there.

After at least three minutes—which felt to me like a month
and a half—she took her hand back from me and wiped her nose
with it. "What happened to him?"

There was no other way to say it. "Apparently someone killed
him."

She stared at nothing, shocked all over again. Her father was
hanging around in the vicinity of the screen door, his suspicious
glower that of a skinny old sparrow hawk. I said, "Let's walk
around the block."

She rose, letting me take her arm. People sat out on almost
every front porch, men guzzling beer from the can, women either gossiping and laughing or scanning the street for their kids
who'd disobeyed orders and strayed from their own front yard. A

few called hellos to Anna, but she didn't acknowledge them. One even asked whether we wanted a beer. Neighborly. Friendly.

When we turned the corner and headed west into the setting orange sun, I wanted to don my sunglasses—but in that neighborhood, one wouldn't dare. In Cleveland, if you weren't driving a car directly into the sun, sunglasses on the street probably meant you were a pimp.

"You've known Earl a long time," I said.

"Since kindergarten."

"Good friends?"

She paused before nodding in the affirmative.

"Where do you work, Anna?"

"Progressive Insurance. I file."

"Earl didn't have a job, did he?"

"No. He—wasn't born to work at a regular job like the rest of us."

"But he's been trying to make money recently."

She didn't answer.

"Do you know about his—photography?"

Her voice was almost a whisper. "He liked to take pictures. He wanted to make money selling pictures he took."

"He took pictures of you?"

She gave her answer some thought. Our walk together was slow and deliberate, as if we were marching down the aisle to the strains of "Pomp and Circumstance" to collect our diplomas. "Sometimes," she finally said.

"What kinds of pictures?"

Her voice was smaller and smaller—and I'd swear she was growing smaller, too. "Like at the park or by the river or the lake." She straightened her spine. "We went to an Indians ballgame, and he took a picture of me in the bleachers, so you could see the whole field behind me." Then all the starch went out of her. "Nobody in their right mind'd wanna buy pictures of me." She tried not to meet my eyes and moved several steps away so I wouldn't touch her, even if by accident.

"Did Earl tell you what kind of pictures he was taking, Anna?"

The hurt emanated from her like the heat of a fierce sunburn when someone falls asleep at the beach. "He started telling me—but I didn't wanna hear nothing about it." Her head quivered atop her neck. "I still don't wanna hear about it."

"Anna, the pictures he took were upskirt photos of girls."

She didn't answer because she was afraid to.

"Did he take pictures of you like that?"

She gasped, her mouth a tight, straight line. Her deathly pale skin had morphed into vivid red smears of humiliation over both cheeks. "No!"

"Did he ask you if he could?"

Speaking through gritted teeth now, trying to chew up her anger and degradation. "I wouldn' let him do nothing like that—an' he knew it, too."

"But he asked you?"

Her silence gave me the answer anyway. I wished I'd refused to stay on the case for Earl's mother. Then I wouldn't have had to make Anna feel disgraced and used. A small, presumptuous ache crept behind my eyes like a bird returning to its nest. Guilt rode my back like a manic jockey—and no sparing the whip.

"Sometimes people we care about do crazy, unacceptable things. Earl tried to make big money, the kind he'd never seen before. He took those upskirt shots to sell them."

A couple of preteen boys—both in shorts and one with no shirt at all, the usual hot-weather summer costume for kids—ran past, jostling us, yelling and laughing as if they were going someplace special. Anna covered her eyes so no one could see her cry.

I spoke softly into her ear. "Those weren't horrible pictures. I don't know if you've ever seen hard-core porn before, but compared to stuff on the Internet, Earl's photographs and videos were just spicy. So don't think badly of him, okay?"

"Think badly of him?" she said through her fingers. "I loved him! I know he was a geek, that he'd never amount to anything. But I loved him awful, ever since we was in junior high school—an' he never even knew it! An' now he's dead because he took those pictures of young girls. How in *hell* can I not think too badly of him?"

It was almost nine o'clock when I got home. Despite my frustration, I was hungry—a guy my size always needs food—but I couldn't summon the energy to go out for dinner, nor to fix anything at home. I could run across the street to the supermarket and pick something up, but it didn't appeal to me. When I first moved into my apartment, the market over there was called Russo's. Then about a decade ago it became part of a large chain, a Giant Eagle. Now it's called Dave's Supermarket. Who can keep track, anyway?

The local landmarks, the ones that seemed to set Cleveland apart, could change and transform themselves in the blink of an eye. The new baseball and football venues were great, but I missed the old Cleveland Municipal Stadium where the Browns and Indians used to play, even though some of the seventy-thousand seats had obstructed views, and there were *never* enough restrooms. What had happened to downtown department stores like Halle's and Higbee's that every child thought was magic because of the elaborate window dressings, and the guy covered in bells, Mister Jing-A-Ling, who made kids laugh every Christmas? Where's the Hough Bakery, with those white cakes nobody's forgotten? What became of the restaurants of the past—the Silver Grille, The Hickory House, the Theatrical, Swingos on the Lake, and that great old steak house, Jim's, which used to be right next to my office on the riverfront and where I'd eaten lunch at least twice a week? And didn't everyone remember our former mayor, Ralph J. Perk, who accidentally caught his hair on fire, and whose wife turned down an invitation to the Nixon White House for dinner because Thursday was her bowling night?

Those things gave Cleveland its character—but then change happened. Sometimes thinking about change depressed the hell out of me. But then I told myself, get used to it.

I opened a Stroh's and sat down at my computer. I had a few emails, and I ignored all of them except for the one from Kevin O'Bannion.

Milan—
I went ahead and worked today—you didn't exactly fire me. If you do, I'll understand. I shouldn't tell people I'm

your employee before messing up and rearranging their faces.
Also, Suzanne said Earl Dacey was dead, but I wasn't sure
you'd walk away from the case or not. If you did, well, I
pissed away today—and if you didn't, I learned a few things.

I got an idea last night and went ahead with it. I bought
lunch today for a sex crimes cop in Mentor. We ate at
Molinari's—Italian, like you can tell from the name, which
isn't a cheap fast-food joint, so I hope you'll reimburse me
anyway. His name is Jake Foote.

I told him I worked for you. He said he never met you but
he's heard of you—and he knows Suzanne. I think they dated
once, but I can't swear to it—just got the feeling.

I asked about sex crimes in his area, and hinted what
Earl did for fun with his camcorder. He said there are more
people than we can imagine—voyeur perverts who love
taking upskirt pictures and videos, hiding cams in women's
restrooms and showers and changing rooms in health clubs,
etc. They even hide cameras inside toilet bowls. God!
Sometimes they're busted—but no police task force is out to
get them because there are more important things to take
care of, like child prostitution.

Probably when you were a kid, you never even HEARD
of sex until you were in your mid-teens. Today, sex is even
in middle schools. The girls who prostitute are recruited by
their own friends; they're told as long as they have sex with
guys their own age, they might as well do it with older men
and make good money. Sergeant Foote made a major bust
at a public school out here two months ago. He collared six
different girls for selling sex—and one of them was only
twelve years old! Jesus, that was hard to hear.

So here's Jake Foote's take. Upskirt pictures and videos are
illegal, naturally, but chances are against going to prison for
it. Most of the photographers are sleazebag sickos getting
their jollies, but would run like hell if any woman actually
wanted to fuck them. But when the subjects are under age,
that kicks it up into a more serious crime. In Earl's videos,
it's hard to tell how old anyone is just by their ass and their
underwear.

After lunch I tootled back over to Beachwood Place
and talked with Carli. Don't get your shorts in a bunch, I
wasn't flirting—at least not much. She said about half her
customers are teens. So where does Earl Dacey fit?

I still don't know if I'm working for you or not—or if
anybody's going to try to kill me. So until I hear from you
one way or the other, I'll just sit around and wait.

K.O.

I saved his email to my computer, printed out a copy for my
files, and wrote back to tell him he *still* worked for me—on slip-
pery probation—and asked him to come by the office in the
morning.

Then I called McHargue. She wasn't in—even gold-shield cops
have to go home sometime—and messaged her K.O. would meet
her face to face at nine A.M. I hadn't mentioned that to K.O., because I didn't want to scare him off. Flo McHargue scares off a lot
of people, and some of them even work for her.

I opened another Stroh's, wolfed down a handful of water
crackers I bought from Trader Joe's and went to bed, thinking
sadly about Anna Barna and her loyal friend from kindergarten,
who'd asked her to let him videotape up her dress.

Everybody gets hurt, it seems, when they least expect it.

CHAPTER ELEVEN

I microwaved a bowl of oatmeal the next morning, melting a spoonful of butter on top of it. I'd heard—probably on some breathless soft TV news show that had run out of anything important to report—that people who eat oatmeal for breakfast feel better all day long. I didn't think it would improve my mood as much as listening to the Lanigan and Malone Show on the radio. Lanigan and Malone never failed to fight like hell over every topic—and both argue with their associates, Chip Kullik and Tracey Carroll, which was invariably good for more than one laugh. Besides, Tracey Carroll has a very sexy voice that gets my attention every morning.

That morning, I listened in the car as they interviewed an author I'd never heard of. I pulled into my parking lot; K.O. was leaning against his front fender, waiting for me. We went upstairs together. He'd dressed up a bit—light blue shirt, khaki slacks, and a lightweight sports jacket—which meant he wanted to impress me so I wouldn't send him home jobless.

"You had an interesting talk with Sergeant Foote in Mentor. How'd you manage that?"

"He was in juvie before he switched to Sex Crimes," K.O. told me. "He was the one who collared me. He stood up for me at the trial, and we stayed in touch after that. If it'd been up to Foote, he would have put those two punks I beat up in jail for life, and given me a medal, because he's got two dogs of his own—rescued greyhounds." He crinkled up his nose. "The judge didn't see it his way."

I nodded. "What did Foote say about Earl Dacey? If Earl took upskirt videos of underage girls, where did he sell them?"

"That's the big question," K.O. said. "Lots of pornographers make their bread off the Internet. There used to be plenty of adult movie theaters around here, but they closed up. Nobody'd pay ten bucks to sit in a filthy, bad-smelling theater watching porn and jerking off under their raincoats when they can do it at home for nothing."

"You do get around, don't you, K.O.? What else do I need to know?"

"No one buys dirty movies when they can find anything they want online. That's where pornographers sell their wares." He looked over his shoulder as we both heard the downstairs door open and footsteps coming upstairs. "Are we expecting company?"

"I think so." I waited until McHargue and Matusen made their entrance. There was a moment when nobody moved—rival cowboys running into each other at the Long Branch Saloon, trigger fingers twitching. Finally I introduced the homicide cops to K.O.

K.O. gave me a dirty look out of the corner of his eye, as if I'd set him up.

McHargue sat in the only available chair left in the room, while Matusen leaned against the wall by the window, the sun at his back making him a silhouette. Joe never took his attention from what his boss was saying.

"So you work for Jacovich, eh? Trying to be a real-life private eye on your own," she said to my assistant.

He shrugged. "It's a dirty job, but somebody's gotta do it."

"Amen to that. It'll take you a while to get started, though—learning all the private eye tricks. Done any law enforcement before?"

"No, but I spent six years in the army, in Iraq and Afghanistan. Does that count?"

McHargue looked momentarily impressed, then said, "So you know deserts and sand. This is Cleveland."

"All I know is, the army sent me there when I was eighteen, so I went there. Now I'm home."

"Cleveland's your home?"

"Close enough."

"What does that mean?"

"It means I live outside your jurisdiction."

McHargue drummed her fingers on my desk, fingernails clicking against wood. "A smart-ass, huh? Just like your boss?"

"Kevin lives in Lake County," I said. "And I'm not his boss. He's doing part-time research for me."

That seemed to amuse the lieutenant enough to elicit an annoyed smirk. "You're going to let the smart-ass part of my observation go without comment?"

"I've learned not to cross swords with you," I admitted.

"Took you long enough. What kind of research is he doing?"

"You can ask me directly," K.O. said. "I'm sitting right here."

McHargue's patented glare would annihilate a row of birds sitting on a fence, but K.O. didn't even blink.

I hoped to intercept her death-ray look. "Lieutenant, you didn't come over to give Kevin a bad time when I'm still here for you to kick around."

"I've bounced *your* head against the wall so often, it's no fun anymore," she said. "So—to business. Does a Ms. Riona Dennehy mean anything to you?"

I shook my head. "Never heard the name."

"It's an old Celtic name," K.O. said. "It means 'like a queen.' Matter of fact, the word *Regina*—as in 'Elizabeth Regina'—came from Riona." All three of us were somewhere between surprised and astonished.

"O'Bannion is an Irish surname," he said, "so I know about stuff like that."

"Good for you," Matusen put in. When McHargue looked at him, he ducked his head, growing smaller like Alice in Wonderland when she drank what was in the magic bottle.

"*Riona* Dennehy," McHargue said, leaning into the unfamiliar first name like a major league pitcher bearing down to throw a high, hard one, "lives in Twinsburg."

"Lots of people live in Twinsburg."

"Well this Twinsburgian—Twinsburgite? God, they *couldn't* call themselves Twinsburgers, could they? It sounds like it comes with cheese and bacon. Anyway, according to Vice, Dennehy is under suspicion for recruiting middle and high school girls into prostitution."

"*Middle* school?" I couldn't help sounding aghast.

"She starts out paying them well to appear in porn movies she finances. After that she eases them into selling their bodies without a camera present. Now, I'm not talking about street hookers who are owned by their pimps and mistreated. These girls live with their parents, but they mostly turn their tricks in the afternoons or on Saturdays. I suppose they tell their folks they're at the library, studying."

"I never imagined it in an upscale suburb like Twinsburg," I said.

"Pick a suburb—any suburb. Twinsburg, Solon, Stow, Lakewood, Rocky River. In the past few years it's become big business."

"Why don't you arrest Dennehy?"

"We need proof." She blew breath out noisily between her lips. "Dacey was found dead in Twinsburg, and since he was gearing up to sell low-level dirty videos, maybe Riona knew him."

"Could be." I shrugged. "Or maybe it's just a coincidence."

"You should have a meaningful chat with her."

"Me?" Automatically my hand went to my desk drawer, where I kept my Winstons until I quit smoking a year ago. I wasn't ready to admit I worked for Savannah Dacey illegally. "I can't stick my nose into open capital crime investigations—according to you."

Her hands gripped the edge of my desk, and she spoke loudly to make sure I heard her. "Riona Dennehy is a relatively wealthy woman. She's got so many lawyers coming out her ass, the police can't even knock on her door unless they have proof—and a warrant. You, however, are not a police officer." She cleared her throat. "I'd just as soon bust Dennehy for murder instead of pimping out minors. That way she'll be an old lady before she gets out. And if the State of Ohio gives her a legal injection cocktail down in Columbus, that'd be even better." Her glance lingered too long on K.O. "Maybe you should send your friend to talk to her instead."

"Why?"

She stood up and moved toward the door, Matusen following her like a well-trained puppy. "Because he'd win her confidence. Dennehy would talk to him before she'd talk to you because she wouldn't believe for one minute an old fart like you is scuffling around for underage pussy." She stopped at the door, so quickly that Matusen almost ran into her head on, and turned back to K.O. "Make it snappy, O'Bannion—time's a wastin'."

"Yes, ma'am." He dripped sarcasm. "By this time tomorrow I'll have memorized your phone number, too."

K.O. and I didn't speak until we heard McHargue's car engine turn over and she left some rubber in my parking lot. Then K.O. said, "I don't think she likes you."

I held up my crossed fingers. "She and I are like this."

"Then she must have been in a lousy mood."

"That was her *good* mood. And since she doesn't like taking no for an answer, it looks like you better go talk to Dennehy."

"Jeez. When?"

I looked at my watch—pointedly. "Don't rush out to Twinsburg. Stop for breakfast on your way."

When he left I moved to the windows to open them and let the fresh morning air in. Before he got into his car, he took off his jacket and hung it on a hanger in the backseat. He'd only been with me a few days and already he was acting more professional. He'd spent a large chunk of his adult life in a war the government sent him to—but his working outfit there had been combat fatigues and who knew what else, since he hadn't shared much about his Middle East tours with me.

Maybe when we grew to know each other better.

If we grew to know each other better.

McHargue apparently had faith in him, or she wouldn't have suggested he enter Dennehy's home which she, as a badge carrier, wasn't allowed to. So K.O. and I were working gratis for the Cleveland P.D. whether we wanted to or not. Maybe McHargue and I help each other out because it's good for both of us.

I doodled on a yellow pad, keeping my hands busy while I mulled over what I'd learned about Earl. My doodles are always the same, and have been since childhood—always old-fashioned gallows with empty hangman's nooses. Fortunately my imagination has veered away from victims actually dangling from the nooses.

Okay—Earl made mildly dirty videos, and the young girls, many of them minors, were victims unaware. I'd talked to a few porn distributors who'd denied any involvement with Earl. I wondered which ones were lying. I wished I could put Earl out of my mind, but this mother still wanted my help—and I understand about parents.

The only good thing that had come out of my investigation so far was a dinner date the following evening with Cisne Kelly. I was planning what to say and *how* to say it casually so it wouldn't sound like I'd rehearsed it—when some more uninvited visitors dropped in, interrupting my doodling.

There were three of them, all dark-haired with olive complexions. Two were somewhere in their twenties—very large, muscular beneath their loose short-sleeved shirts, and not pretty to look at. The third entered my office a step or two behind them—older than his advance guards, smaller, chunky, wearing a shiny gray lightweight suit and a too-thick cornflower blue necktie.

"You're Milan Jacovich," the older man said—a statement.

"I know that."

"You know who *I* am?"

Of course I knew who he was. "How many guesses do I get?"

"Funny," he said. "You're a funny guy."

"I know that, too. You're Jimmy Santocroce."

"Bingo," he smiled. His four front teeth were bonded, looking whiter than the rest.

"Do I win anything?"

"Sure," he said. "You get to sit down—and not lay down."

Cisne, my favorite English teacher even though I barely knew her, would have pointed out he should have said "lie" instead of "lay." I sat behind my desk and Santocroce took one of the chairs opposite me, unbuttoning his jacket so it wouldn't wrinkle in the heat. The trousers were Sansabelt.

"I got things to do," he said, "so I get right to the point. You put a friend of mine in the hospital."

"What friend is that?"

He looked irritated by the question. "Angelo Nicolino, like you didn' know."

"I've never met Angelo Nicolino, much less put him in the hospital."

"Somebody who works for you, then."

I didn't answer.

"He was asking Angelo questions—about some dweeby lurp, name of Earl something. Dancy. Earl Dancy."

"Dacey," I corrected him.

"I don't give a shit about this Dancy. Don't know him, or want to. But I don't like my friends getting hurt."

One hit man stood by the door and the other moved to the window. Both wore their shirttails out, and I knew what those tails covered, especially because the window guy's hip bulged a bit with his weapon.

"So you told whoever works for you to hurt him," he said.

"Do you know what your friend who got hurt does for a living?" I said. "Making films of animals being tortured to death."

"It don't matter—it ain't my business. But he *is* my business. He's my friend—like a cousin." He shrugged broadly. "So who's this guy works for you?"

"He's—a guy who works for me."

"He got a name?"

"Everybody does. Didn't he introduce himself to Angelo Nicolino?"

"Before he beat the shit out of him? Angelo don't remember. He got kicked in the head so many times, he don't remember much—except that the guy works for you."

"Victor Gaimari already told you that."

Santocroce leaned forward as if he'd been pushed from behind, and clenched his fist to shake in front of my face. "Victor Gaimari!" He almost spit Victor's name. "Fuck him in the ass, he should die with a hard-on!"

"Colorful," I said.

"I don't pay no attention to him—and I didn' pay no attention to his uncle when he was alive. Yeah, he called to tell me—but I don't do what he says."

"And what did he say?"

"That you didn' do nothing and I should leave you alone."

"So this is a friendly social call?"

Santocroce relaxed. "Exactly. That's exactly right. You tell me the name of the guy works for you—an' where we find him—an' I'll be so friendly you won't believe how quiet I'll be walkin' outta here."

The one at the door had hardly moved a muscle; the window guy shifted his weight from foot to foot. Both had their arms crossed over their chests, studying me in case they'd have to draw my picture later from memory.

"Walk out quietly *now*," I suggested. "I don't pass out information to just anyone."

Santocroce lost his bullshit smile. "I'm not just anyone—and I'm running out a patience."

"Patience is a virtue."

"I don' got many virtues."

"Is that why you make your living off porn?"

"Do I look like I should work driving a bus?" He levered himself out of his chair. "Stand up, Jacovich."

"I thought getting to sit down in my own office was my privilege."

"Up," he repeated.

There was indeed my own handgun in my desk drawer—but by the time I got it out and ready to function, I'd be toast. Besides, it wasn't the kind of situation in which anyone shoots anyone else. Not yet.

I stood up. Santocroce's hitters stirred themselves and came to flank him. I came around the desk to stand face to face with the old guy—or as close to it as I could get with a man eight inches shorter than I was. "Bad idea, Jimmy."

"I got bad ideas before—but I always go with 'em. So you got one more chance to tell me the guy's name and where he lives— and no hard feelings. Or the boys here'll break your fingers, one by one, so your memory improves. Whaddya think about that?"

"The boys?" I regarded them. "Is that what you call them? The boys? Adorable."

"You're tryin' to be a funny guy again."

"Let's laugh, then," I said.

Santocroce was taking it easy; he had his hired muscle with him, so he didn't expect me to reach out, spin him around, grab his wrist with one hand, and push his elbow the wrong way with my other one. The pain surprised and shocked him, sending him so high up on his toes, he nearly flew out of his shoes.

He grunted—which wasn't good enough for me. I jacked his arm up further—he could almost scratch his head from behind—and the grunt turned into a scream. The "boys" moved forward, both reaching under their shirttails at the same time.

"If you touch that hardware," I said, "when I break Jimmy's arm, they'll hear his elbow snap all the way to Cuyahoga Falls."

Santocroce struggled, so I hurt him some more. "Tell 'em, Jimmy."

He was mumbling under his breath in a high pitch, sounding as if he were crying. I couldn't discern whether he was actually praying to Jesus or just having a conversation, but he said His name three or four times through clenched teeth until I gave his distressed elbow some leeway. Not much, though.

Finally he said, "Back off."

"Don't back too far off, boys" I said. "Take out your weapons—using just the thumb and the index finger—and hold them out where I can see them."

The two men looked at each other, and the bigger one shrugged. He brought his .22 out slowly, holding it the way I'd instructed. The .22 is the kind of weapon gangs use for close-up assassinations.

"Very good," I said. "It looks feminine, holding it like that, but I won't tell anyone if you don't." I looked at the other one. "Your turn."

"Hurry up, Leonard," Santocroce whimpered. "He's fuckin' killin' me."

"Yes," I echoed, "hurry up, Leonard." I asked the other one what his name was.

"Roger," he said sullenly.

What kind of Italian names are Leonard and Roger?

When they both had their .22s between their fingers, I said,

"Drop them—very gently—on the floor right in front of you. Very good—now kick them under my desk. Excellent." I decreased the pressure on Santocroce's elbow, but not enough to suit him.

"All right, then. Now Leonard—I want you and your girlfriend there to go downstairs and wait for your boss."

Leonard looked wounded and defensive. "He's not my girlfriend," he murmured. He had a high voice that didn't match his hulk, but it made him no less intimidating. Victor Gaimari has a high voice, too—and best you not forget that it doesn't fit him at all.

"Don't come back up here—because now I have both your weapons, and one of my own, too. I'd just as soon use them as not. *Capisce?*"

"They *capisce*, they *capisce*!" the old man said, wriggling against me to try easing the agony in his arm, elbow, and shoulder. "Jesus!"

"Get rid of them, Jimmy."

It took him about ten seconds to decide. Then he said, "Go—wait for me downstairs."

The boys looked rankled and out of sorts, but shuffled out as if they were hooked together on a chain gang. I waited until Leonard and Roger were downstairs, then lessened the pressure on Santocroce's elbow.

"I'm letting you loose now, Jimmy. Don't get cute with me, all right? Because one on one, you don't have the chance of a snowball in hell."

He made a noise deep in his throat like the warning growl of a cornered wolverine, but I took it as assent. I released him, and he staggered away, rubbing and massaging his elbow with his other hand.

"You fucking *strunz*!" he said.

"The bully act doesn't impress me. Are you a bully when you make your porno films with little girls, too?"

"They aren't little girls," he protested.

"They aren't grown, either. Are they the ones Riona Dennehy introduces you to?"

"I don't know no Riona Dennehy."

"I'll find out anyway. I never laid eyes on your friend in the hospital. Whatever went down, it's over. If you come around again with your boys, you're really going to get hurt. Not just a sore arm, Jimmy, and that's a guarantee."

Hate shone out of him like the eyes of a bad actor cast in a cheap horror film as a vampire. "You'll get yours," he warned, "you goddamn Polack!"

"Slovenian," I corrected him.

"You don't fool me none." Santocroce flexed his fingers, trying to get blood flowing through them again. "You're like me—an old guy. It's not so hard trying to hurt old guys."

"I'll keep that in mind, Jimmy." His "old guy" crack hit too close to home and hurt like a bee sting. "And if I see you again, you'll be scratching your ass left-handed for the rest of your life." I made a point of checking my watch. "Now run along—and tell Leonard and Roger they suck at their jobs."

He slinked toward the door. I'd humiliated him back with "run along." You just don't tell a mob guy, especially a two-bit one like Jimmy Santocroce, to "run along."

"And you," he said, "better sleep with both eyes open."

CHAPTER TWELVE

I cruised into Vuk's Tavern a few minutes after five. I grew up in Vuk's Tavern—literally. Located in the St. Clair-Superior Corridor, it's where my father used to drink. On Sunday afternoons he'd perch me at one end of the bar where the little TV set has always been, so I could watch a Browns or an Indians game and suck on a parade of ginger ales while he bonded with his Slovenian friends and fellow steelworkers.

Overseeing everything was Louis Vukovich, the owner-bartender. He's close to eighty now, but his looks never seem to change. A big man, broad of shoulder, with large hands, a paunch, electric blue eyes, and a handlebar mustache, he's known to everyone, friend or foe alike, as "Vuk." He's still behind that bar from opening time to last call. The economy has bounced everybody, so he no longer opens at six A.M. but waits until eleven o'clock in the morning—and instead of hanging on until midnight he'll close up when business dwindles, sometimes at nine o'clock. I had my first *legal* drink—a Stroh's beer—on my twenty-first birthday, and Vuk ceremoniously placed it in front of me without a glass and announced that because of my special natal day, the Stroh's was on the house. It was my last *free* drink in that tavern. Vuk runs a business, not a charity.

The tavern has a smell all its own. Whiskey bottles are lined up behind the bar, although most are covered with dust from neglect. What you can smell is beer—mostly Stroh's in this Slovenian-Croatian neighborhood. It's what's kept Vuk's open for half a century.

There are other scents, too, including the disinfectant splashed over everything before its owner opens the doors, and the ghost of stale cigarette smoke from before Cleveland outlawed smoking in public places like restaurants and taverns some years ago.

I didn't patronize Vuk's the way I used to, but I came in whenever I could, when I was "in the neighborhood" and needed the security of being around someone I'd known all my life. I'd cut back on my drinking, but I missed it—not the alcohol itself, but the sociability of taverns.

"Whaddya say, Milan?" Vuk had greeted me that way forever. I don't think he cares a damn *what* I say, but it's a ritual. He set down a Stroh's without asking. If I ever decided to change beer brands he'd have a major heart attack from the shock. "You haven't come around in a while. Where you been?"

"Working hard, like always." I raised the Stroh's as a salute and took a sip. The beer from Vuk's cooler was icier and more bracing than at any other bar in Cleveland. "I'm getting older—sometimes it wears me out to come here and drink."

He made one of those denigrating sounds I can't describe. "You're still a kid, fer crysakes! Remember who you're talkin' to here."

"This kid has joined AARP."

"Who cares? I'm no joiner. So, what brings you here?"

"I'm meeting Ed Stahl."

Vuk scrunched up his eyes and crinkled his nose; it was halfway between a frown and the face you make when you smell something bad. "Him." He shook his head sadly and moved toward the other end of the bar. "That sumbitch never smiles."

Ed Stahl is a damn good writer—and everyone knows it, even though many have disagreed with him and sent insulting e-mails or left profanity on his voice mail. He doesn't need to prove how good he is, but at the bottom of his desk drawer is his Pulitzer Prize medal. He refuses to brag about it, though he boasts about his city all the time.

He's also short-tempered, cantankerous, and opinionated, and he argues about everything. Those who know him would swear he owns only one tweed sports jacket, two astonishingly ugly ties, and one pair of brown slip-on shoes with run-down heels in which he's marched through too many Cleveland winters. But they won't tell him that. His friends also won't mention that *nobody* smokes a pipe anymore, and though he's the only person in Cleveland who'll puff away at it where he shouldn't, sending clouds of obnoxious smoke toward the ceiling, no one has the guts to remind him it's against the law. His horn-rimmed glasses make us all think of how Clark Kent would have looked if he and his alter ego, Superman, had aged.

Ed has an ulcer, but he drinks Jim Beam on the rocks and winces every time it hit his stomach. He was divorced thirty years ago, and if he has a romantically significant woman in his life now, it's a secret to the world.

But Ed is all-seeing and all-knowing—and if you want info about anyone even moderately important locally, Ed's the first person you ask. He'll supply the answers, especially those concerning some sort of scandal.

I'd invited him for an after-work drink while giving him a quick rundown of the Earl Dacey situation on the phone. I let him know about K.O., too, which didn't surprise him—nothing ever did—and ended with a short summary of my visits that morning from Santocroce and his muscle boys, and from the homicide officers. Ed had thought it out carefully before he left his office.

He knocked down a fast Jim Beam, ordered another one, and fired up his pipe, earning baleful looks, but nobody complained when they saw it was Ed Stahl. Then he started on my inquiry. "Jimmy Santocroce," he intoned, handing down one of those immutable truths, "is a moron."

I knew that already, but laughed anyway.

"He never hooked up with D'Allessandro's family—and that makes him a dumb schmuck. Just because he's Italian in a shady business he envisions himself a major mob guy. I don't know why they didn't squish him like a roach, but he's not important enough to be squished."

"Where did he make his money, then? He pays bodyguard protection—even if they aren't so good at it."

The acrid smell of burnt cherries rose from Ed's pipe to the ceiling. "When he was thirtyish, he was a small-time player. He ran a few hookers—black girls he peddled out in Lake County where almost everyone was white and fucking a black woman was an exotic adventure—and he had a teeny-tiny protection racket with small businesses in Collinwood or on East 185th Street, except his business was probably one ten-thousandth as profitable or effective as Al Capone's. Eventually everybody got wise to him and shagged his ass out of that area altogether."

"And Don Giancarlo D'Allessandro never landed on him with both feet?"

"Hookers were never his business, and Santocroce's protection thing didn't earn enough money to bother with. It's like your neighbor's TV playing too loud after eleven P.M.—annoying but not worth the trouble."

"The old man's gone now. And Victor Gaimari isn't as understanding."

"That's because Santocroce's current income has nothing to do with the mob."

"Porn?"

Ed said, "Damn tootin'. Twenty years ago there were porno theaters and adult bookstores all over the place where you could buy dirty movies on tape. You remember them on West 25th Street, or Brook Park Road or Clark Street. Well, most of 'em are gone."

"I never noticed," I said.

He grinned around his next sip. "You don't pay attention. People aren't tired of pornography—they're more into it than ever. But it's on the Internet—you can browse for free, and eventually buy and download whatever kink floats your boat, right from your living room." He observed me. "Don't deny it—you watch online porn yourself, like every other normal human being of both genders and all sexual proclivities."

"I'm jotting that down. 'Sexual proclivities.' Who talks like you, anyway?"

"People who write words of more than one syllable." He waved at Vuk and lifted his empty glass. Vuk came over and wordlessly poured him a refill. The tavern was a public place, but Vuk had little to do with people who weren't Slovenian or Croatian—or people he didn't know. He knew Ed, but Ed didn't drink in there without me, so to Vuk he was still barely more than a stranger.

"Santocroce makes a living putting dirty movies online," Ed

said after tasting his new drink, "and selling ad space to other people with kinks. The bad thing is, some of the participants in his productions are underage—boys and girls both. Now, his name and address are nowhere to be found on the Internet, so even if the FBI chases him, it'd take years to unravel the complicated Web puzzle guys like Santocroce have set up."

"He doesn't sound all that stupid to me," I said.

"The only non-stupid thing he does is hire somebody smarter than him to help him."

"And who is that smarter person?"

"If I knew," Ed said, "there wouldn't *be* any more Internet porn."

By the time he was ready for another drink, I was finished. Beer hits me harder than it used to. So Ed moved on to his next bar—either Nighttown, two blocks from my apartment, or the Tavern Company on Lee Road, just across the street from the Cedar Lee Theatre—both relatively close to his Cleveland Heights home. It was Friday evening, and all the bars were crowded. I hated crowds—so I headed home with one of those early-stage fuzzy headaches. The next morning I had a funeral to attend.

The Catholic church where Earl Dacey's final ceremony took place was nothing like a cathedral, just a homely little church named for an unfamiliar saint, not far from the Dacey home in West Park. There were only about twenty mourners present, including me, Lieutenant McHargue, and Bob Matusen, and of course a teary-eyed Anna Barna.

Savannah was dressed in a black skirt and a new-looking black blouse buttoned almost to the neck, both most likely purchased for the sorrowful occasion. She probably didn't attend many funerals. Neither did I, avoiding them when I could, because I own only two suits. One of them, dark gray, was winter wool, so I chose instead the blue, only a bit lighter in weight, and sat there discreetly patting my forehead, upper lip, and neck with my handkerchief while the priest fizzled on, his canned speech long and boring.

I tried scoping out the mourners, but with the exception of

Anna, I knew none of them. Most were women about Savannah's age, sitting with her in the front two rows on the right, one with her arms about the bereaved parent's shoulders and patting her absent-mindedly like a mother trying to coax her baby to burp.

There were only two other males attending. One was middle-aged, looking as if he hadn't put a tie around his neck in years, sweating profusely in a light gray sports jacket, wet beneath the arms. The other was someone else I didn't know—although I soon would—youngish, well-clothed and barbered, wearing big, expensive sunglasses and not looking as if he were in mourning or even mildly upset about the violent death of Earl Dacey. He was more interested in looking at the other mourners than at the priest, Earl's closed casket, or Savannah Dacey. I was equally interested in him, although unaware that the two of us would soon bump heads like two Colorado mountain goats fighting over a female.

I tried not to nod off, putting up with the endless-seeming drone of the priest, a smallish, elderly fellow with a vague Irish brogue, It was clear that he hardly knew Earl Dacey; his elegy could easily have applied to anyone. I listened to the quiet sobbing of Savannah and the cooing succor of the women surrounding her. I could have sworn I heard one of them utter a soothing "There, there."

McHargue's eyes locked with mine, then she nodded and looked away. She was there not to mourn the deceased but to check out if the person who killed him had showed up at his funeral.

The priest wound up saying Earl Dacey was ensconced in the warm embrace of the Lord. I'm not sure whether I even believe in the Lord anymore, but if He's indeed up in heaven, does He really cuddle Earl so warmly without a few disapproving words to him about his voyeuristic photos and who knows what else? Or perhaps the priest knew nothing about Earl's peculiarities and had no idea he might not end up in heaven at all.

Half the mourners filed out as the organ bleated, only a few kneeling and crossing themselves first. I didn't kneel. I can't remember when my last real confession took place, probably when I was still in high school.

On the sidewalk, where it was even hotter, Savannah's eyes were fire red from crying, and the tears made her mascara run down her cheeks like rivers printed on a map. Her female friends surrounded her, touching her and clucking. I battled my way through them.

"I'm so sorry, Savannah." I managed to get my arm around her and touched my cheek to hers. She spoke quietly into my ear, "Don't fail me, Milan; I'm counting on you," and I had to retort with a whispered "Shhh" so the Cleveland homicide cops wouldn't catch on that Savannah was paying me to break the rules.

"Are you coming to the cemetery?" one of Savannah's supporters demanded, hands on hips as though challenging me to follow the party to the grave site.

Enough was enough. "Sorry, I can't." I took the grief-stricken mother's hand and squeezed it gently. "We'll be talking."

The moment I stepped away from her, the women surrounded her again, taking up the space I'd so recently vacated. I couldn't even see her anymore.

I headed around the corner to where I'd parked my car. McHargue and Matusen were waiting for me.

"I thought you resigned from this case," she said.

"I'm paying my respects—just as *you're* doing."

"We're doing our *work*," Matusen said.

"On a Saturday? Wowie!"

McHargue said, "If we don't solve murders between Monday and Friday, we're shit out of luck, huh?"

"One thing's for damn sure," I said. "Earl Dacey is out of luck."

When I drove by the front of the church on the way back to the Flats, McHargue and Matusen were still there, standing near the curb. Matusen wasn't saying much—he never did when his boss was around. But McHargue was talking earnestly to the youngish guy with the short haircut.

On Collision Bend, it was relatively quiet. River traffic was busy, boaters and their guests sucking up every moment of summer. There was nothing doing in my office, so I collected the mail that had been squeezed through a slot in my door and shuffled through it. Bills—always bills. There was a check from a late-paying client who'd been dodging me for the past four months. The rest were ads—a ton of them. Between the snail mail delivered to my office and apartment, at least one tree must have died every year so I could get harassed to buy things I didn't want in the first place.

I flipped open my laptop and logged on. I knew there would be even more ads for me online, and various organizations asking for donations. The political party I almost never vote for had gotten hold of my e-mail address and put me on their list. I put them into my spam every day and even e-mailed them begging to be removed from their list, but it didn't stop them.

Late the previous afternoon K.O. had e-mailed me. I'd forgotten I'd sent him on a sticky errand. I needed time to read his e-mail carefully before going home to shower and make myself look relatively presentable for my first dinner date with the lovely Cisne Kelly.

I sat down at my desk, angling the laptop so there wasn't much glare from the windows, and clicked on Kevin O'Bannion's latest electronic missive.

Friday
Milan:
Very interesting morning. Stopped for breakfast at Jack's Deli. I think I was the only customer in there who's not Jewish and doesn't belong to AARP.

From there I drove to Riona Dennehy's in Twinsburg. She lives in an upscale development, houses all look pretty much the same from the outside. It's off Route 91, not far from Tinker's Creek, where they found Dacey's body.

I knocked on her door at 11:30. When she opened it she looked as if she might be going out. Not real attractive, in her fifties, dressed in a light blue pantsuit and dark blue blouse, platform heels, about 30 lbs overweight.

I figured she wouldn't talk to me if she knew I worked for a P.I., so I kind of made up a story. I told her I'd heard she produced local movies for distribution.

"Where'd you hear that?" she said. She looked suspicious as hell.

"Around," I said.

"WHERE around?"

I told her I was looking for work.

"Work? You always knock on strange doors looking for work? What kind of work?"

"I want to be an actor."

She checked me out and looked like she didn't believe me.

"How old are you, anyway?"

"Twenty-four. I can show you my driver's license if you want."

"You can buy phony IDs anywhere. Don't bullshit me, sonny." She considered that. "Have you done any acting?"

"Just in high school," I said. "Some amateur theater. Little theater."

"Not that kind of acting. Look—you heard I produce movies, right? Well then you know what kind. You're not gonna be a movie star doing sex films."

I told her I was just trying to make some easy money doing something I liked to do anyway.

"O.K. then," she said, "Let's see what you've got to offer the public. Drop your pants and show me your dick. I don't hire actors with small dicks."

"Then put five on the table," I said. "I don't go around flashing. This is business."

I know how tough I am—this suburban pimp didn't have to tell me. (Is there a feminine word for pimp? Pimp-ess?) "Maybe I just came to the wrong place," I said.

"Maybe. Who sent you, anyway?"

"Nobody sent me. I'm trying to connect. Do you know a guy named Earl Dacey?"

When she heard that she jumped to her feet and said, "What about him?"

"He's dead."

"I know." She walked toward the window. "I read it in the paper."

"He didn't act in any movies for you, did he?"

She laughed. "Geeky kids with acne don't appear in my films."

"So you knew him," I said.

She chewed the inside of her cheek. "No. I met him. Once, for about half an hour. He had video clips and photographs he was trying to sell."

"Did you buy any of them?"

"Of course not. Cheap amateur voyeur crap. They weren't worth a nickel."

I asked her if she had any idea who killed him.

"How the hell would I know?"

I said they were both involved in the porn business, and maybe he crossed somebody or something.

"Hey, this isn't criminal activity here. Adult films are a legal business."

"Not when they're made with minors," I said.

"I don't know anything about minors," she said. "Anybody in my pictures is at least eighteen. Hey—what did you hear about me, anyway?" she snapped. "Why are you sneaking around asking me about minors? Are you a cop? Let's see your badge."

I told her I wasn't a cop.

"Then get your ass out of here—or I'll call somebody to escort you out."

I said that sounded like a threat.

"Royce!" she yelled, and a few seconds later a guy came down from upstairs. About six feet tall with a shiny oiled skull and a complexion like milk chocolate. Sweatpants and a T-shirt 2 sizes too small for him to show off his six-pack and muscles. Guys who are all muscled can't really fight for shit, but I headed for the door while he watched me from the stairs. I didn't know what he might try—and I didn't wait around to find out. I wasn't in the mood for a fight.

So after all that, here's what I think: Riona Dennehy knew Earl but not well. I don't like her but I believed her. Makes sense: He wasn't important enough to anyone in the porn business to make someone mad enough to kill him.

Earl lived in a spare bedroom in his mother's house, didn't own any nice clothes, drove a car older then he was, spent money shooting dumb videos. If nobody gives a damn about him, who killed him?

Anyway, that's what I thought about. If you want to talk
it over some more, email me or call me—I'll be home all
weekend.

Except tonight. I'm going out with Carli. Wish me luck.

K.O.

I wished us both luck. Saturday might be special for both of
us. I hoped so.

I checked my watch. Time for me to go home, shower (again),
and select the outfit that would make me look my first-date best.
I was closing things up when I heard the footsteps on the stairs
that previewed the first-time visit of Special Agent Jeffrey Kitzberger.

But you know all about that.

CHAPTER THIRTEEN

riving out to Lake County, I still simmered over Kitzberger's invasion of my office. His mug shots were of people involved with producing and distributing indecent films. Apparently that's what the FBI—or at least the local office—were after.

Good for them, I thought. I was as much against pornography as they were—and even more infuriated by the use of underage children in porn and prostitution.

But I hated bullies, too—and that persona was what made Kitzberger tick. Maybe it just came with the badge. Our brief meeting probably put me on Kitzberger's fecal scroll, but who cared? It wouldn't be the first time, either.

I put it out of my mind and concentrated on my evening. I hadn't been on a boy-girl date for almost a year, and feared I'd forgotten how. I wasn't bringing flowers or a gift because in the twenty-first century, first dates were casual. No limousine, no corsages, no elegant dress-up—I wore gray slacks and a dark blue dress shirt, and I suppose I stewed over my look, even flipping down the visor in my car to check my appearance in the mirror. I was fifty-nine years old with nothing left to prove, no dreams driving me on, but damn it, Cisne Kelly was a very attractive young woman—and I use the word *young* advisedly. She was no child—probably in her late thirties—but to me, that was young.

So why was I on this first date, anyway? Everyone makes a fool

of themselves more than once in their lifetimes—but I was terri-
fied of making myself an *old* fool.

I'd chosen Gavi's for dinner in downtown Willoughby. It's been
around for a couple of decades, one of the best Italian restaurants
anywhere in the area. I didn't pick up Cisne at her house—we
decided to meet in the Gavi's parking lot and go in together. I got
there first, five minutes early. It's my habit.

Things worked out perfectly. Cisne showed up one minute
early—and I was impressed all over again. She looked lovely in
her fitted black jeans, a silky black blouse with a white scarf at
her neck, and her hair loose and hanging nearly to her waist in
gentle dark-blonde waves. I tried not to notice everyone else noticing her.

The waitress gave us menus and handed me a fairly lengthy
wine list. I didn't know the first thing about wines and was
scared I'd do something astonishingly stupid and louse up the
evening before it got started. Cisne, however, gave me her wide
smile. "Shall we get a bottle of wine, Milan, or are you a whiskey
drinker?"

I'd never learned about viniculture—so my first instinct was
to use Bela Lugosi's accent, saying, "I never drink—*wine.*" I managed to control what there was of my sense of humor. Besides, she
might not have seen Lugosi as Dracula and the joke would be lost
on her. I said, "Let's have wine, if you prefer."

I opened the wine list and stared at it for too long, not com-
prehending, and then passed it across the table to her. "It's your
choice. Pick something good."

Those blue eyes looked amused. "I get the feeling you aren't a
wine snob."

"That's why you're choosing."

"Well, then . . ." She scanned the list. "Somewhere in the middle—not as pricey as a new Cadillac and not as tacky as wine-in-
a-box. Red or white?"

"It's an Italian restaurant."

"Red it is, then." She ordered a Zinfandel from Napa Valley,
California—which sounded good to me. But then what did I
know?

Then she said, "You're a beer drinker?"

"My drinking—anything alcoholic—has slowed to a crawl."

"Mine's always crawled. I can count on the fingers of one hand how many alcoholic drinks I've had on my own in my whole life."

"It sounds as if you're more Spanish than Irish."

"The eyes and hair are Irish," she admitted, "and the temper. The rest? Who knows?"

"And you've never been married?"

"Once—in my early twenties. It lasted less than two years, and after our nasty divorce, I reverted to my maiden name."

The waitress returned with the Zinfandel. We clinked, and I said, "To you, Cisne."

"To both of us. *Sláinte.*" She sipped. "Not bad."

It didn't taste like Dr. Pepper, so to me it automatically seemed "not bad."

"And you?"

"And me what?" I said.

"Married, divorced, in between?"

"I'm now divorced for longer than I was married. Two grown boys I don't see nearly as often as I want to. Involved with my work."

That seemed to surprise her. "No romance?"

"You're the first woman I've been out on a date with since Bush Two was president of the United States."

"That's why you were nervous when you invited me. Still nervous?"

"A little bit."

"I don't bite—or not very often, anyway."

"You might have noticed—I'm older than you."

"You're bigger than me, too. So what?"

"We might not have the same tastes," I said. "For instance, my musical appreciation stops somewhere between Dick Haymes and Rosemary Clooney."

"I have no idea who Dick Haymes is—but I know about Rosemary Clooney. She was George Clooney's aunt. I also listen to Carrie Underwood. What else?"

I thought about it for half a minute. "With the exception of Clint Eastwood—who's much older than I am—I'd rather watch Bogart or Cagney than anyone who's made a picture since 1975."

"What's interesting about you other than your outdated favorites from the New Deal era? Why did you become a private investigator—besides looking good in a trench coat?"

"That's not as easy a question as you might think." I studied the ceiling for a while. "Some people do things that piss me off, even if it's not personal. In my job, I can often do something about it. Besides, you've never seen me in a trench coat."

"I have a great imagination."

"Is that why you're an English teacher?"

"I hardly remember why. I spend more time entreating St. Kat girls not to be snobs and bullies to each other than I do teaching English."

"Are all your students like Carolyn Alexander?"

Cisne stopped smiling and shook her head. "Carolyn has more problems than I'm equipped to solve."

"Oh?"

"She showed up at school the morning after you met her—with a big purple bruise on her cheekbone and a lip that had been split."

I winced. "What happened?"

"She *said* she tripped and fell down the stairs at home. But for the rest of the week she wore long-sleeved blouses or shirts. No teenagers wear long sleeves when the temperature is near ninety unless they have bruises and finger marks on their arms."

"Is she abused at home?"

"I doubt it. My guess is it was her boyfriend."

I had to stop and think for a moment. "Shane?"

"Shane Ward," Cisne said.

"From—uh—Mac. Immaculate Heart of Mary."

"Immaculate Conception," she corrected me. "If she says she fell down the stairs, there's nothing I can do. I told the principal about it, but he snapped at me not to bother with anything happening away from school."

"Father Laughlin? Priests only care about what happens at school?"

"He doesn't like students—or teachers. He doesn't give a damn what happens to them if it's not during school hours on school property."

"How do you square that with being Catholic?"

"It's been a long time since I even thought about Catholicism. When they start letting women be priests, I'll consider it again."

"I gather you don't share these thoughts with Father Laughlin?"

"I share little of anything with him. But I do care about my students—that's why I asked around about your voyeur cameraman after I met you." She took another sip. "One of the reasons, anyway."

"What were the others?"

She rested her chin on her hand. "You're the most clueless man I've ever met, Milan."

"I am?"

"I'll confess. I'm not dying of loneliness. I'm not in love with you—not after two very short conversations—and I'm not desperate for a Saturday evening date, either. I find you attractive and interesting—and probably a nice guy. For me, that's a biggie. Unlike teens dipping their pinky toes into unfamiliar waters, I'm bored with outlaws."

"Unlike Carolyn Alexander?"

She lifted her shoulders and then let them fall again. "Shane Ward isn't exactly an outlaw. Very rich family, good grades in school, and an outstanding athlete. I understand why Carolyn set her cap for him."

"Is this the first time he's hit her?"

"I don't know. It's the first time I've seen the bruises."

"And she won't admit it?"

Cisne shook her head. "Without proof, we're at a dead end."

"Well," I said, "I can assure you I'm harmless."

"You don't hit women?"

"Never in my whole life. Oh, wait," I corrected myself. "I did, once."

She looked serious. "That's not funny."

"It wasn't at the time, either."

"What did she do to get you so mad at her?"

"I wasn't mad, exactly. She had a nine-millimeter automatic pointed at my heart. I punched her in the jaw instead—which made her drop the gun."

Now she looked genuinely concerned. "Guns?"

"My job is almost as dangerous as teaching English."

"Are you carrying a gun now?"

"Nope—I didn't think you're dangerous. So if you try to shoot me, I'll have to whack you in the jaw, too."

She rolled her eyes. "You're the funniest man!"

"Whoa—nobody ever accused me of that before."

"And the most interesting man, too."

"What's so interesting about me?"

Cisne said, "I spend every day talking to stuck-up teenage girls, and on the rare occasion I interact with any male on the premises, it's always a priest—usually one with a cranky personality. And then one day I'm heading out for a walk in the sunshine to get whining sounds of adolescent angst out of my head, and there you are. When I found out what you were looking for, I took advantage of the opportunity to get you together with Carolyn. Not because of her, but because it was a chance to get to know you even better."

She smiled at me over the rim of her wine glass. "Are you happy you asked me on a date?"

I pretended to mull that one over. "I'll tell you after dinner."

And what an enjoyable dinner it was . . .

It was a pleasant evening after a hot day, so driving home I had the car windows down and what's left of my hair blowing in the breeze. There were too many Saturday ideas bouncing around in my head, shouldering one another aside like customers in the crowded West Side Market. I hadn't mentioned Earl Dacey's death to Cisne, but I couldn't forget his funeral—and his mother, more determined than ever to keep me on the investigation even while stepping on the toes of Lieutenant McHargue. Then there was K.O.'s e-mail about his visit to Riona Dennehy, a woman who made a living enticing children into selling their bodies. I was hearing again in my own head Cisne Kelly's offhand remarks about the mean-spirited Father Laughlin, and her report of Carolyn Alexander's mistreatment. And let's not forget Special Agent Jeffrey Kitzberger, who'd already put a giant crimp in my Saturday. All worrisome.

What didn't worry me was the lingering taste of Cisne's goodnight kiss. It wasn't like in the movies—sexier than a friendly kiss, but far from passionate. Kisses are always pleasant—but I'd never kissed anyone before whose lips were as soft and as giving as Cisne's.

The next day was Sunday, a relaxing day—no work. That meant I wouldn't have to worry about Kitzberger, or Savannah, or K.O. and his meeting with Riona Dennehy, or about Earl Dacey's misadventures and death that had brought so many problems to my doorstep. I was ally ally oxen free—at least for twenty-four hours.

That meant I could spend all day Sunday thinking about Cisne's lips.

CHAPTER FOURTEEN

When I woke up Sunday morning, I did so smiling—and I can count on my toes, with one whole foot unused, how often that happens to me. Another shining moment in a happy life? Not exactly—I have good days and bad. My first date with Cisne Kelly had been a good one indeed. Our kiss goodnight in the parking lot of Gavi's became several kisses, each a little longer than the one before. I'd be more specific, but I lost count.

I threw on my ratty bathrobe with green, yellow, and black stripes—a Christmas gift years ago from my sons—and collected the Sunday *Plain Dealer* from the hallway. I fixed a large bowl of oatmeal and some green tea. Then I inserted an Oscar Peterson CD into my stereo system and settled down to read.

It was easy getting through the sports pages—the Indians were victorious Saturday night, newsworthy in itself. The front page—more reports of political corruption in Cuyahoga County—wasn't relaxing, but I'd grown used to it. Every time a local politician is interviewed by the press, they always begin by saying, "It wasn't *me.*"

I was heating my second cup of tea in the microwave—I know tea purists never do it that way, but I can't find the time or the energy to boil water first, pour it over the tea bag, and then wait three minutes while it brews—when the phone rang.

"K.O. here." As brusque as ever. "How was your big-deal first date last night?"

"None of your business. How was yours?"

"Peachy-keen. But this morning kind of threw cold water on everything."

"Wasn't waking up together as much fun as going to bed together?"

"We didn't go to bed together," he snapped. "I went online this morning for research."

"On what?"

"Crush films," he said.

My stomach did a double flip. "I don't want to hear that this early on a Sunday."

"I didn't want to think about it again—but it bothered me."

"What bothered you?"

"That some pissed-off person was going to come around and cut off my legs."

"They've already been around, K.O., to my office. They talked tough and then folded up. Don't worry, I took care of things."

"I'm sure you did—but I found something on Google that'll amaze you. Did you know making and selling crush films showing the mutilation, torturing, and killing of small animals is legal?"

"*What?*"

"In the spring of 2010 the Supreme Court approved it by eight to one. Freedom of speech."

"Nothing the Supreme Court does surprises me anymore. But what does this have to do with Earl Dacey?"

"Nothing. It has to do with me putting Nicolino in the hospital." He cleared the frog from his throat. "I could go back to jail."

I hadn't read the U.S. Supreme Court decision on crush films, but if it was as K.O. said, he could wind up in prison. In an indirect way, it'd be my fault.

"I'll talk to my lawyer, K.O.," I said. "But not on a Sunday. Nobody does anything on Sunday."

That was forty-five minutes before FBI Special Agent Jeffrey Kitzberger showed up again, this time swooping down on my apartment like the U.S. Army attacking Kabul.

He was full of surprises, Kitzberger—wearing a light-colored tan suit with a discreet darker brown pinstripe. His tie was plain—

bright red; I suppose he learned how to wear ties like that from watching Donald Trump. His shoes were different from yesterday's but also tan, shining with fresh polish, and his cheeks oozed Brut cologne. I didn't think men had splashed Brut on their faces since 1977.

Need I remind you of my own host outfit of a green-and-yellow-striped bathrobe and thong sandals?

He reintroduced himself, flipping his badge open so I could see it one more time. "We got off on the wrong foot yesterday."

"Same foot today," I said. "This is my home. I live here."

He smirked at the bathrobe. "I can see that."

"I've done nothing illegal, so you have a hell of a nerve busting into my apartment without being asked."

"I wouldn't bust in on the Lord's day," he said. "I should have explained more clearly what I'd wanted. I showed you photographs of various individuals and asked if you knew any of them."

"You can ask if I prefer Coke or Pepsi—but I won't answer without a subpoena."

He smiled a phony smile. "I'm a Pepsi man myself. May I come in?"

I hesitated long enough for him to add, "I'm not 'busting,' I just knocked on the door like everybody else—hoping to be invited."

In twenty-four hours he'd changed from Sergeant Friday to Mister Rogers. I stepped aside and he walked in. "Nice place," he said, checking out my furniture. "Lived here long?"

"Shall we get this over with?"

His face fell as if his feelings were hurt. I wondered if they taught *that* look at Quantico. Then he regarded one of my chairs—hopefully.

"Sit down," I said.

"Thank you." He settled himself comfortably. "Nice music—piano jazz. Old stuff from before your childhood? Is that why you play it?"

"Beethoven is from before my childhood, and I enjoy that, too."

He lifted one condescending eyebrow. "You disapprove of the FBI, don't you?"

"Not unless they're in my living room."

"I just wanted to talk—and you wouldn't be in your office on Sunday." His hand hovered near his jacket pocket. "Can I show you those photographs again?"

I took a spot on my sofa. "I remember them. Vividly."

"Then you can tell me about them."

"I doubt that," I said. "Those people aren't exactly my best friends."

"But you know who they are—and what they are."

"They're either with the mob or they're pornographers—or both. And that's *all* I know. Pornography is legal in this country—or haven't you heard?"

He tried not to frown but failed. "Are you into porn yourself? Do you hang out on porn sites on the Internet?"

"No—but it's legal. There are other legal things in this country I'm not into, either. But you don't care about my list." I leaned toward him. "What do you want from me?"

He was growing less convivial by the second. "The kid who got killed—Dacey. You're involved with him."

"I never set eyes on him. He disappeared, and his mother hired me to find him. Unfortunately somebody else did first. Who said I was—involved? Lieutenant McHargue?"

"What do you think?" Kitzberger said.

"I *think* she's probably as much shot in the ass talking to FBI guys as I am."

"You have an attitude, Jacovich."

"It's *Mister* Jacovich to you, Special Agent Kitzberger, unless we either get to be good friends or you get an arrest warrant for me. And I'm not the one with attitude. You are."

"So you don't give a damn if we stop these smut peddlers?"

"I give a damn you don't push me around by flashing your badge. I'm not impressed."

"Are you impressed there might be children involved?"

I nodded.

"You've talked to these scumbags?"

"Some."

"So—go talk to them again."

That got me up on my feet. "*What?*"

"They know you. They'll talk to you, especially if you bring up kiddie porn. It's important—to this country, and to children. So get off your anti-FBI attitude and poke around some more. You have my permission."

My hands curled into fists in spite of myself. "Your *permission*? You stroll uninvited into my home on a Sunday and you give me *permission*?"

"Don't take everything personally. I'm not trying to piss you off."

"Try again."

He sucked up much of the air in the room and let it out as if he were tired of the whole business. "I know you have relationships with the mob. No, don't deny it; let's not waste each other's time. But if you don't bend a little and help us out—if you don't start asking questions for us that we can't ask on our own, I guarantee you that with one phone call from me the FBI will come after you."

"They can't pin anything on me."

"That's not the point. We'll bounce you around so badly, and let this whole town hear about it—they'll be so far up your ass that not even a colonoscopy will find them again."

I took a menacing step toward him. He laughed. "You look too ridiculous to start a fight wearing that circus bathrobe. Besides, I'm twenty years younger and can wipe the floor with you." He pulled out the stack of photographs and waved them in my face like a picador enraging a bull. "These people are rat shit. They know you aren't after their asses, so they'll talk to you."

"And?"

"Then you talk to me, I talk to the Justice Department, and pretty soon they're cooling their heels in the Graybar Hotel. That'll make everyone happy."

I looked his virginally unwrinkled outfit up and down. "I don't have the wardrobe to do your job. I have my own agenda."

"Is Earl Dacey your agenda?"

"Among other things."

"What if Dacey was involved in child porno?"

"I'd be surprised."

Kitzberger spread his hands out. "*Get* surprised. One lousy phone call to me won't kill you."

I glared at my apartment door after Kitzberger's supercilious exit. He was an insufferable smart-ass with a snot-nose attitude and a one-step-from-God complex shared by lots of FBI agents—but he only *thought* he knew what might or might not kill you.

He also knew how to push my buttons, the son of a bitch! The abuse of children was one of those things that got me hard and deep. So I'd get involved in his investigation whether I wanted to or not, because—well, because it was the thing to do.

I had to be careful. I still worked for Savannah Dacey—against the rules of the Cleveland Police Department. I could lose my license. The FBI was only a hundred times worse. For me to poke around their territory and then squeal to them was dangerous enough, but getting K.O. involved was another thing altogether. His brave service in the U.S. Army fighting not one but two unnecessary wars wouldn't begin making up for his early years in juvenile jail—not to the FBI it wouldn't.

As far as I knew, Earl Dacey was an amateur peeper, taking upskirt shots for his own enjoyment, but someone put it in his mind to try and make money. And since some of his victims were high school students, the word got from Flo McHargue to the FBI—and now I was in the goddamn middle of it! My job, like it or lump it, was to figure out who was pulling all the strings.

I couldn't sit around in my bizarre bathrobe much longer. I spent the rest of the day in gym shorts and a T-shirt. My mind was too full of Earl and Special Agent Kitzberger and everything else I should have put aside for a Sunday off—except it never works that way.

Close to dinnertime, K.O. called again.

"I didn't have plans today," he said, "so I bit the bullet and watched the rest of Earl's DVDs. God!"

"Anything different?"

He laughed. "Different-colored panties, some with designs—and one, probably an older woman, wearing pantyhose. Didn't they go out of style already? Anyway, I noticed one thing. Remember, I told you that first video was taken at Great Lakes Mall?"

"Sure."

"Well, most of the others were taken there too. Not all—there were some from Beachwood Mall—but six of the nine were taken at Great Lakes. Now, Earl lived on Cleveland's West Side. Why do you suppose he took so many videos way out in Lake County?"

"Maybe he didn't want to get recognized in his own neighborhood. Lake County was far enough away that he wouldn't get spotted by the cop who walks the beat down his street."

"That's one reason," K.O. said. "But it keeps bouncing around in my head—why would he spend all this time at a mall about forty miles away from his house."

"So it's troubling; what are you going to do about it?"

"Maybe *you* should do something about it."

"And what might that be?"

"Well, if I were you," K.O. said, "I'd go out there tomorrow and introduce myself to Carol Shepard."

K.O.'s phone call and Kitzberger's visit left me with a plateful of problems. Instead of watching TV or wending my way out somewhere to a summer festival—there were many different ones each summer weekend—I stayed home, scribbling thoughts on three-by-five cards and reminding myself that my paying job was helping Savannah Dacey discover what happened to her son. It wouldn't bring him back, but it could help lay to rest the ghost that otherwise might haunt her for the rest of her life.

On Monday I was out and about at ten thirty, wearing a sports jacket over an open-collared dress shirt. It's more formal than usual for me, but it bestowed on me a gravitas I don't have. My first stop was Helene Diamond's studio on Superior Avenue. Climbing the steep stairs was no different than the last time; I had to stop outside the door to catch my breath.

Helene and her daughter Ruth were alone in the studio; no "talent" hung around waiting for cameras to roll. Then again, it was pretty early in the morning for that sort of thing. Helene was at a desk, papers spread out in front of her. Ruth dusted, straightening posters on the wall.

Helene wasn't annoyed by my presence. "I have nothing interesting for you today—but if you want coffee," she jerked her head in the direction of a coffeemaker on a filing cabinet, "help yourself."

I didn't want coffee, but it seemed polite and friendly to pour myself half a cup. "I have some more questions, if you don't mind."

"If I *do* mind, will you stop?"

"If you throw me out, I'll go quietly—but I haven't had my coffee yet."

"If a question ticks me off, out you go. Otherwise . . ."

"You said the porn shot here is legal."

"We call them adult films. Yes, they're legal. They passed a law last century saying it's okay as long as it has artistic content."

"Artistic?"

"It's got to have a story," Helene said. "Like regular movies in a theater or on TV. They don't start out with everybody naked—one or the other is lonely or disturbed, so stripping down and getting it on is justified in the first few minutes."

"So there's a script?"

Ruth piped up, "I write them." I turned and looked at her; it was the first time I'd heard her voice. "And we always cast people who can act."

"That surprises me," I said.

"Half the actresses working legitimately have at one time or another done things on film you'd never imagine—even some local actresses you see in plays right here in Cleveland."

"It's a dangerous way to make a living."

"Not so much. This is a profession like any other. We always let them see a script, or at least an outline, beforehand—and we never ask them to do anything they're not comfortable with. Also," Ruth said, "we make sure everybody's been to the doctor so nobody worries about—catching anything. And we pay well."

"How well?"

"They'd have to work at WalMart for a month to earn what we pay for one night."

I took a sip of coffee; it was strong enough to remove chrome. "Did you ever think about writing a real screenplay, Ruth—and having it shown by the Cleveland Film Society?"

Ruth laughed. "You make it sound easy."

"So—"

"So," Helene said, "we're legitimate—and as long as we stay

that way, we make a decent living and don't get hassled by the cops. We don't even have to schmear them."

"Schmear them?"

"You never heard that expression? Where've you been living, in an underground cave? Or are you just resolutely gentile?"

"I thought schmear meant putting cream cheese on a bagel."

She laughed. "Close enough. The other meaning is a bribe. We don't bribe cops because we don't do anything illegal and they don't bother us."

"You wouldn't kid me, would you, Helene?"

Ruth said, "Mom'd kid the pants off you if she could. But she's telling the truth."

"So have we convinced you we've never done business with that geeky guy—what's his name? Earl?"

"Earl," I said. "And you won't be doing any more with him."

"Busted?"

"Dead."

"Aw." Helene looked sad. "That's a damn shame. What happened?"

"Somebody killed him."

"Oh my God!" Ruth whispered. Helene turned pale and put her hand to her face—it was a mother's concern.

"Did someone else in the porn community get mad at him?" I asked.

"For what? The worst he could be is a pain in the ass, and that's no death sentence."

"If he's cutting in on someone else's territory—"

"Get it through your head," she said, "that he wasn't cutting in on anybody. It'd be like an eight-year-old kid making book on horse racing. Nobody'd pay any attention."

"Okay," I said, shifting into Kitzberger's domain. "You're square—and you're small time in Cleveland. Who isn't? Who might deal with underage porno?"

Helene glanced at Ruth, then down at her desktop. "I don't mess with that."

"Somebody does."

"You see a picture or video shot up somebody's skirt, who knows if it's a twelve-year-old girl or a fifty-year-old woman?"

"I'm not necessarily talking about Earl."

Her skeptical lips pursed. "If not Earl, why all these questions?"

"I have other reasons." I said, trying to sound heavy.

"Well, they aren't mine," Helene said. "I'm not squealing on anybody, because I know almost all of them. Anyone doing kiddie porn in Greater Cleveland is a stranger to me."

I looked at the daughter. "Ruth?"

She half smiled. "Despite my job here, I'm familiar with the real film industry—so here's a great quote from producer Samuel Goldwyn, who said, 'Include me out.' Okay?"

I stood up. "If that's the way you both want it, I *will* include you out. And by the way, Helene—your coffee was rotten."

CHAPTER FIFTEEN

arol Shepard was nowhere to be found when I arrived at the security office of the Great Lakes Mall, but I recognized Leon from K.O.'s photograph. He was about six feet two, and almost as wide as that, broad in the chest, shoulders stretching the fabric of his security uniform. Clipped onto his belt was what people in my generation referred to as a walkie-talkie, although today they must call them something else. His neatly trimmed beard and mustache didn't disguise his youth—he was probably about twenty-three. His demeanor was pleasantly serious, as was his voice.

He remembered speaking with K.O. and posing for the picture. He was taken with my business card, though.

"Does that mean you're an actual private eye?" He tucked the card into his shirt pocket. "Like in the movies?"

"Afraid not—they always smoke cigarettes, get beaten up, and get the prettiest girls."

He grinned. "Doesn't that ever happen to you?"

"Not all at once."

"How come that other kid with the phone camera doesn't have business cards?"

"He's only been on my payroll for a few days," I said. "I'll wait to see if he works out."

"He asks good questions. Are you here to take more pictures?"

"No, but I want to ask about the guy who *was* taking pictures—from his shopping bag. You said somebody called you about him, but he ran before you got hold of him."

"Yeah, the girls who work at Macy's. I just saw the back of him scooting away. He saw me coming—but I'm hard to miss."

"Had you ever seen him before?"

"Maybe," Leon said, "but I never talked to him. Lots of people carry shopping bags—I don't pay much attention. I look more for shoplifters than pervs. Ms. Shepard, my boss, says that's what we're here for—catching thieves."

"And that's what she told you to do? Look for shoplifters?"

"Pretty much, yeah." He glanced at his wristwatch—shiny and gold, almost as big as a saucer. "I should be out walking the mall. If she finds me in here she'll raise hell."

"Does she raise hell a lot?"

"Ooh-wee!" he grinned.

"Can I walk with you a little? I won't get in your way."

"Suit yourself," he said.

We wove in and out of the patches of sunlight shining through the skylights. Most shoppers gave us a casual glance—we were both big men. The mall was less crowded than I remember, even that early in the day. The recession crunch that started in 2008 had washed businesses over the side all over Ohio. There were too many vacant stores and not enough people to shop in them. But Great Lakes Mall was hanging on; there were several malls in Greater Cleveland that had closed up, now gathering dust and yesterday's blowing newspapers and, at night, shadow people you don't want to think about.

"Is this a full-time job for you, Leon?"

"I work days, Thursday through Monday, and go to the U. of Akron evenings."

"Good for you. What's your major?"

"Prelaw," Leon said. "I want to be a lawyer. I don't know what kind of lawyer yet—just an honest one."

"An honest lawyer? That'll be lonely. Tell me—you said you never confronted the video guy. You never faced off with him."

"Right."

"What if you *had* bumped heads? What would you do?"

"The procedure around here is we'd get his name and address and then ban him from coming back to the mall. If he does, then we call the police."

"You can't arrest him yourself?"

Leon allowed himself a small smile. "I'm no cop—not on ten bucks an hour."

"Is that the same thing Ms. Shepard would do if *she* caught him?"

He peered into the Gap store in case someone was shoplifting. "She's not a cop, either. She's an administrator."

It was almost noon, and in the food court customers were lined up before several fast-food counters. A young girl in an aggressively ugly uniform was handing out samples of Chinese cuisine on a toothpick. I inquired, and found out it was bourbon chicken. I didn't taste it.

"Leon, you probably have things to do," I said, "but I'll wait for Carol Shepard." I held up my empty hands. "No camera—no sneaky pictures."

He moved away with a small wave, and I walked in the other direction as if I had a specific destination, thinking about the mall's security. According to Leon, Carol Shepard was vexed over petty thieves but hardly aware of perverts and voyeurs with cameras.

I stepped out of the path of about fifteen senior citizens walking in a pack for exercise, more comfortable in an air-conditioned mall than on the street when the temperature hovered close to three digits.

I couldn't help noticing an attractive teen in a short skirt barely hiding very shapely legs stopping to window-shop, and I wondered if another person like Earl Dacey came here to take upskirt photographs and videos. If I found one, he might have known Earl as a colleague. Every scrap of information could help—it was a long shot, but between an angry Savannah, a demanding Lieutenant McHargue, and a pushy and threatening Fibbie, I had little choice. Discreetly—*very* discreetly—I followed twenty feet behind the young woman.

I stopped when she went into the ladies' restroom.

Feeling like a disgusting deviant and total damn fool, I skulked back to the food court and bought a cup of tea from the Asian stand, sat at a table, and watched other people eat.

At one o'clock I returned to the security office. Carol Shepard had finally arrived, dressed like she had been in K.O.'s snapshot, only this time her blouse was a muted red and her skirt gray. She was moving papers around on her desk. I wonder why people with desks always riffle through papers, stacking and stapling them. Is there a Paper Shuffling 101 course in business school?

I introduced myself and reminded her of her conversation with K.O. last week. She didn't look any more pleased than she had in her snapshot.

"I told him all I knew about that creep, which isn't much," she said. Her soft sniff was a preamble to my dismissal. "I've no time to chat with you or repeat what I told your partner."

"Apprentice," I said.

"What?"

"Mr. O'Bannion is my apprentice. He's not my partner."

She pointed her pretty nose at the ceiling. "I don't care if he's your father."

"You told him strange guys hang around young girls in this mall all the time. You've never caught one doing something wrong?"

She tossed her head. If her hair were as long as Cisne's, the toss would have been very dramatic—but since it was a short-cropped tousled cut, the move was ineffective. "I can't march up to someone and demand he show me his shopping bag. This mall and I would get sued three or four times a week."

"So you instruct your staff to watch more for thieves, then?"

"Thieves cost merchants money," Carol said, "not pervs. This is a business—about profit and loss."

"And women who are unknowing victims don't count as loss."

"No, they don't. Listen, if someone takes videos up my skirt and I don't know about it, it costs me nothing. So if my security guards only looked for sickos, the stolen merchandise would fly out of here under people's raincoats, and then the price of everything would go up. The shoppers wouldn't like that, and neither would you."

"By your reasoning, Ms. Shepard, we should stop paying so many police officers with our tax money, too, because we probably won't get raped or murdered, and if somebody else does, well, it's not our problem and we shouldn't have to pay for it. Have I got it right?"

She perched a pair of glasses on the end of her nose, and pulled a stack of papers in front of her. "I have things to take care of."

"Young girls come here from schools like St. Katherine's and St. Bonaventure, don't they?"

She sighed, perplexed that I hadn't disappeared.

"But you don't seem to give a damn about deviants taking advantage of them in your mall." I pronounced the last word the way I might have said "empire."

"I don't have *time* to give a damn," Shepard said, biting off words like they were celery sticks. "We want to make money and get ahead."

"No matter what?"

She nodded emphatically. "No matter what."

She was some piece of work. I ran a hand over my face. "You ought to know Riona Dennehy," I murmured, almost to myself.

Something happened to Carol Shepard's face. It grew white, taut, almost twisted, and her gasp was audible. "What about Riona Dennehy?"

I didn't think she'd hear my mumble—but I got over my surprise. "You know her personally?"

She stammered, stuttered. Finally she managed to say, "I've met her. She's a good customer here. A regular customer."

"Where? In what stores?"

"Um—all of them. All the ones in the mall."

"Macy's? Dillard's? Sears? How do you know her, then? I'm sure people who work for those stores know her, but how do you?"

She took her glasses off, licking her lips as though her mouth had suddenly gone dry and there was no Biotene in sight. "She—joined our customers' club. She bought gift cards to use anywhere in the mall."

"You don't issue those cards—you're security. How do you know who buys gift cards and who doesn't?"

She stood up angrily. "I've said I have things to do, and I'm going to do them now. That means you're leaving. You're not a cop and I'm sick of answering questions. If you're not out of here in thirty seconds, I'll call someone to show you out—and not gently, either."

That someone must be Leon, I thought—and it probably wouldn't get rough at all, because he and I were already best buddies.

Exaggeration: I didn't *have* any best buddies, with the possible exception of Ed Stahl. Maybe it's because I'm an insufferable prig, but what I do for a living—crossing swords with unpleasant, unscrupulous, and sometimes evil people—alienates almost everyone with whom I come in contact. As I drove slowly back to Cleveland, I looked back on the contretemps with Carol Shepard. She was never going to like me, and half the fault was mine. Maybe I ought to enroll in a course and improve my social skills.

But then there was Riona Dennehy—the connection surprised me.

Bob Matusen was waiting for me in my parking lot, leaning on the front fender of his car and drinking a Diet Coke to go with his cigarette. His jacket was off, his tie pulled down with the top shirt button opened, and his sleeves rolled up to his elbows. His face shone with Cleveland summer sweat.

"Having a late lunch," he said. "I picked up a Reuben sandwich at Inn of the Barristers before I came over. Finished mine, but I got one for you in case you were hungry." He reached into his car and presented me with a paper bag. "I didn't know you were out of the office, so I've been here an hour. Want to eat this upstairs," he pulled at his wilted collar, "where it's air-conditioned?"

We went up, I unlocked the door, and then I headed straight for the air conditioner control. "Give it a minute or two and tell me what you're doing here. I'm finished with your murder case."

"Earl Dacey's? Sure," Matusen said cautiously, "but I thought you'd be interested in the postmortem."

I sat behind my desk and removed my Reuben sandwich from the bag. "No french fries with this?"

He raised both eyebrows. "You actually like cold fries?"

I took a bite. The Reuben was pretty good, even after being bagged for an hour in the car—and I didn't miss the limp, cold french fries at all. "Did the killing take place in Cleveland?"

"The coroner doesn't know where he died, but it wasn't on the bank of Tinker's Creek. They found patterns of scuff marks on his shoes indicating he was killed and then dragged across a sidewalk or street somewhere, and taken to Twinsburg for, ah, disposal. Forensics also found carpet fibers on his clothes, which means he was put into somebody's car."

"What kind of car?"

"Someone's working at finding out. The official line is that although there were several blows to his head and body with some sort of bat or club, what killed him was a horrendous blow to the top of his head, splitting his skull wide open."

"A horrendous blow, eh?" I tried not to smile—most homicide cops don't use words like *horrendous* very often. "The coup de grâce."

"What's a cootie-grah?"

"Look it up."

Matusen wasn't interested enough. "They found a little scrap of thin blue plastic in his hair, at the back of his neck." He showed me the dime size with his fingers. "It probably came from one of those plastic shopping bags they pack your stuff in at the supermarket."

"Blue, hmm? Giant Eagle, I'd imagine."

"Everybody has Giant Eagle plastic bags in their house. The bad guy probably covered his head with it before braining him and didn't notice that little piece."

"More likely," I said, "they put the bag over his head after he was dead so they could haul him away and dump him without getting blood and brains all over their car."

Matusen said, "You gonna eat the rest of your sandwich, Milan?"

Amazing—homicide cops talk about food and sandwiches in the same breath as a blood-and-brains killing. "Bob, you didn't bring me lunch to tell me the results of Earl Dacey's autopsy—especially since I'm not working on it at all." I opened a desk drawer, looking for a napkin that wasn't there. Finally I wiped my hands on a tissue.

"You're too damn smart for your own good." He popped the

knuckles on his right hand. "The word is that the mob is mad at you."

"Where'd you hear the word?"

He shook his head; he wasn't going to tell me.

"Well, it's not true."

"Then how did I hear it?"

"I just asked you the same question."

"I'm also told you put somebody in the hospital."

"I didn't put anybody anywhere," I said. "I none too gently escorted people out of my office recently, but if they're in the hospital, it's either because they had a nervous breakdown or they ran their car into a tree. And look out the window—not a tree in sight."

"You threw Angelo Nicolino out?" Matusen said.

"I never laid eyes on Angelo Nicolino. And I never *sent* anyone to hurt someone in my life; if I want them injured, I do it myself."

"At your age?"

"If anyone cares to take their best shot, send them over."

He shook his head. "I'm tryin' to help you. You can't take on the whole mafia."

"The mafia's not even annoyed with me. Why would they be?"

"Maybe because you stick your nose where it doesn't belong for the FBI."

I wasn't thrilled he knew about that. "The FBI is supposedly on our side. Why do you ask? Curious?"

He rolled his eyes back in his head like an adolescent girl. "You're not supposed to be in our way. That's the rule. P.I.s don't investigate capital crimes."

"You think the mob iced Earl Dacey and now they're after me?"

"I don't think nothin'." He fanned his face with his flattened hand, creating no cool breeze whatsoever. "I clock in, I clock out, I do what I'm told, and keep my mouth shut. I'm just askin' questions."

"Are you finished? Asking?"

He considered it. "More or less."

"Then thanks for the sandwich, Bob," I said. "Tell McHargue thanks, too."

I didn't thank him for McHargue's message to watch my step.

After he left I stared out the window for too long at the lazily flowing river. The FBI thought I was mixed up with a dead guy who was involved in child pornography. The P.D. thought the mob was mad at me. And if the mob really *was* mad at me, including Victor Gaimari—then no matter which way I turned, my ass was grass.

It was too hot anyway. I closed up the office and went home early. Besides—sauerkraut on a Reuben sandwich always makes me burp.

CHAPTER SIXTEEN

I t was close to six o'clock. During the summer, little on television keeps one's mind alive, so I chose one of my old movies on DVD—*Chinatown*, one of the best movies ever made about a private eye. Jack Nicholson was great in that film—but I wouldn't want anyone cutting off half *my* nose like Roman Polanski did to him.

I was close to the end of the story—where John Huston sticks a gun in Nicholson's face and demands the return of a telltale pair of glasses—when the phone rang. "How's tricks?" Suzanne Davis said when I answered.

"You're interrupting one of my favorite movies."

"You don't have to watch the rest of it—the butler did it."

"Thanks for the spoiler."

She paused for too long. "How's it going with K.O.? Is he doing a good job?"

"He's a hard worker—and a bright guy. He's good."

"Uh—have you heard from him today?"

"No. I don't even know what he was up to."

"I talked to him about half an hour ago. He said he was down near your office—he wanted to see you—but apparently you went home early."

I felt myself frowning. "What was he doing at my office anyway?"

"You'll have to ask him. He sounded lousy, if you want to know the truth."

"Lousy how?"

"Unusually quiet. You know why?"

"No. He didn't give you a hint?"

"No—but I could tell."

"I guess if he wants me, he'll call me," I said.

"Or drop by your apartment."

"You think he will?"

"I'm guessing he will. Stick around tonight—unless you have a date or something."

"No date," I said, looking for a notepad to write a reminder to call Cisne. Maybe I should have sent her flowers.

"I think K.O. might be in some trouble."

"Suzanne, all of us are in trouble most of the time. It comes with the job."

"Tell me about it," she said. Then: "Listen, Milan, if K.O. needs anything, let me know soonest, will you?"

After I hung up, I allowed myself to worry. Kevin O'Bannion was just a kid I barely knew—but in the few days since we met, he'd already hospitalized a guy in tight with a splinter group from the mob in Cleveland, an act that sent three mugs to my office to punish *me* for his assault. God only knew what he'd done now.

When I dialed the phone and heard Cisne Kelly's musical voice, it lightened my heart a little.

"I should have called you before this," I said, "to say how much I enjoyed spending the evening with you."

"That's okay. According to those rules—set down by whoever they are—yesterday, 'then,' was too soon to call me after a first date. And I've only been home from work for about an hour and a half. So you're still on my good list. How are you?"

"It's been a tough two days for me."

"Sorry to hear that," she said like she really meant it. "I know your profession is a difficult one. Can I help with anything?"

"It's too long a story," I said.

"Is it a secret?"

"Not if you read the *Plain Dealer*."

"I don't. What did I miss?"

I decided it wouldn't hurt anything to come clean with her. "That young man who was taking upskirt pictures of young girls—"

"Yes—did you find him?"

"I didn't, but the police have. He's dead."

She grew quiet.

"Someone killed him."

"My God. Who?"

"I don't know—yet."

"Are you looking for him? Or her? I thought the police did that."

"They are," I said. "I was hired by his mother to find him. Now that he's gone, I'm on the sidelines."

"It'd be horrible if you actually came face to face with a killer." I didn't bother telling her some of my old job-related adventures. "Have you any idea who did it?"

"I have a list a mile long, but I don't think any of them are killers."

She didn't say anything, and I couldn't blame her. When your recent date—the one with whom you spent fifteen minutes making out in a parking lot—tells you all about a murder, there isn't a hell of a lot left to say.

"Cisne, this isn't easy. I don't want to upset you. Would you prefer I don't call you anymore?"

"I didn't say *that*," she said, and I was relieved to hear the lilt back in her voice. "Of course I want you to call me. I want to see you again."

"Me, too."

"Are you saying that *you* want to see you again?"

"No," I said, flustered, "I'm saying—oh. You're being an English teacher again."

"It's in my DNA. Besides, I like teasing you."

"When can you do it again in person?"

"Assuming nobody's going to shoot you, how about next weekend?"

"I'm too old to shoot. Saturday night?"

"As long as we don't go to another dinner and be polite. Let's do something fun. Pick something for Saturday and call me the day before to let me know about our date."

"So you'll have time to plan your wardrobe."

"Among other things," she said—and I thought about *that* for the next twenty minutes or so until my doorbell rang.

"It's K.O.," came the voice over the speaker from downstairs.

It took him longer than I expected to climb the stairs. When I opened the door to admit him, I saw why.

His left eye was swollen half shut, dark red and on its way to purple. Around his left nostril was crusting dried blood. There was an angry bruise on the middle of his forehead, and I noticed both hands were bruised and cut around the knuckles. As he walked past me into the living room, he leaned a little bit toward the left. Bruised ribs, maybe even busted. The front of his shirt and the right pants leg of his jeans were bloodied.

"Sit down, I'll get you a drink."

He grimaced and lowered himself onto the sofa. "Just water, please."

When I came back out with his drink, K.O.'s eyes were closed.

"Are you conscious?" He opened one eye, nodded imperceptibly, and reached for the water. It was cold, and he held the glass against his eye.

"What happened?"

"Give me a second."

I waited. He shifted around, trying to get comfortable, wincing with every move, and carefully touched his nose to make sure it had stopped bleeding. Then he focused on me. "This all has to do with you," he said.

"You got beaten up because of me?"

"Sort of," he said. "By the way, I didn't get beaten up. I did the beating."

"Really? Frankly, you look like shit."

"You oughta see the other guy."

"What other guy?"

"His name's Royce. I don't think you know him personally."

"Okay, then. Tell me."

He tried vainly to make himself more comfortable.

"I spent this morning working for Suzanne, just looking stuff up and doing research—which is okay by me. I hope it's okay with you also. Between the two of you, I'm making a living—and racking up hours for when I apply for my own PI license. You knew that, didn't you? Okay.

"So I had to come downtown to Cleveland and go through some files at the County Court House. I made notes and phoned them in to Suzanne—you won't care about her case, so forget it. Then I dropped by your office to see if you needed me for anything else today. If not, maybe we could of grabbed an early dinner or something as long as I wasn't getting in your way.

"I didn't see your car in the parking lot. I thought maybe you'd gone home early—but I decided to wait for a while. I didn't notice the other car in the lot.

"When I got out of my car, he got out of his, too. The sun was in my eyes, so it took me a few seconds to recognize him. His name is Royce, and he's Riona Dennehy's bodyguard and muscle. He's built like he spends too many hours in Gold's Gym because he's ripped—but I think he gets off looking at himself in the mirror because Gold's doesn't build guys for fighting, just for posing. Maybe he's her chauffeur and housekeeper, and for all I know, her favorite lay. When I interviewed Dennehy, she summoned him to make sure I left. His arrogant walk was that of a guy who belonged there.

"I never told Dennehy I worked for you, never mentioned your name—I tried convincing her I wanted to be a porn actor, but I guess my emoting was lousy because she didn't believe it. So—there's Royce, in your parking lot, probably waiting for you and as shocked to see me as I was to see him. I wonder why he was looking for you.

"But it didn't take him long to put the pieces together. He starts by saying, 'What the fuck you doin' here?'

"Same question," I says.

"I saw his eyes working. He's not the smartest guy I ever met, but not the dumbest, either. Finally he said, 'You work for this Jacovich guy!' He pronounced your name wrong."

"Like everybody else does."

"'What's it to you?' I said.

"He shrugged, hands in his pockets. 'I came here to talk to him—but you'll have to do—for starters.'

"The next thing I know, I'm flat on my ass on the cement. When he took his hand out of his pocket, he had brass knuckles or something—caught me right under the eye.

"Before I could get my bearings—before the birdies went away—he'd kicked me twice in the ribs with steel-tipped boots. When he tried a third, I grabbed his foot and twisted, hard. He went down.

"I scrambled over and kneeled on him—or knelt; which is right? Well, anyway, I landed hard on his chest with my knees and it blew the breath right out of him. Then I started in with my fists. I hit him five or six times—real good ones—before he got his brass knuckles around and smashed me in the ribs, right where he'd already kicked me. It hurt like hell and rolled me off him. Pretty soon we were both back on our feet.

"So here we are, dancing around like welterweights, throwing punches that weren't landing. He couldn't punch fast enough because of the knucks, and I couldn't get close enough to hit him without his braining me.

"Eventually I figured it out. When he came at me, I kicked out and, I think, wrecked his kneecap with my shoe. The pain made him drop his hands, and then I hit him several times—I didn't count—but some good ones in the mouth and one in his nose which, I think, broke it. Oh yeah, he caught me one in the nose, too—which is why it started bleeding.

"That's when I grabbed his right arm and twisted it up behind him, clawing at his fingers until he dropped the brass knucks.

"We slugged it out for a while longer. He's a hard sonofabitch— hard head, hard stomach. I knocked out some teeth—but one of them got imbedded into my fist."

"I hope you don't get rabies," I said.

"I got too close to him at one point because he got me in a bear hug. He's pretty strong in the arms and shoulders, and he was squeezing the life out of me. I could hardly breathe.

"I extended my hands on either side of his face and clapped

him hard on the ears, and he screamed and let go in a hurry. He put both hands to his ears—exposing his belly like a cat falling asleep in the sunshine. It must have been very painful.

"He took a few steps backwards and I went to work on his body. Probably his workout days at Gold's strengthened his gut, but there wasn't much anyone could do when someone's hammering his ribs and kidneys. It took me less than two minutes to put him down.

"He rolled over on his hands and knees and tried getting up. That's when I let him have it, right under the chin with the toe of my own shoe. His teeth clacked like castanets and he rolled over on his back, out cold. Blood ran from his mouth, but he was still breathing, which was OK—I didn't want to kill him or anything. I left him there in your parking lot—I figured he'd wake up sometime."

"Thanks," I said.

"So I drove up out of the Flats. When I was on Carnegie Avenue at East 30th Street, I pulled into the McDonald's parking lot and called Suzanne, but she didn't know where you were. I didn't tell her I'd been in a fight—I didn't want her worrying—but she got the idea anyway. She's a tough woman, which is why I like her so much.

"I wanted to call Carli, just for her sympathy—to lay my head in her lap and let her take care of me and soothe my wounds. But we're nowhere near that after just one date. Besides, I don't want her seeing me like this.

"Finally I called 911 on the land line inside Mac's and requested an ambulance be sent for a seriously injured man unconscious in your parking lot. I guess Royce won't be pumping iron at the gym for a while. And he won't be smiling much, either.

"But Jesus, Milan—I fucking ache all over!"

"Let's get you to the emergency room," I said.

"No hospitals!" He shook his head angrily. "If I give them my right name, they'll want to know *how* I got banged up, and then they'll be all over me like a cheap suit."

I'd been to the ER more often than I could remember, but K.O. had been there a few times, too. "Well, someone should patch up that eye before you lose it. And if your ribs are broken you'll need to be taped." I looked at his hands. "You'll have to deal with your own knuckles—unless Mr. Royce has rabies. I'll call my own doctor. He'll take good care of you, no questions asked. And he lives about five minutes from here."

I called Dr. Ben Sorkin, an old pal from my Kent State days. I knew the number by heart.

"For a change it's not you that got hurt, Milan?" Ben said over the phone. "I'm shocked—*shocked*."

"Can you see him now, Ben?"

"In about half an hour, if he lives that long."

I passed the message along to K.O. "Can I do anything for you in the meantime?"

He looked right at me—with effort. "Can you think of a reason why Royce, who never even heard of you, was sent to your office by Riona Dennehy, who never heard of you either, to knock you around?"

"I think I can," I said. "Stay comfortable until we have to go."

He closed his eyes, but he wasn't sleeping—probably just trying to escape the pain.

"Can you listen?" I asked.

"Every word."

"Good. Dennehy practically admitted to you that she does underage porn—and convinces young kids to turn part-time hookers to make some money. True?"

The sound he made was as close to "Uh-huh" as he could get at the moment.

"But she doesn't think of you with me.," I said. "Maybe here's a connection. You talked to Dennehy but both of us talked to Carol Shepard—the security boss at the Great Lakes Mall. And when I mentioned Dennehy's name to her, Shepard practically went postal. Could it be those two women are in cahoots?"

K.O.'s eyes flew open. "Maybe—but she was a hotshot at Kent State, and twenty-five years younger than Dennehy. How did they get together in underage prostitution?"

"Shepard spots pretty young girls in the mall, and if they're malleable, and hungry for extra money, she turns them over to Dennehy."

"How sick is that?" K.O. mumbled.

"Shepard doesn't give a damn, just so she gets a piece of the action, Dennehy gets another piece—probably bigger—and then young girls are doing porno and turning tricks."

He sat up. "How much money can Shepard take off the top?"

"A rich old scumbag might pay a few grand for a shot at a fourteen-year-old virgin—even more if they're younger."

"Jesus," K.O. whispered.

"Guys like that come from all walks of life. They're not crazy-eyed toothless deviates who hide in the bushes. They have good jobs, nice families, and go to church." I couldn't help a dissatisfied sigh. "Often they're the ones who pray the loudest."

K.O. massaged his sore, swollen right fist with his left palm. "If somebody heard you talking about loud-praying guys with dirty secrets, they'd want to kick your ass."

"If everybody heard everything being said in this world, we'd all be furious with *someone*—and that would mean all-out war."

"But you do get enraged about certain things, don't you?"

"Don't *you*?"

He tried to grin. "Point taken."

"Now—if we don't get you patched by Ben Sorkin, you'll perish right here on my carpet." I went over and helped him stand up. "No arguments. That's an order."

"An order?" he mused, leaning most of his weight on my arm as we moved toward the door. "If it's an order, that must mean I'm still on the clock."

CHAPTER SEVENTEEN

During our visit with Ben Sorkin, K.O. got more than some tape around his cracked ribs. In addition to providing a cleanup and codeine tablets to assuage K.O.'s headache, Ben poked and manipulated the swelling around his eye, wrote a prescription, and gave him a tetanus shot.

K.O. also got a lecture. I'd suffered many from Ben Sorkin and had grown used to them, but it made K.O. more acerbic than usual.

I took him back to my apartment. I suggested Nighttown or the Mad Greek for dinner, but he just wanted to go home. He was in no condition to drive to Lake County, so I insisted he spend the night where he was. Ever since I moved from my ex-wife's home, I had maintained a spare bedroom in my apartment for my boys when they visited on weekends. Now that they're both grown, they don't spend overnights with me anymore. But I haven't bothered remodeling my spare room, changing it from their bedroom to something useful—because I can't think of anything else to do with it.

Tough and swaggering as K.O. was (or at least thought he was), he staggered into the bedroom, kicking off his shoes but otherwise remaining dressed. He virtually collapsed on the bed and fell asleep almost immediately. By nine o'clock he'd curled into a semi-fetal position. I didn't put a blanket over him; it was too hot. I switched on a night light, and left the door open a few inches. It was starting to feel as if I had another kid.

I hadn't eaten since lunch, and wound up with a peanut butter and jelly sandwich, accompanied by potato chips—not exactly a decent dinner, but the stand-up meal served its purpose. For those of you taking notes about me, on the rare occasions I spring for peanut butter, I always buy the crunchy variety. I don't guarantee how good you'll feel eating PB and J right before you go to bed, though.

I didn't sleep much. My so-called apprentice had been in another violent fight, the second one in less than a week, but this one had been meant for me. I was grateful for his help, naturally—but I couldn't help wondering why I had been targeted. Royce, whoever he was, might be the puzzle piece to connect the porn makers and distributors with Earl Dacey—but no matter how many times I ran over it in my head, I couldn't make the pieces fit.

When K.O. hauled himself out of bed at eight o'clock the next morning—a long sleep—I was buried in the *Plain Dealer*, Lanigan and Malone nagging each other on the radio. I'd brewed green tea for myself and coffee for him, and he drank it, sullen and obviously still hurting. His swollen eye had turned vivid Technicolor overnight.

"Want oatmeal?"

He shook his head, not even looking at me. I thought about telling him a nice healthy breakfast was good for him and could jump-start his day. Instead, I gave him more coffee, which he drank very hot, rubbing his hand over his beard stubble. I offered him the use of a razor, but he declined. Finally he said, "I have questions."

"Awake enough to ask them?"

"Royce came all the way from Twinsburg to beat you up," he reminded me. "But until we met in your parking lot, he didn't know I was with your company, or that I knew you. Neither did Riona Dennehy, by the way."

"So?"

"So—why? Why did Dennehy decide it was you who deserved a rough-up."

"I don't know."

"I think I do," he said. "I talked to Carol Shepard when I started this case. She's a small-time monster to people like me who don't flash money at her, but she seemed okay as far as what she said about Earl Dacey. Then *you* confronted her, and all of a sudden Royce—who works for Riona Dennehy, whom you haven't even met—shows up at *your* office to hurt you. He was surprised to find me there, but decided to pound lumps on me instead. It didn't work out for him very well."

"What's your question?"

"I have three. What do Dennehy and Shepard have to do with one another? And why do we bother with porn people like them in the first place?"

"And your third question?"

"Is there more coffee?"

"Drag your bruised ass into the kitchen and find out for yourself."

When he came back with his third cup, I said, "Okay. I don't know how Dennehy and Shepard relate to each other. I want to find out. Yesterday you looked up stuff for Suzanne at the courthouse in Cleveland. Today, do the same thing for me in Lake County."

"At Painesville?"

I nodded. "Go home—clean yourself up and look more or less respectable before you hit the county offices. What you can't find in the files you might find online—everything about those two women. Birth, education, jobs, awards, board memberships, real estate holdings, anything like that. Personal stuff, too—families, boyfriends or husbands, past and present. See if either of them have police records or unwanted publicity. I want to know what color they paint their toenails, what they've had for breakfast for the last twenty years, and what they use to brush their teeth when they finish eating it."

"I get you," K.O. said, annoyed. "What do they wear to bed, right? But why?"

I fidgeted in my chair for a while, wishing I had coffee to drink, too. "I'm working on another—inquiry."

"Gonna tell me about it?"

I considered Special Agent Kitzberger meeting up with K.O.

What would happen then? Whatever it was gave me the creeps—it would be more trouble than it was worth. "Maybe later."

He raised his shoulders and closed his eyes for a second. "It's your ballgame."

I busied myself washing cups after he left. If I pressed Dennehy and Shepard myself, I might get answers, or at least a direction in which to search. But if no clues were forthcoming, I'd hit a brick wall.

When I got down to my office an hour later, the voice-mail indicator was blinking like crazy. I listened to all the messages and then started returning calls.

"Why aren't you getting anywhere?" Savannah Dacey demanded. She wasn't crying all the time anymore; now she sounded perpetually pissed off. "My son is dead and you don't have a damn thing to tell me. Why the fuck is that?"

The profanity coming from her mouth took me aback. I knew women cursed, but I didn't expect it from a recently bereaved mother. "No one's lining up outside my door to confess. It takes work, digging and asking questions—and most people don't want to answer them."

"You're a cold man, Milan," she said. "I didn't think you were when I met you, but now I think you are. There's no warmth to you."

There was not much warmth to Savannah either—once she stopped inexorably flirting with me.

"I'm an investigator," I said. "I'm tough and cold because no one opens up to me if they think I'm warm and cuddly."

"You don't care about Earl—you never did," she moaned. "Or about me, either."

"I stayed on this case even when it's illegal for me to do so, and I could lose my license because of it. Does that mean I don't care?"

"It means," Savannah said, "that you're in it for the money."

I wasn't able to pull the phone away from my ear before she slammed hers down. I toyed with the idea of calling her right back to suggest what she could do with her money, but I was too tired to—even this early in the morning.

The next message was from Anna Barna. I hadn't expected to

hear from her again. The number she left for me was answered by an operator from Progressive Insurance, where Anna worked.

"Mr.—Jacovich," Anna said when she finally came on, speaking not much louder than a whisper. "I thought of a few things, an' I prob'ly oughta tell you." Then she lowered her voice even more. "Not on the phone."

"Shall I meet you at your house when you've finished work?"

"No!" Too quick, too resolved. "Um—my father hates it when people come to the house. I take a fifteen-minute break here at work at about two thirty—could you come then?"

Progressive Insurance has a large facility in Mayfield Heights near the Cuyahoga County line. That meant a relatively long drive from my office for fifteen minutes' worth of conversation, but I saw no way out of it. I made the date—wondering what exactly Anna wanted to tell me that she hadn't already.

I went "up the hill" from the Flats to Sokolowski's University Inn for lunch. They serve authentic home cooking, especially if your "home" happens to be somewhere in Eastern Europe. I love their potato soup, but it was too hot for soup, so I chose the city chicken instead. Nobody in the world makes gravy like the University Inn.

I had to announce myself to several different people at Progressive Insurance; most of those who worked there had no idea who the other people working there were. It took about five minutes until Anna Barna found her way down to the lobby.

"Thanks for coming," she said.

"Where can we talk?"

We wound up in a little room surrounded by drink and snack machines with bright colors and flashing lights, luring passersby to eat junk food like Sirens enticing passing sailors to smash themselves to bits on the rocks.

I fished in my pocket for change. "Can I get you something to drink?"

She shook her head. We sat down. Three people at another table didn't seem to notice us. They probably worked in a different department, or different wing.

"I should of told you this before," Anna said, rubbing her hands together as though anointing them with lotion after doing the dishes. "Earl was scared about those pictures—scared to death."

"Why?"

"Well, one day he was videotaping some high school girl without her knowin' it, 'cuz she was wearin' one a those plaid skirts—an' her boyfriend caught him doin' it—saw Earl's camera in the shopping bag." She looked miserable. "He beat Earl up pretty bad."

"How bad?"

She stared down at the table, hoping the haunting ghosts tormenting her would go away. "Well—um, he punched him in the stomach an' almost knocked him down—an' then punched him in the face, too. Earl had a split lip that looked pretty bad."

"What else?"

"I guess that was it, because the guy tried to take away Earl's shopping bag an' his camera—an' Earl grabbed it and ran like crazy."

"Where did this happen, Anna?"

"Um, I'm not sure." She pronounced the word "shurr," the way Valley Girls used to in the seventies. "I think it might have been Great Northern Plaza—in North Olmsted?"

I nodded.

"At Dillard's, maybe. He went in there a lot last spring. But after that—after he got beat up—he never went anyplace on the West Side to take pictures. He said it was too close to home, so he stuck to places on the East Side—in the suburbs."

"Anna, why are you telling me?"

"'Cuz," she said, "teenage girls can be meaner'n anything. They were all bullies—mean to Earl when he was in high school, and it kept on after he grew up—so he was super-scared of them." She lowered her voice even more, and I leaned forward to hear her. "He was scared of just about everybody. All men or boys."

"Was he scared of your father, too?"

Her eyes widened fearfully.

"You knew Earl since you were little kids playing together. Why would he be afraid of your father?"

Her chin was low on her chest, and her next words were aimed toward the floor, but I managed to make them out anyway. "*Everybody* is scared of my father."

Anna Barna's father's first name—I looked it up in the phone book—was Josef, with an *f*. He was home when I knocked on the door, and I got the feeling he was always home, probably because he hadn't a single interesting thing to do if he left his living room.

"Huh. Cop again," he said through the screen door. It wasn't a snarl, nor even a growl; it was more a sound of deep disgust. "Anna's not here."

"Actually, I came to see you."

"So you're seeing me. Now fuck off."

"I just need a minute of your time."

His eyes narrowed. "Minutes cost money," he said.

"You want me to give you money?"

"If you wanna talk to me. I'm old now, an' I got no more job, so if you take up my time you gotta spend."

I considered ripping the screen door off its hinges and kicking Josef Barna to the curb, but my better instincts took hold. I dug into my pocket and fished out a ten. He shrugged.

"Does that thing have a twin brother to go with it?"

Reluctantly I gave him another ten. "You're a hard man, Mr. Barna."

"Goddamn right, and don't you forget it," he said.

"I'm not sliding them under the door. If you want the cash, open up."

Resentful, he unhooked the door and stuck his hand out for the money. I didn't have to shove too hard to force my way inside.

"Goddammit!"

"Settle down, Mr. Barna. You'll get the money after we talk."

He shook his head stubbornly. "Before!"

"I hope," I said, "I don't look that stupid. Shall we sit and be comfortable?"

"No!"

"As you wish. I assume you heard about Earl Dacey—that he died."

His expression didn't change at all. "Too bad."

"You knew him since he was five years old. He was your daughter's friend."

"So? He was no friend of mine."

"Was he your enemy?"

"He was nothing one way or the other. Just a little shit hangin' around."

"And you never had a conversation with him?"

"Sure—like 'go home!'"

"He's been Anna's friend for twenty years and all you ever said to him was 'go home?'"

He aimed a tobacco-yellow finger at my chest. I hoped he wouldn't poke me with it; I don't like being poked. "My wife died when Anna was born. Then it was just the two of us—and I never had nothin' to say to her 'cuz I don't know how to talk to kids. I never talked with her friends, neither, so they stopped comin' around. Now Anna tells me Earl got killed—so like I says, too bad. Too bad he was a little geek freak, too—but it don't mean nothin' to me one way or the other."

"He was killed—beaten to death with a baseball bat."

He inflated his chest and doubled his fists in front of him. He was too skinny to intimidate me or anyone else, but he gave it his best shot. "Are you sayin' it was me?"

"You brought that up—not me." I tried not to let him know I was thinking it. "Anna was his friend. Did they have other friends in common?"

Barna actually jumped, and then seemingly suffered a slow leak—not like a tire blowout on the highway but a quiet loss of air and pressure from his chest that deflated him. He'd spent three decades trying *not* being a father; now my questions were catching up with him. "You seen Anna, right?" he sighed. "She's no beauty, you gotta admit that. And she's quiet—so she never had no friends except Earl. He didn' have no friends neither, 'cuz he was a geek. Nobody around here likes guys takin' dirty pictures. If he'd took any of my girl I'd a killed them both. I swear to Jesus I woulda."

"You knew about the pictures, then?"

He swallowed hard and turned his head away, not letting his

eyes meet mine. "I didn' *know* about 'em. I never seen any—but you hear stuff."

"From where?"

"*Around!*"

"Around where? I didn't think you got out much."

"I got friends," he snarled. "Plenty of friends—in the neighborhood. Stan Majkrzak, for instance—he's my friend for a lotta years." Resentfully he said, "I guess you already talked to him."

"Was it Stan who told you about the pictures?"

Barna chewed the inside of his cheek as if it were bubble gum. "I don' remember."

"You said if Earl took dirty pictures of Anna, you'd kill him. Did you mean that?"

That rattled him; his answer was a whisper. "I never killed nobody. I wouldn't of—but I might of knocked the piss out of him." He ducked his head. "Shit, that sounds like I done it."

"In that case, Mr. Barna," I said, "if I were you—and if the police come around—I'd watch my mouth."

Driving back to my office, I couldn't stop thinking about Barna's longtime friendship with Stanley Majkrzak—and Stan telling him about Earl Dacey's photographs. I'd follow up on that—if Stan let me in again.

I was mad at myself, too, that I'd wasted part of an afternoon on a hunch that went nowhere—but I was even more annoyed with Barna. Poor Anna had spent her whole life in the home of a man who never knew how to talk to her—and when he talked *about* her, he made sure the word was out: she was unattractive, socially inept, and had no friends. I'd bet dollars to doughnuts that during her existence, Barna never told his daughter he loved her. He hadn't forgiven her for her mother's death a quarter of a century earlier—hardly the fault of a newborn babe.

Then I began thinking of my own boys—grown men. Many times when they were little I told them I loved them—but to my shame, I couldn't remember the last time I'd spoken the words to them. Worse, I couldn't recall either of them saying it to me. I wonder if either of them ever said "I love you" to *anyone*.

It's a strange generational thing. When I was a kid, the *L* word was rarely used, except perhaps when Clevelanders discussed how much they "loved" Jim Brown when he played football in orange and brown. Most people of my age hug one another—but the younger crowd doesn't. They hardly shake hands as we did; they bump fists instead. And they don't make love anymore, or even call it "having sex." They "hook up."

The world changes too rapidly for me.

I called Savannah from my desk, hearing six rings before she answered.

"What is it, Milan?" The words were a sigh. "I'm burned out."

"Just a quick question," I said. "About Stanley Majkrzak."

"Who? Oh, yeah, Stanley. Well, he was Earl's friend."

"He wasn't your friend, too?"

"Not really. A few years ago, he asked me out a lot. I think he was hot for me, the old sleazebag. We even went out to dinner and a movie once—not a very good dinner, either, at some coffee shop place. But he wasn't my type, so it didn't come to anything more than that one date. Earl, though—he saw him a lot."

"Why?"

"I dunno. They was far apart in age. Earl never said much about him to me—except he *thought* Stanley might go into some kinda business with him and make lots a money."

"He didn't say what business?"

"Nuh-uh," she said. "I thought it was all pie in the sky, because Stanley never made money since he quit working. Listen, I'm no gold digger—but if I get romantically involved with any man, he's gotta have a few bucks in the bank. For security."

"Your security or Earl's?"

"Like I say, I don' know what was goin' on with he and Earl."

"Nothing about Earl's photos and videos?"

She paused to sip whatever she was drinking—probably lemonade or iced tea on a hot afternoon. Her gulp was audible. "Stanley might've liked those dirty pitchers. If some girl sat down opposite him, he'd always try to look up her dress. God knows what else he might be into."

"It sounds like you don't like him much."

The next hesitation was longer than the first. When she finally answered she made no attempt to keep vitriol from her tone. "Till we find out who killed Earl—I don't like *anyone!*"

*   *   *

Stan Majkrzak must have been surprised to find me at his door again this late in the day. I don't think he expected me to return; as a result he wasn't quite as kind and accommodating as he had been the first time.

"I was getting ready to cook dinner," he said crossly. He didn't invite me all the way in, so we stood awkwardly in his front hallway.

"You know Earl Dacey is dead."

"Everybody knows. It was on the news a couple a days ago."

"You also know he took dirty videos—and you told him you weren't interested in seeing them."

His lower jaw was extended, shoulders squared. He gave me an affirmative nod.

"You and Earl were going into business, weren't you? To sell those pictures and videos."

Stanley was trying to look intimidating, but his upper body shook a little. He lapped at his lips, trying to wet them. "You're a damn liar," he managed to growl.

"Earl didn't have money—he never had a job—but he needed *some* cash, to buy videotapes and film. He couldn't ask his only other friend, Anna, for money—he had already proposed taking upskirt pictures of her, and she turned him down flat—so he came to you. Am I right?"

Stanley reached out to put his hand against the wall, leaning on it. "I just gave him a couple a hundred bucks. As a loan."

"A loan," I said, "or an investment?"

I thought he would fall down. I took his arm and led him to his sofa, then sat on the other end. "Stan, somebody murdered Earl. If you don't want to be a suspect, come clean with me."

He breathed heavily, and I feared he was having a heart attack. He waved me away for almost half a minute, then said, "Can you get me a drink of water?"

I fetched one from the kitchen. He nodded his thanks and drank half of it slowly. Finally he settled against the back of the sofa and started talking.

"It was a kind of investment," he said around deep breaths. "I didn't need the money. My car is all paid for, an' so's my insurance for the next two years. I don't live a glamorous life—as you can see—so I didn't care how much money I made."

"Why, then?"

He considered. "You know how old I am, Mr. Jacovich?"

"Milan," I said. "Call me Milan."

"Awright, Milan, I'll tell you. I'm gonna be seventy-six years old in November."

"You don't look that old."

"Save the bullshit. I got a mirror. You got any idea when was the last time I got laid? *I* can't even remember. It was in the last century, though."

"Lots of people have a sex life clear into their eighties or nineties."

"Yeah, but I always liked young women." He raised a cautionary finger. "I'm not talkin' about children, now! I'm no—um—pedicure." I didn't correct him, and tried to suppress a smile. "It's the older teenies and twennies—the grown-ups—is what gets to me."

"I still don't understand—"

"What pretty girl that age would ever look at me? Or even a not-so-pretty girl. Not even *look* at me!" Stanley rubbed his hand across his eyes. "As it is, I'm way better off than Earl was; I don't think he ever had sex in his life. That's why he started taking obscene pictures—it was his sexual outlet. And me? I enjoyed his enjoyment of it, 'cuz that's the best I can do at my age. Don't get me wrong, when I was married I never even looked at another woman—even after my wife got sick—because she was a real good looker when I married her. That was when she was nineteen, I think." He wrinkled his nose. "After she died, I could afford hookers if I wanted—but that makes me disgusted."

"Stan, if you just want to look at pictures and videos, there are millions of them on the Internet. Do you have a computer?"

"Sure—but that's professional stuff. Boring. Earl was shooting real people—right here in Ohio—and I got the kicks out of it 'cuz it was him doing it. He was my friend—he was getting a blast, an' so did I."

"If it thrilled you so much, why didn't you take videos yourself?"

His eyes widened. "Are you kidding? I mighta got killed. Listen, Earl got caught a couple a times—boyfriends or something that were shopping with these girls—and one of them roughed him up so bad he fell over, an' another one chased him clear outa the mall. If he'd a caught him he'd a beaten him senseless. So if Earl was scared all a time—can you imagine how scared I woulda been?"

"He went through all this," I said, "and didn't make any money?"

"Nah—he tried. Nobody was innerested. So when I say it was an investment, it wasn't for the money. For me it was the only fun I could get anymore."

"But he never sold them—never made a nickel from them. Didn't that piss you off?"

"Sorta—but not really."

"Not enough to lose your temper and kill him?"

"I'd never been that mad at anyone in my whole life," he said, shocked. "And Earl—he was nearly fifty years younger than me, an' a hell of a lot bigger, too. I couldn't of beat him to death if I tried."

"You didn't buy his pictures and videos?"

"He always let me see 'em, an' promised when we made some money he'd make copies so I could have 'em for my own. But that never happened." He sighed with the desperate aloneness of an elderly man who let himself get lost in the disintegration of his own time. "I guess now," he said—it nearly broke my heart—"it never *will* happen."

CHAPTER EIGHTEEN

I should have gone straight home, but I stopped by my office to close things up. I knew it was a mistake when I saw Agent Jeffrey Kitzberger waiting comfortably in his Cadillac for me, wastefully burning gas to keep himself air-conditioned cool.

"I was ready to give up on you," he said, unfolding himself from his front seat and adjusting his sunglasses. His designer shades were expensive, probably some Hollywood brand I'd never heard of that would cost most working people a week's salary.

I wasn't glad to see him—but then I never was. "Are you stalking me?"

He didn't smile; Fibbies must be trained not to. "You're not my type." He tucked his briefcase beneath his arm. "Shall we go upstairs?"

"It's the end of a long day, Special Agent Kitzberger. Can't this wait until tomorrow?"

"Afraid not. At the Bureau," and he pronounced the word carefully as if it were sacred, "we don't have such a thing as the end of a day." I slammed my car door, and his dark glasses masked his amusement at my anger. "I won't take up much of your time—I hope."

He'd come back again like a bad penny I'd done nothing to deserve. My trek up those steps was akin to scaling Mount Kilimanjaro—or some other mountain in a place where it's as hot as it is in a Cleveland July.

As soon as I unlocked my office door, he strolled past me and settled into a chair as if he'd been there a hundred times before. "You have an attitude problem with the FBI."

I sat behind the desk. "I have a problem with *some people* in the FBI—like I have one with *some* parking lot attendants or small-minded fanatics or pencil pushers with a pissant title that makes them feel they have some authority."

"Then apparently you have a problem with me."

I put it as politely as I could. "Let's just say our personalities don't mesh."

"I can live with that. Frankly, I don't care if you think I'm the anti-Christ—just so you have the answers I want." He took a leather-bound notebook and a fountain pen from his pocket. A fountain pen! It hovered over a blank page like a scalpel before the surgeon makes the first incision.

I took my time booting up my laptop, and brought up a file. "I couldn't find out much, because I don't have a badge like you do to scare anyone. I hardly knew what to say to ordinary pornographers, much less those involved in kiddie porn. Think of another question."

"I'll keep asking this one. Who are the porn peddlers in Greater Cleveland?"

"Write them down because I'm not making this a habit." I waited as long as I could, just to bug him. "Start with Wade Applegate. WACO Distributing. He distributes. That's small potatoes for someone like you."

He wrote in his notebook—very carefully, small and neat. He must have won penmanship prizes in grammar school. "What else?"

"Helene Diamond. You have her mug shot. She produces adult films, but as far as I can tell, she's legit."

"Legit?"

"That's your law, not mine."

"Not *my* law. If we operated under my law, I'd line up every one of them against the goddamn wall." He stroked his chin thoughtfully, like a bad actor trying to indicate deep thoughts. Finally he said, "Next?"

"There's a guy I know of but haven't met yet—Stuart Eisen. From what I hear, he's also a distributor."

"I know of him, too. He's clean, at least when it comes to kiddie porn. Next?"

"This might get your attention. Are you aware of Jimmy Santocroce?"

Kitzberger nodded. "Is the pope Catholic?"

"From what I've read about the pope, I'm not so sure."

That sent Kitzberger's eyebrows scurrying up toward his hairline, even behind the dark glasses. He chose not to comment. "Did you visit Santocroce?"

"No, he visited me, here in the office. He admitted that he sometimes uses underage girls for his porno films—and he brought some friends with him."

"What friends?"

"Their names are Leonard and Roger."

"*Last names!*"

"It wasn't a formal introduction. Maybe you can trace their last names through these." I unlocked my bottom drawer, bringing out the guns I'd taken away from Santocroce's *boys.* "Take them with you."

Kitzberger examined them, then slipped them into his briefcase. "Why did Santocroce visit you with hit men tagging along?"

"One of his shirttail buddies got hurt and he blamed me for it."

"Which buddy?"

"Another name you may or may not know—Angelo Nicolino."

"So what's he into? Kiddie porn, too?"

"I don't think so," I said. "Not now, anyway. He produces and sells crush films."

Kitzberger didn't blink an eye. "The Supreme Court is taking care of that. It's none of my business."

"Doesn't it creep you out that they torture and kill small animals on film for sickos' amusement?"

Kitzberger shrugged. "I'm not an animal person. Dogs slobber all over your clothes—and there's no way I'll clean out a cat litter pan. So I don't care about animals one way or another. Where do you fit with Nicolino?"

"He got hurt and wound up in the hospital."

"Is that why you beat him up? Because he produces these scrunch films?"

"*Crush* films. I never laid eyes on him."

"Then who was the culprit?"

"The culprit? Jesus, have you been reading Charles Dickens? 'The culprit?' Ah, strike that," I said, "you probably don't read anything except FBI field manuals."

He looked piqued. "Who was the muscle—the beater-upper?"

I didn't want Kevin O'Bannion getting involved with the FBI. Not that they'd prosecute somebody for beating up somebody else—that's small-time crap for the federal government—but I didn't want K.O. butting heads with Kitzberger just yet. I'm short on the diplomatic front, but K.O. was totally bereft, and he'd get himself into such trouble with Kitzberger that his life would be one long nightmare. On the other hand, I wouldn't knowingly lie to a Fed. I was sure the FBI already had a file on me, and I didn't want them adding "He lies through his teeth" for that.

So what I said was, indeed, the truth. "I wasn't there. I didn't see it happen."

"Are you being honest with me, Jacovich?"

"Are you aware that if you use my last name like that again I'm going to rip a hole in your chest and remove a lung, fed badge or not?"

"You aren't tough enough."

"Maybe not," I said. "But unless you shoot me right now, I can hurt you very badly. I reminded you about your FBI manners the first time we met. I guess it didn't take."

He considered. "Then I apologize—*Mister* Jacovich." He shook his head. "You're pretty thin-skinned."

"You bring that out in me, Special Agent Kitzberger."

"You wear me out."

"Ditto."

He snapped his notebook shut. "I assume you've finished?"

"Not quite," I said. "Have you ever heard of Riona Dennehy?"

"Riona—is that a Polish name?"

"No—Irish. This Riona lives in Twinsburg. Middle-aged, fairly well off—and I suspect she's involved in making porno with underage teens—and possibly turning them out as part-time, highly paid hookers."

He opened his notebook again and wrote down just about everything I'd just said—probably in less-interesting language. "When did you talk to this Dennehy?"

I've heard the expression "pregnant pause," but I'd never before been guilty of it myself. Kitzberger cocked his head, waiting patiently for the fat lady to sing.

"I've never met her either," I said. "Or talked to her on the phone."

This time he took off his sunglasses. "Were you texting her? Or did you and she chat about child prostitutes over Skype while you sipped your morning coffee?"

"Again—somebody told me. That's all you get."

"Somebody," he murmured. "Do I get to guess?"

"Go back to your office on Lakeside Avenue and do your guessing there."

"It's no guess. We know all about you—and who your friends are."

"The FBI doesn't have enough to do investigating terrorists so they spend their time creating a dossier for me?"

Kitzberger lowered his head like a bull ready to charge. "One for you—and one for Victor Gaimari. Do you think I'm too dense to know you and Victor are bosom buddies?"

"If you know that, ask Victor. It's not part of his business—or mine, either. I let you lean on me and I told you all I know about child pornography—not much. Threaten me all you want, if that's what floats your boat. But float it somewhere else. You're not welcome here."

Kitzberger arose slowly, making sure his pants hadn't been creased. "I'm concerned over your patriotism, Mr. Jacovich," he scolded.

"I don't see an American flag in your lapel, either," I said. "You should wear one—it'll impress the hell out of everybody."

"I don't want to impress anyone. The FBI's only job is to serve the citizens of the United States." He crossed his arms defensively across his chest—and that made *me* concerned over his jacket and shirt getting wrinkled. "But you don't seem to like them."

"I don't like the people of the United States? Oh, come on! I *am* one."

"That's not what I meant."

"The U.S. Congress is *supposed* to serve its citizens, too—and I don't like them, either." I threw him a lazy mock salute. "It's been magical knowing you, Special Agent Kitzberger, but *adiós*—and don't come back."

He strolled almost to the door, then looked over his shoulder. "Not without a warrant I won't."

I grumbled at my desk for almost an hour after Jeffrey Kitzberger left, trying to calm down. It's easier these days not to lose my temper—I've grown more mellow with age. But guys like that bring out grievances long suppressed. I felt as strongly against minors in porn films as anyone—but working for Kitzberger got me almost as mad as Jimmy Santocroce blustering into my office with mouth-breathing hurt-givers.

I'm not *that* mellow.

So, I thought, he'll submit his report to his higher-ups, all the people on whom I've squealed will get busted and probably sent to prison, Kitzberger will earn a medal or a promotion and a round of polite applause, and my name will never be mentioned. If he doesn't tell anybody where he got his information, hopefully nobody will look up my dossier and see what a terrible human being I must be.

I finally noticed an e-mail from K.O. Here's what it said:

Milan:

Per your request: I spent half the day poking around in the county seat records at Painesville. You've probably been there before. The historical courthouse isn't so quaint when you're down in the basement getting dirty and sweaty, sneezing dust and trying to find out something bad about someone else.

Carol Shepard lives in a nice thirty-seven year old house in Chardon—three bedrooms, two and a half baths (What is a "half-bath?" Is that for when you just want to wash from the waist up?). Anyway, Shepard owns it outright—paid in full when she moved in three years ago.

When she was twenty—she's twenty-nine now—Carol Shepard was arrested for prostitution in Mentor. Don't get the idea she was a streetwalker. She advertised discreetly online, and in some Cleveland alternative weeklies like The Scene. This was before Craig's List and Twitter, but she got her name and her contact numbers out there. Her professional name was "Autumn." Wow. When she got hauled into court she pleaded that she was trying to earn enough money to stay in college—Kent State, majoring in business. Isn't that your college too, Milan?

She charged anywhere from three hundred bucks to two grand per trick, depending on the length of her dates and the sexual demands made on her. Those prices were expensive a decade ago. Later newspaper articles, both in the News-Herald and the Plain Dealer, mentioned that she sometimes marketed herself as a dominatrix. (No further explanation is necessary to you, is there?)

She was represented in court by a high-priced Cleveland defense attorney, Peter Beaulac. She pleaded No Contest to Judge Charles Abkern, now deceased, and was sentenced to two years probation and two hundred hours of community service. I have no idea what community services she performed; your guess is as good as mine. I wasn't sure at first why she got a slap on the wrist instead of jail time, but it didn't take much digging to find out. Lawyer Beaulac and Judge Abkern were good buddies; they even co-owned a Browns season box on the 40 yard-line until the judge died two years ago. Beaulac still owns his share.

Chew on this for a while: Carol Shepard rarely got punished for anything. For instance, she wasn't kicked out of school for her pross bust. She wasn't on any sort of scholarship, so either her parents or somebody else paid her tuition. Maybe she worked her way through college on her. I'm wondering if Peter Beaulac signed the checks—out of his law firm, probably.

So she completed her two years at Kent without anyone

knowing much about her—and then disappeared. No job anywhere in Northeast Ohio.

She came back strong, because four years after she ducked under the radar, she was in Lake County again, opening her own business. She calls it "Young-at-Heart Entertainment." (Those hyphens are hers, not mine.) I guess she keeps her day job at the mall so nobody will think twice about her having money in the bank. Now she buys ads in the alternatives again, and heavy-duty on the Internet, too. But here's the best part: she has a partner in the business—Mrs. R. Finnegan Dennehy—of Twinsburg, Ohio. Sound familiar?

Being an entrepreneurial type—did I spell that okay?— Mrs. R. Finnegan Dennehy opened her own business at about the same time—home-based in Summit County. It's called—here it comes—"Young-at-Heart Festivities." Some coincidence, huh? Dennehy's partner in that particular company is listed as one Carol Jessica Shepard.

What do we make of this?

Maybe Dennehy's into a lot of shit and sent Royce after me so I wouldn't talk it up where anyone could hear, but it had nothing to do with Earl Dacey. Surprised that she was linked with Carol Shepard, it made me poke further. I hope it won't piss you off.

I called Jake Foote again—the Mentor cop I had lunch with. The one who busted me a million years ago when I went to Juvie? He's got access to all kinds of computers. He can look up just about anything in the United States within seconds. So I asked if he'd check on both women—especially on Riona Dennehy.

She was born to lace-curtain Irish parents in New York City, name of Finnegan, but left home when she was sixteen and went out to Los Angeles. Prettier forty years ago than she is now, she worked an escort service for a while in L.A.—even serviced more than a couple of actual movie actors, or so the story goes, until she set up her own shop in a place called Brentwood and started advertising in some of those local weekly papers more gross than the ones in Cleveland. Apparently she didn't have the California connections Shepard had here, because she got busted and spent nineteen months in the slammer. When she got out she headed east, for Chicago.

She didn't get caught until about eight years ago. Not so young and pretty anymore, she graduated from hooker to madam. Madams aren't bothered by the local cops. They factor in the bribes they pay off as a necessary business expense. So for whatever reason, her arrest was expunged. Is that the right word—expunged?

She also got married—for a while. Hubby was Aidan Dennehy—big manufacturer with a monster mansion on the South Side of Chicago, near the Museum of Science and Industry. He was in his late sixties when they married, and didn't survive more than three years. His will left most of his fortune to his three grown children; Mrs. Dennehy only got just over two mill. Poor baby, huh? Don't you feel sorry for her?

So Dennehy aimed for big money on her own—recruiting teenage girls to sell themselves while they were still in high school. You know, girls lie to their parents all the time about where they go, who they're with, and what they do. The cost of a young teen for sex is more than double for an adult, and the ballgame Dennehy ran brought in a ton of money. Her business was growing out of hand, so she hired someone younger and prettier to help her in the recruiting department—Carol Shepard. Shepard had hooked for her for a short time, and they were friends. But peddling minors for sexual purposes goes beyond pimping. Both women got arrested.

About Chicago politics: the charges were dropped. Foote didn't have time to find out why—he'll look for reasons if you want. It won't cost you anything—maybe another lunch—because it's as a favor to me. Weird because I owe _him_ more favors than I can count.

Dennehy and Shepard were advised to find another city more to their liking, so they skeedaddled from Chicago and wound up in Greater Cleveland. Shepard's childhood was here and she knew her town well. To make sure nobody connected them, they moved to different counties—Shepard to Lake County, Dennehy to Summit. Both bought their homes outright for cash. Dennehy doesn't work at all anymore, at least not at a regular job. Shepard got hired at Great Lakes Mall; she has people under her, like Leon, and the mall is a good place to meet teenies who like to spend money on clothes and cosmetics and don't yet know how to earn it.

This is way past what Earl Dacey had in mind. Apparently both women knew him, but wouldn't bother with a not-so-bright geek with a camera in a shopping bag. I wasted my time and your money on Dacey. Sorry—that's how the cookie crumbles.

Jake Foote's heard of you—you get your name in the papers a lot—and he sounded interested. He says he wants to meet you, too. Maybe when this is all over, we can set up another lunch.

I'm seeing Carli again tonight, if that's okay with you. Or even if it isn't. Not asking your permission, just politely telling you how I'm spending my evening. Meantime, boss, what do ya want me to do tomorrow?

K.O.

More to worry about. I was pelted with stones from every direction, because my life had somehow gone off the tracks. I started out looking for a missing guy whose mother didn't know where he'd gone. That turned into chasing a murderer without getting the Cleveland police rightly furious with me. A marginal mob guy with two bungling muscle men busted into my office to beat me up—and a black guy with a shaved head whom I've never even laid eyes on showed up to do the same thing, but was dissuaded by the assistant I hadn't planned on hiring in the first place. Then, along came an arrogant FBI agent forcing me to ferret out local dirty filmmakers—without getting paid for it, either, which made me an unwilling volunteer. And now, thanks to K.O.'s superb probing, I found myself in the middle of a child porno and prostitution setup that was much more sophisticated than I'd ever imagined.

So how was *your* day?

CHAPTER NINETEEN

O nce home, I kicked my shoes off at the door. Wiggling my toes inside my socks, I headed for the refrigerator. The Stroh's was ice cold, and I drank half the bottle in one long swig. Then I padded into my favorite spot in the apartment, the bay, took my seat by the window where I could look out into the pleasant twilight of the Cedar-Fairmount triangle, and leaned forward to turn my air conditioner on HIGH.

I kept thinking about all the junk K.O. had dug up concerning Carol Shepard and Riona Dennehy. I knew enough to do the "right thing" and tell the FBI all about them—they were, after all, purveyors of porn and underage prostitution—although rather than talk to Kitzberger again, I'd prefer a root canal.

I checked my watch; it was ten minutes past eight—too late to call the Feds and spill my guts. I'd wait until morning.

Something else about K.O.'s message stuck in my head. While I was vegetating in my chair watching people have a good time and enjoy cocktails across the street at the Mad Greek, K.O. was seeing Carli. I finished my beer, breathed in and out a few times to wake up my brain, and dialed Cisne's home number.

"I've been thinking about you, Cisne. I wanted to call you every day since we saw each other."

"So," she joked, "a serious hangnail prevented your calling."

"Even old-timers like me don't have dial phones anymore. I just plumb forgot to call—or was too wiped out. Forgive me?"

She chuckled, but it was almost a reluctant laugh. "Sure. We have our own lives."

"Is anything wrong?"

"Not between us. But I've been through the meat grinder today."

"Trouble with your principal again?"

"Father Laughlin? He's no Bing Crosby in those old movies. He's a total pain in the ass, so today was no worse than yesterday. But I had a suspicion—I approached him with it but he nearly bit my head off, so I followed through on my own." She stopped and took a breath. "It wasn't pleasant."

"Want to talk about it?"

"It's not your area of expertise."

"I'll try my best."

"Well," she said. "You remember Carolyn Alexander. She wasn't in school again today. It got me worried. I called her house but there was no answer. Both parents work, but if no one picked up the phone just after noon, it meant she wasn't sick but out somewhere, or she *was* home and didn't want to talk to anyone. So after classes, I drove over there. She was home, all right—and when she answered the door I could tell somebody had beaten the crap out of her again."

"Twice in one week?"

"Her bruises are new—there's a big ugly one along the right side of her jaw. The other eye is black too, and bloodshot. And oh yeah, she now has a cast on her left hand. Two broken fingers, she said—from falling down the stairs again. But I know she's lying. I'd never visited her home before—a big, sprawling ranch house. One level. No stairs."

"Are you sure it isn't her parents abusing her?"

"It crossed my mind," Cisne said, "but her father's out of town on business. He owns a medical supply company—they make all sorts of instruments and things. Don't ask me what they are—science isn't my strong subject. I remember her telling me they live in the area because Cleveland is one of the major medical centers of the world, but that he's off to New York or Japan or Europe all the time and she hardly ever sees him. And her mother—she's almost tiny, anyway—is on so many boards of nonprofit organizations in Lake County, she probably doesn't have the time, strength, or inclination to beat up her daughter."

"So you're convinced it's the boyfriend—Shane, is it? The big-shot athlete?"

"Shane Ward. I can't prove it, or do a damn thing about it—but I'm certain it's him."

The English teacher in her would have said "It was he," so I could tell how upset she was. I glanced outside. Passing in front of the wide-open windows in the lounge of the Mad Greek Restaurant was a teenage couple. The cute blond girl wore shorts and a bright blue halter top, and flip-flops. The guy, whose deathly white skin probably hadn't seen a sun ray all summer, sported a baggy T-shirt on what looked like its third straight day of wear and khaki shorts hanging so low on his hips that most of his boxers were displayed to the rest of the world. They looked adoringly at each other, except he was holding on to her—and not in the embrace of a love-struck twosome. His hand was firmly cupped around the back of her neck, as though he feared she'd try to run away and then he could increase his pressure and cause a great deal of pain to stop her.

I tried to tell myself lots of kids walk that way together.

"Why doesn't Carolyn just dump his ass? She's pretty and rich. She can have anyone she wants."

"If that were true, Milan, no teenage girl would ever get hit by her boyfriend more than once. But you'd be amazed how many girls put up with it—even the pretty, rich ones."

I was thrown off balance. I hadn't called Cisne to talk about one of her students being slapped around by her boyfriend. But that's the way life is. We never know what's just around the corner.

Cisne wanted to go back to Carolyn Alexander's house to urge her to talk about what happened. That didn't surprise me. What did, however, was her asking me to go with her.

"From our last meeting," I said, "I don't think she's that crazy about having me around."

"Well, she doesn't have much respect for me—and probably her parents don't, either. I'm just an employee. You're a large man and you *look* official. Besides, she doesn't know what a private investigator really is."

"She's too young to know about all those private-eye movies, hmm?"

"So am I. Come with me, Milan. At the very least, it'll make me feel better."

So we made a date for the next day; I'd pick her up at St. Katherine's and we'd drive together to speak with Carolyn Alexander. I wasn't looking forward to the conversation. Talking about men beating up women makes me uncomfortable when it's not my business.

Who knows what it is, exactly, that affects your sleep? I thought I'd toss all night, but I fell dreamlessly asleep early, woke up once at about three A.M. to pee, and arose the next morning rested and energetic.

When I went out to my car, it was cooler than it had been—the morning temperature in the high sixties. It's always a nice July day when you don't sweat.

It could have been a great day—until I sat down at my desk, brought up K.O.'s last e-mail on my laptop, and tapped out the number of the FBI headquarters. It was downtown, a big building on Lakeside Avenue that looked as if it should be the headquarters of an international manufacturing company. That's where Special Agent Jeffrey Kitzberger hung out; I imagined him in his stuffy government office, probably looking out his window at beautiful, blue Lake Erie as he picked up the phone and I heard his voice—assaulting my ear like fingernails on a blackboard.

"I didn't expect to hear from you so soon," he said, bright and cheery at ten o'clock in the morning. "You must have been a busy bee."

"The faster I work, the quicker you'll be out of my life," I said. "I have information."

"Regarding kiddie porn?"

"Regarding whatever you think it's regarding."

"Good. I'm going to record this conversation, if you don't mind."

"I mind like hell," I said.

"If I tell you I'm doing it, it's legal."

"And if I tell you where you can stick your tape recorder, or whatever gimmick you've got there, that's legal, too."

"You don't expect me to sit here and take notes like somebody's secretary, do you?"

The weight of the world was back on my shoulders. Screw him. "I *expect* you to be in my office in about twenty minutes."

"Why don't you come over to my office instead? We can talk here."

"You'll record what I say—without telling me. Right?"

"What do you mean?"

"What do I mean?" I said, feeling good about it. "What part of 'be in my office in twenty minutes' don't you understand?"

It took him thirty-five minutes to get from FBI headquarters to my business in the Flats—at worst a ten-minute drive—but he was deliberately late, just to bug me. It did, however, give me plenty of time to delete K.O.'s e-mails from my laptop. On the off chance the FBI would "borrow" my computer, I didn't want K.O.'s name all over the place.

When Kitzberger finally arrived, he was frowning—not enough to wrinkle his suit, which was today a dark blue, but I still think he was mad at me.

"I shouldn't be running around after you," he said. "I have other things to do."

"So do I," I told him. "I don't work for you. Whatever I have for you is a favor—which means if you want it, you can drag your ass over here to get it."

He sat, this time not fussing with his pants, both feet on the ground and knees together, like an elderly lady having tea with the parson. "This better be good."

"It is what it is. You can decide just how good it is."

He took out his annoying notebook and his old-fashioned fountain pen. I wonder if it ever sprung an ink leak and ruined one of his suits. I hoped so.

"I'm waiting," he said.

I gave him everything K.O. had dug up, mainly the connections between Riona Dennehy and Carol Shepard. As I talked and he wrote, I saw I was finally gaining a scintilla of control. When I finished, he closed the notebook and capped the pen. "Is that all?"

"I thought it was enough—the exploitation of children for sexual purposes."

"It's very serious," he said.

"I agree. What I don't understand is why you came to me in the first place. I don't know these people—and I've never been involved in a porn case."

"I know that," Kitzberger said. "But you are involved with people in the Cleveland community who are—not always on the level. I'm talking about your friends."

"My friends are not in that business."

"Maybe not," he said, "but they know everything."

"They should go on *Jeopardy!* then."

"There's not enough money for them on that show." He stood up, putting the notebook in his pocket. "Thanks. Your government appreciates your help."

"What? No Medal of Freedom?"

"Just our thanks."

"Fine," I said. "Then I'll thank *you* not to bother me again. You're a bully—never mind the well-pressed suits and the expensive shades. You're also a lazy ass."

"Really?" He seemed surprised—no one had ever called him that before.

"Don't harass people you don't know with all sorts of made-up shit when they work their asses off for you—for nothing." He was about to reply but I chose not to let him. "If you come back to this office—*not* my home—don't bring mug shots. Bring a warrant— or I'll kick your ass so far out of here you'll need an airplane ticket to get back."

"You're an old man, Mr. Jacovich. Don't overreach yourself or you'll get hurt."

"If I get the first punch in, I won't get hurt at all."

"You think you'll get in the first punch?"

"If I don't—I'll at least make sure your fountain pen runs all over your suit. So I'll say bye-bye to you now, Special Agent. I hate long goodbyes, so don't even think of asking me to say it again."

He paused in the doorway. "Some unwanted advice: watch yourself. If you stepped on the wrong side of the line, you might take a long vacation—in Leavenworth."

"As long as I don't have to share a cell with you." I pulled a file from my drawer and opened it as if I were studying for a test, ignoring Kitzberger until he wasn't there anymore.

Then came another morning kick in the ass—my biggest surprise in years. Kitzberger, on his way out, almost bumped into Victor Gaimari coming in. I feared one of them might tumble down the stairs.

Victor's eyes flicked from Kitzberger to me before he said "Milan." Just one word, my name, sounding serious as hell. That's all he needed to say; I could tell from his tone and manner and the set of his mouth that he was angry. For the head of the Cleveland mob to stand nose to nose with an FBI agent probably made him even more unhappy. Why this meeting had to happen in *my* office, I have no idea.

Kitzberger, on the other hand, looked joyful enough to turn cartwheels. "Mr. Gaimari, isn't it?" he said. "Victor Gaimari? Nice to meet you. I'm—"

"I know who you are." Victor ignored the offered handshake. "Milan, if you have a few minutes—"

I nodded. "Special Agent Kitzberger was just leaving."

"That's good," Victor said. He slithered around Kitzberger, moving gracefully enough not to touch him. He wound up at my desk but didn't sit down.

The FBI guy considered a response, then moved out of the doorway, letting the door shut behind him. I waited until his footsteps had faded, then waited some more until I heard his car start up.

Victor didn't sit down. "When you asked me for names," he said—no hello, how are you, no chitchat, just ice cold, "I didn't know you'd spill them to the FBI."

"I didn't spill their names to the FBI."

"Then why did you want them in the first place?"

"I told you—at John Q's. There was a guy running around taking porn pictures with a videocam."

"Did you find him?"

"Not exactly," I said. "He's dead."

"Killed?"

I nodded.

"Then what was that FBI agent doing up here?"

"It's a long story."

"Condense it."

I was wearing an open-collared shirt. Had I been wearing a tie, I'd have been tugging on my too-tight collar. "Why don't you sit down, Victor? Let me get you something to drink."

He shook his head. "This isn't a social call."

The hair on my arms rose and quivered. Not a social call? My relationship with Victor Gaimari had been social since 1987. Not a best-friend type of thing, but civil and sometimes even warm. Not now, though. For the first time within memory, Victor made my whole body and mind go on guard.

"Kitzberger came to me," I said defensively, "with a pocketful of photographs of Greater Clevelanders one way or another involved in porno. Most of them were people who'd been on your list, the one you gave me."

"How did that happen?"

"I don't know. I visited some of them—and some others, too. I suppose one of them is connected—high up—and they complained. That complaint got to Kitzberger, so he walked in here and flashed the photos. He wanted me to find out more about who's involved in child pornography, and to let him know the details."

"And did you? Let him know?"

"He already had the pictures, so I didn't have to tell him anything."

Victor inspected the cuffs of his dress shirt. "How did my name come up?"

"Not from me. He knows we're friends, so he brought your name up."

"You admitted you knew me?"

"Victor, he's a Fed. He knows more than the two of us put together. Of course I admitted I knew you. Why wouldn't I?"

"Why indeed?" Victor moved over to the window and looked

out at the slow-moving river. The gulls wheeled around in the sky, occasionally swooping near the water, and Victor watched them as if fascinated. "I wonder why people call them seagulls?" he mused quietly. "They aren't anywhere near the sea."

I didn't have an answer.

"What did you tell Kitzberger that brought him up here again?"

"Things that have nothing to do with you."

He tore his eyes away from the birds to look at me. "Are you sure?"

"I have a job, Victor—finding out what happened to Earl Dacey. None of it has your name on it."

"I'm not comfortable with you and the FBI having sleepover parties."

"I'm not, either—but he pushed his way into my life, and I tried being a good American citizen."

Victor spent some more time studying the view, looking at Progressive Field, and I wondered if he were as big an Indians fan as he was a Browns lover. Then he said, "We go back a long way, Milan."

I nodded. "We started off badly."

"And then we got civil to each other."

"And friends, after a while," I said.

"My uncle, the don—he cared about you."

In my own way, I'd loved Don Giancarlo D'Allessandro. I was sad when he died, probably shed a tear or two where no one could see me. I still miss him.

"He cared for you as much as he did anyone who's not Italian. Family. Italians are big on families." He walked across the room until he was directly opposite me, his well-manicured hands resting on the back of a chair. "You aren't family. Not our family, anyway."

"Not anybody's family. Just my two sons."

"We helped each other out over the years. When we needed one another."

"That's what friends do."

"When you stop and think about it," Victor said, "I helped you more than you helped me—right up to that list you asked me for." His brows lowered into a frown. "The one that's gotten me into trouble."

"How so?"

"Don't be dense! The FBI doesn't imagine for a second that I'm only a stockbroker. They know what I do. Over the years the D'Allessandro family developed an uneasy understanding with them—not with that jag-off who was just here but with the former SAC. He retired two years ago, but I had no problem with them. Until now." He turned his back on me and shoved his hands into his pockets. I don't think I'd ever seen Victor Gaimari with his hands in his pockets in all the years I've known him. "Now every morning I have a stack of messages from people you've been talking to—and bullying. You scare the hell out of them—make them nervous. That's fine for you. It's got nothing to do with me, but it's rubbing off on me and I'm sick and tired of it."

I started to answer him but he turned and put up a hand, palm out, to stop me—as if I were a bus heading right toward him. "Milan," he said, "we have to rethink our relationship."

And that was it. He only stayed another three minutes or so before leaving without a handshake or even a verbal goodbye, telling me to stop contacting him whenever I needed help with my business assignments. No more chummy lunches at Lola or John Q's, no more dinners at Giovanni's or La Dolce Vita, no more chatty phone conversations, no more trips to his office in Terminal Tower. Whatever status I'd enjoyed as "Honorary Italian"— which I hadn't been aware of anyway—had been revoked. I was finished.

What it boiled down to was Victor Gaimari and I weren't friends anymore. That's the way he wanted it.

It felt strange—almost like someone you care about suddenly dying. It wasn't that I called him once a week, or even once a month. It wasn't about going with him to ballgames or parties. I didn't turn to him for advice on love and romance, nor for help with finances—his legitimate occupation.

It was just that he was—*there*.

Now he wouldn't be anymore.

The loss of a friend, through death or other causes, leaves a large hole where they once resided. I thought about those I'd been close to over the years—my ex-wife, Lila, who grew tired of our marriage and has slowly but surely moved far from my life. My parents and my kindly old Aunt Branka, who communicated with one another in the Slovenian tongue, are long gone, shadowy memories of an early life I outgrew. My best pal since we were both ten years old, Marko Meglich, head of police homicide, who died in my arms while trying to save my life—God, was that more than a decade ago? His passing still hurts every day. Lovers, like Mary Soderbergh and Connie Haley and Nicole Archer and others I barely remember anymore. Friends from my childhood, from high school, people with whom I'd shared much—now off tending to their own lives and pursuits, and away from my influence. Cases that involved adolescent pals like Matt Baznik, Sonja Kokol, and Alex Cerne had turned them from me in anger—I didn't hear from any of them now. Even my sons are grown and as far away from me as Kathmandu.

With the exception of cantankerous Ed Stahl of the *Plain Dealer*, Suzanne Davis, who plies her P.I. trade up north in Lake County, and crabby, mustachioed Vuk, who owns the bar that served me my first legal alcoholic drink and where I hardly ever drank anymore, I apparently didn't have a real friend left in the world.

CHAPTER TWENTY

The morning crawled toward lonely afternoon. For the most part, I usually worked alone anyway. But now a part of me felt forcibly removed—like an arm or a leg.

I wasn't up to going anywhere for lunch. I'd have to leave pretty soon to collect Cisne outside St. Katherine's, but I had time to make one more phone call—to my new assistant. When K.O. answered, it sounded as if he were someplace with lots of other people—making me even more aware of my solitude. "Sounds like you're in a crowd," I said.

He hesitated, probably embarrassed. "I'm upstairs in the food court at Beachwood Place."

"Looking for guys with shopping bag cameras in the food court?"

"I'm waiting for Carli. We're having lunch together."

"Bravo for you."

"I'm not working, so lunch won't come out of your pocket. So—you called?"

"I did," I said. "Your digging up background on Shepard and Dennehy was great. It got me off a hook. You ought to give the same report to Lieutenant McHargue at Cleveland HQ down-town."

"Why? None of it took place in Cleveland proper."

"Maybe it did. Besides, you'll get a gold star in McHargue's book."

"So why should I throw a party just for one of her gold stars?"

"After this," I said, "she'll like you more than she likes me."

"Why don't *you* do it?"

"Because I'm paying you to. Be discreet when you talk to them. Don't mention *why* you found out all this stuff. And for God's sake, don't tell them that you beat up Nicolino. *Or* Royce."

"What if they ask me? Should I lie?"

"Don't lie to the police—but stretch the truth if you must. I'm sure that, being Irish, you're good at that."

"That's bigotry, Milan. The Irish crack."

"No—it was said with affection for everyone connected to the Emerald Isle."

"Like Slovenians?"

"No, like leprechauns."

"I'd argue with you further on that, but here comes Carli so I gotta go."

"Don't hang up yet."

"Jeez," he said, "I'd say goodbye first."

"Good. After lunch, head out to Lake County and look up police records for a Shane Ward."

"Wait, let me get my notebook out." He put his phone down to rustle around in his pocket. Then I heard the K.O. and Carli greeting; he said "Hey, babe," and she said, "Hi, Kevin." Already she's calling him Kevin. They talked more in too-low-to-hear tones. Finally he got his phone back up to his ear and said, "Carli says hey."

"Tell her hey," I said.

He did. Then he said, "Shane Ward? What's his deal?"

"He might be eighteen now, so I'd need whatever he did when he was a minor."

"What do you *think* he did?"

"Let's just say he was a naughty boy—and his father is a big-shot contractor. I'm meeting with Cisne Kelly, but it's not a date—it's work. One of her girls at St. Katherine's keeps getting beaten up, and Cisne thinks it might be her abusive lover, Shane. We're both going to visit her and try to find out."

"What'll you do then?"

"If it is Shane, I'll probably look *him* up."

"And beat the crap out of him?"

"I'm too old for that."

"I'm not too old," K.O. said. "If you want me."

"He might be tough. He's a star athlete."

"At what? Checkers?"

"You're not going to hit him. Just find something on him if you can—preferably something violent."

"Ah, he *is* naughty. I'll see what I can do. Meantime," he said, "I'm having lunch with the prettiest girl in Greater Cleveland, so I'm gonna say goodbye now."

K.O. and Carli. *Kevin* and Carli. It sounded cute, either way, and they were a cuddly-looking couple—at least when K.O. was looking at her sap-eyed rather than growling at everyone else. I hoped it would come to something between them. People that age stay in love for approximately twenty minutes before they flounce off into the sunset, hurt, angry, bored, or searching for something better. But what the hell, it's a *good* twenty minutes, and that's more than most of us get, anyway.

St. Katherine's was quiet, probably gathering its strength together for when the bell rang and young girls would be freed for another day. I stood outside the car, breathing the air, which was fresher and cleaner in Lake County than in Cleveland, relaxing the tightly knotted muscles in my shoulders that had arrived, hooked on, and solidified during my difficult morning. Then five minutes before the final bell sounded, Father Laughlin came marching through the front door, heading right toward me.

"Well, well," he said, "if it isn't the policeman who's not really a policeman."

I kept myself from observing that he was a priest who wasn't really a priest. He *was* one, actually—he just didn't act like one. Instead I said, "Afternoon, Father."

"Hanging around here getting another good look at all the girls?"

"If you think so, why don't you call a policeman? A *real* one."

"If I were big enough I'd throw you out of here myself."

"Out of where?" I said. "I'm parked on a public street."

"You think you can do anything you want on a public street?"

He rotated his head, tormented by the tight collar. "Lusting after girls that are still children?"

It had been too lousy a day already; I refused to allow a nasty, sawed-off priest make it worse. Has anyone ever been enraged with you without even knowing you, without your having done a single thing to bug him? This time the principal just hit me the wrong way. I flipped open my cell phone. "Sorry to upset you, Father Laughlin. I'll call up the bishop right now and we can get everything straightened out?"

Many of my assignments have been dangerous, but I've learned from each of them. This one taught me that when a priest decides for no particular reason to be extremely unpleasant, even the threat of calling the bishop to complain about him can scare him right out of his turned-around collar. Laughlin's face went white as a sheet; he looked around in near panic for a savior, then gave it up and scurried away toward the faculty parking lot, screaming over his shoulder, "You'll burn in hell for this, you know!"

I found myself smiling as I watched him go. After the first shout, he never looked back at me.

The bell rang inside the school. I counted to fifty before the first girls burst through the doorways, looking happy to be out— it was summertime, and most of them had expected a more fun-filled eight weeks, not makeup classes and homework to turn their summer into a bad memory.

The nuns and civilian teachers exited last, Cisne Kelly among them. Her hair was up in a bun again, but the "teacher look" couldn't disguise that adorable smile, which brightened when she saw me. I can't tell you how much I wanted to kiss her right at that moment, but it would have been frowned upon in front of the nuns.

"Thanks so much for coming, Milan," she said. We shook hands instead, with her squeezing mine more warmly than if I were a stranger. "It's so thoughtful of you."

"Let's pretend I'm a caring person, and forget I'm here because I wanted to see you again."

"I'm worried." She opened her purse, rummaged around inside it, then closed it again. I guess she was nervous. "Carolyn is extremely bright, when she's not all hung up about her 'love affair.' So I wanted to see her today but I wouldn't go alone, just in case—um—anybody else was there."

"She'd probably be reluctant to talk to me, though, so I'll keep quiet if I can. I'll be there for support."

"You're so nice . . ."

Few people *ever* say that to me. Maybe I'll have to rethink who I really am. "Come on, we'll take my car."

On the way there, I said, "If Shane keeps beating Carolyn up, why does she stay with him? I don't get it."

"Some girls aren't comfortable unless they have a boyfriend—especially one who's handsome and popular and rich like Shane. It gives them such status with the other girls in school." Cisne shrugged. "We still raise kids the way we did a hundred years ago; like it or not, this is a male-dominated society."

"It is if we allow boys to abuse girls without consequence. I imagine this couple is sexually active?"

"I'd say so, but I'm not supposed to ask. More than half the St. Kat's girls are experienced. My only job, according to Father Laughlin, is to teach them to read, write, and speak English, and that's it! We shouldn't deal with personal problems—just educational and religious ones." Cisne shook her head, mad at herself. "I should have hung in there for my Ph.D so I could teach college, where I wouldn't have to worry about anybody."

"Sure you would—but they'd be adults, and you could talk directly to them." I checked my speedometer, making sure I hovered around thirty-five miles per hour; I didn't want to get stopped by an overeager Lake County mountie aching to write a ticket. "I wonder if Shane's parents know how he treats Carolyn."

"I don't know. It's hard enough for me just handling girls."

It took about seven minutes to get to Carolyn Alexander's house—an elegant, sprawling cream-brick ranch at the crest of a gently sloping hill. There hadn't been much rain here through most of the summer, so the grass wasn't as lush and green as it should be—but there wasn't a weed or blade of crabgrass in sight. The driveway was crescent shaped so nobody would have to go to all the trouble of putting their car in reverse to get in and out. It would be another two months before we'd see fallen leaves on the driveway; in July it was spotless. Someone took good care of this place. By the garage door on the left side of the house was a Mustang convertible—bright red, brand new, with the white top up. On the bumper was one of those stickers reading CHOC. I've never understood that one.

Cisne looked envious. "It's Carolyn's car. They won't allow her to drive when nobody's home, so her mother keeps the keys until Carolyn needs them. But Carolyn has her mother eating from the palm of her hand when she wants something, so that Mustang gets used more often than it's supposed to."

"Shall I park at the front door," I said, "or wait for the valet?"

I stopped about ten feet past the entryway and got out. The doorbell resembled a brass sculpture affixed to the wall. The chimes inside sounded like church bells announcing the Angelus.

Carolyn Alexander opened the door, wearing a white T-shirt and blue shorts. Looking surprised, she said, "Oh, hi, Miz Kelly," but then she glanced over at me, mumbled "Oh Jesus!" and disappeared from the doorway at a dead run. She didn't get away before I noticed both blackened eyes and a gash on her chin, just to the left of center—probably not requiring stitches but pretty painful looking. I wondered if it might scar. Red bruises like finger marks ran up and down both arms, with similar bruises on her neck. There was a horrendous black-and-blue contusion on her left leg—just about the size of a shoe.

She hadn't closed the door in our faces so I didn't know what to do next—go inside or stand out there in the sunshine. I raised an eyebrow at Cisne.

"Be patient, Milan," she whispered.

It was ninety seconds before Carolyn returned—as long as it took her to don a long-sleeved blouse over her T-shirt and long khaki slacks instead of shorts. A pair of gigantic heart-shaped sunglasses covered her eyes.

"Sorry," she said, ducking her head. "I didn't know you both were coming. I didn't want you to see how I look. C'mon in." I thought she spoke strangely, until I observed her right eyetooth was broken off.

The living room was sprawling, one entire wall of glass looking out onto a well-landscaped backyard. I estimated the place covered at least two acres, possibly more. The furniture, paintings, sculpture, and throw rugs indicated an imaginative interior decorator had furnished it in Southwestern modern—not my taste, but sumptuous. Carolyn ushered us into the family room, with a TV set almost as large as most of the movie screens at the Cedar Lee Theatre in Cleveland Heights—the theater that shows relatively obscure art films and indie flicks to neighborhood movie fanatics. Even I go there sometimes, preferring those films to the multiplex studio releases that after fifteen minutes all look and sound the same.

There was only one window in the family room—a large one, covered by dark brown drapes absorbing the light from outside. It didn't surprise me that Carolyn didn't want to be seen in sunshine. She indicated Cisne and I should sit on a light beige sofa with deep pillows. She perched very slowly on the edge of a chair opposite, with her back to the window.

She said, "You didn't have to come over here. I'm okay, as you can see."

"What I see," Cisne said, "is that you're in a hell of a lot worse shape than you were the last time you got bruised. And how many days ago was that?"

I couldn't see Carolyn's eyes through the sunglasses, but her chin dropped near her chest. Humiliation made her shoulders slope. "I fell downstairs again. I do that a lot—just clumsy." She tried to smile but it hurt too much. "That's why I never tried out for cheerleader or anything, because I'm uncoordinated."

"I'd like to see those stairs."

"Not here. Naturally. It was at a friend's house."

"Which friend?"

"You don't know her," Carolyn said too quickly. "She doesn't go to St. Kat's."

"Where does she go, Carolyn?"

"Um—she's in college. She goes to Lakeland."

I knew Cisne had strict rules to follow, laid down by Father Laughlin, so she couldn't press Carolyn for details. But they aren't my rules—I pay no attention to Father Laughlin. I said, "Carolyn, how long will you continue letting Shane beat you up whenever he feels like it?"

"He doesn't!" she said, her voice too shrill.

"Well, somebody does, because we don't believe that crap about falling down the stairs."

"It's the truth!"

"We saw finger marks on your arms and neck—and that bruise on your leg the size of Shane's shoe. And you walk like something is broken inside."

She wanted to deny it, but couldn't. I think the words "broken inside" actually made her shudder.

"Don't you realize," I said, "that if he continues, one of these days he'll kill you?"

"He won't kill me!" she said, now getting angry—at me. Why? I'm not the one who beat her within an inch of her life, but I was there to absorb some of her fury. "You don't know a fucking thing about it!"

"With that bad a temper, he can't control himself. You know what that is, Carolyn? Being a spoiled *child*."

She gasped.

"And if spoiled children continue to be spoiled and pampered, they'll never stop doing wrong things because nobody tells them not to. That's why he might kill you—and I'll bet the farm he'd get away with it."

She put up her right hand to cover her eyeglasses, as if she were crying—or maybe frightened. I wanted to put my arm around her and make her feel safe and secure, but I didn't dare touch her. I just said, "It'll be okay, Carolyn. Don't cry."

Her eyes narrowed and her mouth grew hard. Her head, previously drooping onto her chest, was now held high, her chin aggressive. She was the big shot once again, the school princess, the doyenne of the Mean Girls. "I—don't—cry," she said evenly. "Nobody ever saw me cry since I was four years old. Not my parents. Not my teachers. Not my friends. Not Shane—and sure as hell not *you*." She angrily folded her arms across her chest.

My mouth was getting dry; I wished for a glass of water, but I doubted I'd get one. "Be as mad at me as you want to—but maybe you can live with it and maybe you can't."

That shook Carolyn up a little—but not nearly enough. "Look, I—appreciate what you're trying to do—but it'll just make things worse." She looked at her wristwatch. "He'll be here pretty soon. He's playing baseball over at Mac. If you're here when he comes over, I'll just get it again."

"Not while *I'm* here."

She made a sound through her nose and angrily tossed her head, as if I'd suddenly begun speaking Lithuanian. Then she glanced pointedly at the door. "It's never while *anyone* is here," she said.

"Now what?" Cisne said as we pulled out of Carolyn's driveway. "Are we going to talk to Shane?"

"Not we," I said. "Me. I'll take you to your car."

"You're not acing me out of this, Milan! I'll never forget how she looks right now. Besides, it was me that dragged you into this in the first place—so you're not going to get *all* the credit. I'm coming with."

"You're not supposed to say 'I'm coming with.' You're an English teacher."

"Yeah, well I'm also a Clevelander, and that's how I talk sometimes. And if you get into a fight with Shane, I'll be there to call the police."

"Cisne—I won't fight with an eighteen-year-old because he could take me apart. I'll just talk to him—a man-to-man talk."

"I've heard words like *fuck* and *shit* before."

"Me too—but it's fingernails on a blackboard when you say them."

"We don't have blackboards anymore, Milan. It's the twenty-first century."

The twenty-first century doesn't have Frank Sinatra or Bette Davis, either—or manners or thoughtfulness or calling your elders "sir" or "ma'am." Maybe I've lived too long.

"You involved me in this, Cisne," I said. "That means you aren't tough enough to get the job done. I am, and I'm doing it all by myself—and you're not tagging along or following me in your own car. My job, my rules. If you don't like that, I'll just skip it and go home."

"Wow," she said, but her eyes danced, "you *are* tough, aren't you?"

"Just on days that end in *y*. The rest of the time, I'm a pussy-cat."

The goodbye kiss wasn't nearly as sensual as the ones after our Saturday date, but I did, after all, drop her off in front of St. Kat's. I had no time to think about the kiss, to rate it or judge it, because I was headed somewhere and mulling over other things—like what the hell I was doing here in the first place.

It wasn't an organized baseball game. Immaculate Conception was closed for the summer, so there were no bases or nets to protect onlookers from foul balls, and the grass wasn't as green as it is in springtime. Nobody on the field wore uniforms, just jeans or shorts with T-shirts of various colors and patterns, and only half the players sported mismatched baseball caps. There weren't coaches at first or third base, and as far as I could tell, there weren't nine men on either side—just a bunch of late-teen guys getting together to hit the ball around.

That's what summer is supposed to be for.

Cisne had described Shane physically, but I'd have picked him out anyway. He was over six feet tall, broad shouldered and V-shaped in a white baseball shirt with red sleeves, semi-curly black hair drooping wetly over his forehead, and no hat at all. He was handsome in that late-teen fashion, eyes so dark they appeared almost black, heavy brows that seemed locked in a frown, and a downward slope at the corners of his mouth spelling out arrogance, entitlement, and cruelty.

When I drove up, he was playing between shortstop and third base. To look at him one might think he was in the major leagues. He crouched near the ground, knees splayed, head down but staring fixedly at the opposing batter at home plate, punching his glove with his fist, chattering encouragement to the pitcher. I got out of my car and leaned against the chain-link fence, watching. The breeze kicked up, a late-afternoon cooling, a nice respite from a long and too-hot summer. August was coming fast, and it would grow miserable again, hard to take a deep breath that didn't burn your throat, but when one lives in Northeast Ohio, one accepts the climate, which changes from hour to hour. I wished I were at Progressive Field enjoying the Indians, eating a hot dog and drinking a beer, and not on the sidelines of a dusty diamond in Lake County. As I watched the pickup game, suspicious thoughts about Shane came upon me unawares, and the hair at the back of my neck quivered and stood up straight. Another one of those moments I wished I still smoked cigarettes.

Twenty minutes later the game was over. I didn't know how many innings they'd played, didn't know nor care who won. As everyone bumped fists with each other and collected their own equipment, I wandered over near the yellow Hummer that looked more like one of General Patton's tanks than anything else. I think it cost more than my entire annual income.

Shane approached his car, his glove hooked on his belt and his bat over his shoulder.

"Shane Ward?"

The look he gave me was not a pleasant one, nor was it angry—but one reserved for a mosquito buzzing around his nose. He brushed the hair off his forehead. "You want something?"

"My name's Milan Jacovich." I extended a business card to him, but he didn't take it, didn't even look at it. I said, "Last week I had a nice long conversation with your girlfriend, Carolyn, at Borders—I think you came by and picked her up when we were through."

His upper lip curled. "That was you?"

"I was with one of her teachers, too—Ms. Kelly."

"Holy fuck," he said as casually as one might say "Gee whiz." "I didn't think you were such an old guy."

"Is that why you hit her? Because you thought she was flirting with me?"

He stood up as straight as he could. He wasn't as tall as I was, but his stance was athletic and threatening. "What are you, her father or something?"

"You know damn well who her father is."

"Then it's none of your business."

"Guys beating up women *is* my business."

He wanted to flatten me, but a quick reconnaissance around the lot let him know there were still people around to see it. Instead he opened the door of his Hummer and angrily tossed his equipment inside. "That's between her and I."

"Well, it fascinates me, a big guy like you beating her so badly that she can't go out of the house. Why the second time?"

He was getting more angry by the second, grinding his teeth together. "You really care, old man?"

"I asked."

"Because she was still pissed off at me for the time I hit her the week before and she wouldn't put out for me. Is that what you want to know?"

"Thanks for telling me, Shane. Now I'll tell you something." He looked uneasy but stuck his chin out, waiting.

"If you make her cry again—I'm going to make *you* cry."

"You're too fucking old for that kinda threat."

"Don't tempt me! You don't just beat up on young girls—you want to hit anyone who doesn't do exactly what you want. Isn't that why you chased that pervert with the upskirt camera all the way out into the parking lot at Great Lakes Mall—and didn't you threaten to kill him?"

Now he looked frightened, shaken. He doubled up a fist and actually shook it in my face. "Shut your fucking mouth."

"If you aren't careful, you'll kill Carolyn, too. Then the law's going to put you away somewhere and throw away the key. A pretty boy like you, I don't even want to think what your life's going to be like in prison. There are no girls for you to punch around—just big, hard, mean, vicious men who will love how young and pretty you are."

The torrent of profanity that spilled out of Shane's mouth didn't shock me, as I'd heard all the words before—but not so many of them with just one breath, spraying saliva with every word. When he finished, purple in the face, he threw himself into the Hummer and blasted off, leaving heavy streaks of rubber sizzling on the road.

I started my car and headed off in approximately the same direction, aiming for the Route 2 freeway. The sky was still vivid summer blue, and wispy clouds were dotted near the horizon as decorative touches. Late in the afternoon the sun burned out of the west, making me squint. I was in a rural stretch of Lake County; except for Mentor and Painesville, it was all bucolic, with farms and forests on either side of the road. I knew there were wineries in this vicinity, too; I'd even visited a few in my almost forgotten past—one of my long-gone romantic partners was much more into wines and wineries than I was. Now, of course, I couldn't have located them without a map.

I dropped the visor above me to shield myself from the relentless sun. Because of the glare, I didn't see the Hummer waiting by a side road, didn't realize whose it was until it roared out onto the highway and rammed my car on the driver's side. When they were created for military use, the Hummers were designed to do things like that, but one wouldn't expect it on two-lane road in rural Lake County.

The driver's door crumpled toward me, badly bruising my left arm, and I was thrown sideways. Without my seat belt, I would have flown out through the windshield and probably wouldn't have survived. As it was, my body moved like a puppet's, and the pain in my twisted back traveled from my waist up to my neck as my head attempted to detach itself from the rest of me. My hands were wrenched from the steering wheel—the two driver's side wheels had left the ground and I wouldn't have been able to steer anyway. My car tumbled into a broad ditch beside the road, releasing the air bag, which billowed out and smacked me right in the nose.

My head jerked back, slamming into the headrest; the fiery pain that had crawled up my spine proceeded to drop back down again. The gas tank in my car was located on the driver's side as well, and before I could even look around I smelled gasoline, leaking. That usually presaged a fire. It had all happened so fast that I didn't even think of why the Hummer hit me. Now I had to get out of the car he'd deliberately rammed—before it caught fire.

With great effort I shoved open the mangled door and, ignoring the agony in my head, shoulders, and back, I fumbled to release my seat belt. Finally I pulled myself out, and stood there, bent over and groaning. My cell phone fell from my pocket and lay there in the weeds. I started to pick it up, but Shane Ward had jumped from his Hummer, and now he raced down into the grassy ditch toward me, swinging his baseball bat at my skull.

Before everything exploded into fresh agony and plunged me into the black depths I'd visited far too frequently in my past, my worry as the bat closed in on me was how I'd been warned against any more concussions.

And the last thing I saw, from my stumble-down angle in the ditch, was the rear bumper of the Hummer. It bore a sticker, ironically asking the question I suppose the driver wanted answered—just after he rammed me off the road and milliseconds before he tried knocking my brains out with a baseball bat: WHAT WOULD JESUS DO?

CHAPTER TWENTY-ONE

I don't know how long I was unconscious, but when I pried my eyes open I was in a spacious, well-furnished basement—a family room big enough to hold a hundred partygoers. On one wall was a well-stocked bar, on another a large stove, grill, and a huge refrigerator. Scattered all over the wallpapered room were a pool table, a poker table with chairs, and three gigantic TV sets so that the entire county could come over on Sundays in the fall and watch a football game from one of several long, comfortable sofas. One of them was where I'd been installed until I decided to wake up and join my hosts.

Shane Ward sat on one of the bar stools slugging on an Edmund Fitzgerald from the Crooked River Brewing Company just around the corner from the West Side Market. Excellent beer—and an eighteen year-old was drinking it with relish.

The man I assumed was his father enjoyed an Edmund Fitzgerald too. He was well tanned and polished, in his early fifties, and his turquoise-blue silk polo shirt made him look very much at home in his basement rec room. On the floor between them was an enormous dog, close to two hundred pounds, sitting perfectly still—probably part rottweiler and part battleship, and his eyes met mine unflinchingly. His tail wasn't wagging, and he didn't blink. Maybe he was hungry and had the idea I was his dinner.

Shane's father smiled pleasantly from his bar stool. "How are you feeling?"

"Just how I look," I said. The front of my shirt was blood-soaked. I ran a hand over my face. My nose—bloody from the impact of the air bag—had stopped bleeding but nobody had wiped my face clean. The rest of my body hurt, too, from being twisted and bounced about—but it didn't hold a candle to the grinding, throbbing pain in my head. A Masai warrior—a seven-foot-tall tribesman in Africa—must have driven a spear through the back of my skull at close range.

"I'm Scott Ward. Can you sit up?"

I tried. It hurt.

"You can still talk, can't you?" Scott Ward took my wallet off the bar, flipping through it, looking at the business cards, the credit cards, the driver's license, even the snapshots of my two sons. I felt violated. "Milan Investigations. That's your business, Mr. Jacovich?"

He mispronounced my given name as badly as he had my surname.

"I own several businesses," he said. "The biggest one—in Lake County—is Ward Builders. You're from Cleveland so I don't imagine you've heard of it."

"The president of the United States *isn't* from Cleveland, and I've heard of him."

He flipped the wallet shut. "You have eighty-seven dollars in cash."

"Quaint of you to count it for me."

"We hardly need your money." He jovially slapped Shane on the back. "We have more than we need—but that's how most wealthy people are. When they get rich, they look to get *more* rich. I knew that from the time I was three or four years old."

"Lucky you," I said.

He nodded his assent. "I believe you're right. And when Shane finishes college, he'll be a full partner in all my companies. It's his birthright, you know? We've been best buddies since he was born; that's how it's always been." Then, over his pleasant smile, his eyes grew cold and dead. "I take care of him any way I have to."

He turned my wallet over and over in his hands. "Are those pictures of your two sons in your wallet? I'm sure you take care of your sons—protect them—watch their asses—like I do with Shane. That's a father's job."

I hauled myself up to a sitting position and battled the dizziness. The timpanist from the Cleveland Orchestra was playing a symphonic solo on a drum inside my head. I closed my eyes for a second, then opened them right away. I knew about concussions, and feared going back to sleep. "Why am I here, Mr. Ward? Why did I almost die on the road? What's the deal?"

His eyebrows lifted. "Interesting you'd use the word *deal*. Because I'm a businessman, too—I make deals all the time. I want to make one with you."

I gently ran my hand over the back of my head, sucking air through my clenched teeth from the pain. Shane's well-swung baseball bat had left a large, boil-painful bump, but no blood. "In a deal," I said, "each party gives something. Isn't that how it works?"

He nodded sagely. "I agree. I'm sorry about your car. I'll buy you a new one—whatever kind you want—to compensate you." He rewarded me with a businessman's beaming faux smile again. "I like those silver-colored Hondas like yours—but whatever you choose is okay with me."

"Silver," I murmured.

"That's not enough, I realize, because you've been through a lot. So part of the deal is cash, too—no checks, no credit cards, no taxes to worry about. Cash in the sum of twenty-five thousand dollars."

"That's a lot of money. Should I guess why?"

"For nothing," Ward said. "For your silence."

I decided to give him his silence—for the time being; I'd prefer hearing his explanation.

"Shane's not a bad boy," he went on, fairly shimmering at his offspring. "But he gets mad sometimes. Don't we all get mad when things don't go the way we want them to? Well, as soon as he starts college this fall—he's going to Brown University—he'll enroll in an anger management class to straighten him out."

Shane needed an anger management class. He looked as if he wanted to cut me up in little pieces and feed me to the alligators—assuming the Wards kept alligators as pets.

"I know," Scott Ward said, "he got a little rough with that gal of his—and we'll work on that so it won't happen again. I mean, what the hell, he's off to college and he won't ever see her again—that Carolyn girl—so it's no big deal. I'm just surprised you're involved, Mr. Jacovich, because it's none of your business."

I waited a beat too long. Then: "What I get paid for is my business, Mr. Ward."

"Invading Shane's private life—well, that *could* be dangerous. My money is his money to do with whatever he cares to—and Carolyn is *his*, bought and paid for. He spent lots of money on her—and time—so when she wouldn't put out for him anymore, he lost his temper. You're a man, so you understand, I'm sure. And when you showed up and began pushing him around about it—"

"I never laid a finger on him." I looked at Ward's number one son. "Did I, Shane? Or were you just not paying attention?"

"It's Milan, isn't it? Mind if I call you Milan? Anyway—you have kids, so you get it, don't you? Shane was furious when he found out the kid was shooting videotape up his girlfriend's skirt, so when he chased him out into the parking lot and saw him jump into his old beat-up car, he wrote down his license. That's how he found out where he lived." Scott Ward shrugged helplessly. "He just wanted to whack the shit out of him—teach him a lesson. Well, wouldn't you? Wouldn't your boys?" He leaned against the bar—the front edge of it was upholstered in what looked like leather. "As it happens, it's a good thing he's gone. It's one less sick, deviant erotomaniac in the world. Shane getting him out of the way did us all a favor."

I couldn't answer even if I had wanted to. I had no saliva, hardly any breath, and for a minute my brain didn't work properly enough to choose the words I wanted to say. I'd driven up to Lake County to stop Shane Ward from beating up his girlfriend again. Now I'd heard from his father that Shane killed Earl Dacey.

I swallowed hard, trying not to sound dry and thirsty. "So Shane keeps punching up Carolyn because she won't fuck him, he runs my car off the road because I tell him to knock off the violence toward women, and he beats Earl Dacey to death with a baseball bat and then dumps him in Summit County. And you want my silence for twenty-five grand?"

"And a new car," Scott Ward said.

I shook my head. "Sorry, Mr. Ward, but that's not a good deal."

Scott Ward sighed. "Ah, shit. Well, I figured you'd want to negotiate, so all right, then—thirty-five thousand. That's over and above whatever car you choose."

He rose from his stool and walked around behind the bar, stooping down for a moment so I couldn't see him. I could see Shane, all right—he probably would have hated me even if his father had offered me thirty-five cents instead of thirty-five grand, but as the price rose higher, his fury at me doubled back upon itself. He showed me his teeth as if he wanted to bite the life out of me.

Scott Ward reappeared behind the bar with seven stacks of money in his hand and laid them out one by one. "That's five thousand each, Milan—thirty-five in all. As soon as you decide what car you want, call me and I'll get the car dealer on the phone within minutes." Again he smiled, but it was less and less a happy smile. "You'll have to buy it here in Lake County—I get a good discount—but there'll be no trouble. When I make a deal, I stick to it."

I studied the money spread out on the bar. I hadn't seen that much cash all in one place in my lifetime—and I've lived a long while. Not that I was tempted—there wasn't enough money in the world to tempt me. But I did enjoy looking—and fantasizing.

"So what do you say, Milan?"

I took in one Ward and then the other, father and son—they even looked alike—supercilious, entitled, cruel. I couldn't decide which one I liked least. "Not interested."

"You fucking scumbag cocksucker!" Shane almost screamed, his eyes slashes in his face. He began rising, fists clenched, but his father put a restraining hand on his arm.

"Easy," Scott said, "we're still negotiating. Never interfere with a deal in the making, son, you don't want to screw it up. Stay calm." Then he added sternly, "And watch your language. Be an adult."

He turned back to me. "Milan—don't be a schmuck, okay? I know Shane's made mistakes—big ones—but he's my boy. He's hardly more than a kid. Let him grow—and learn. He's my *boy!*" He ran his hand through his hair. "I'll spend whatever I must

to save Shane's ass—I don't care *what* he's done. All right, Milan—the money goes up to fifty. Cash. Plus car. I don't mean you
should buy yourself a Ferrari or something, because everyone in
Cleveland'll think you're an asshole, but this is lots of money I'm
waving in your face so Shane can go to college and get on with his
life. I assure you it'll be a great life—with no more problems. I'll
see to that."

"No more problems?" I said. "Does that mean up until now
you've been a lousy father?"

Defensively: "I've been a fantastic father! Not paying enough
attention, that's all. But that'll change. Shane is a Ward and it's
my number one job taking care of him, keeping him from harm.
All you have to do—or *not* do—is don't say anything, that's all."
He waited for my acceptance, but it didn't come. "Sixty thousand
bucks—cash, along with the car. Pretty close to a hundred K—
and that's my final offer."

What could I do with sixty thousand dollars? Pay off my bills,
buy things I've always wanted, like a giant TV screen that won't fit
in my apartment—maybe I'd even travel. As for the new car—my
old Honda had eaten up ninety-two thousand miles. Wouldn't it
be great to drive home in one with only six miles or thereabouts
on the odometer?

As far as protecting my sons, I'd never really had to. They grew
up to be good people, even after living half their lives with their
mother and her boy toy Joe, and me not in the picture that much.
So of course I'd protect them—but not by lying for them. Not letting them get away with murder.

Literally.

"Sorry," I said to the father. "It won't do."

He was losing his deal-making personality quickly. "That's not
right, Milan! I'm offering you a fortune and it won't cost you anything."

"Sure it will. Honesty. Integrity. Conscience. Guilt."

"You'd have nothing to be guilty about, and it saves Shane everything—his career, his happiness, his *life*."

"What about Earl Dacey's life? What about Carolyn Alexander's happiness?" I lightly touched the fast-swelling bump on my
head again. It still hurt like hell. "What about my skull?"

Now all pleasantness, all artificial heartiness fled from Scott Ward's face. "I frankly don't give a flying fuck about any of that. I only care about Shane—and I'll go the full nine yards to protect him."

"What does that mean?"

He reached below the bar again, to wherever he'd gotten all that money. This time he brought up an automatic pistol and squinted one eye shut to aim it directly at my chest. "That means," Scott Ward said, "that we have to kill you."

CHAPTER TWENTY-TWO

In Northeast Ohio it gets dark late in the summertime. On this particular evening the Wards waited until after ten o'clock to get things started. Now, at almost eleven, the yellow Hummer rolled east along I-90. I had no idea of our eventual destination, but things didn't look good for me no matter where we were going.

I was in the rear seat, uncomfortable with my hands secured behind my back with duct tape—too tight and getting tighter with every bump or patch of rough pavement. They'd taped me up shortly after Scott Ward pointed the gun at me. I might have suffered another concussion, but that wasn't my biggest concern. We'd stayed in the Wards' rec room for a long time, and nobody offered me food, drink, or a trip to the bathroom. Scott talked to me when he felt like it, but Shane was statue quiet and as menacing as a cobra. At five o'clock he'd turned on a TV set to watch Dr. Phil's show.

Dr. *Phil*, for God's sake!

I kept drifting in and out of consciousness. Neither of them appeared worried about it; maybe they thought I'd die right there in their basement and save them the trouble. During my feverish sleep I heard the doorbell ring, but I couldn't stay awake long enough to identify the visitor.

The Ward men weren't anxious to leave their home until it got dark enough so no one could see me being roughly escorted to Shane's eighty-thousand-dollar pussy wagon, stumbling as I went; it's not easy walking with your hands tightly bound behind you. Shane threw me roughly into the backseat and warned me to keep my head down. Then he let the rottweiler into the front seat next to him.

Scott Ward took his son aside and whispered to him for more than three minutes. Then he came over and actually apologized to me—in his own way. "This is too bad, Milan, but it's your fault. I offered you a way out—and a nice fat bonus, too. But you turned it down, you dumb shit. Now you can't blame anyone but yourself."

"What if I took your bonus and turned Shane over to the cops anyway?"

"It'd be your word against ours—and you'll lose. No proof that Shane did anything worse than chasing that degenerate out into the parking lot. No real proof that he ever laid a violent finger on that little bitch-slut piece of ass of his—and she knows better than to shoot her mouth off to the police. Your car? Well, just after Shane rammed you, your Honda went up in flames—and there won't be anything left of it when the cops find it. The fact that I offered you money can't be proven—we're talking cash. I'd have bought your new car for cash—and the auto dealer wouldn't mention my name when anyone came around to ask, because the car'd be in your name. And by the way, if you did talk to the cops about Shane *after* you pocketed the money from our little deal, I'd have to make a call—and you'd vanish into thin air."

"Just like he's gonna tonight, Dad," Shane said wickedly.

I sat up, or tried to, and Shane brutally shoved me. My forehead struck the back of the front passenger seat and I blacked out again, but only for a few minutes. I woke up struggling not to see double—but there wasn't much to see besides fireworks going off behind my eyes. We were on the road.

On the ride, not much was said. The few times I spoke to Shane, he either shut me up or stared mutely ahead at the road disappearing beneath his headlights. For all his bullshit, he wasn't very sociable. He was careful, driving just under sixty miles per hour, making sure no highway cop stopped him to write a ticket—not with me trussed up in the backseat.

After nearly an hour, we passed a sign welcoming us to Ashtabula County. I finally asked, "Where are we going, Shane?" That made the sleeping rottweiler, a loud snorer, raise his head and glare over the seat at me.

"Don't matter to you one way or the other."

If Cisne were riding with us, she'd have corrected his grammar. "It *doesn't* matter," not "It *don't*." I was glad Cisne hadn't come along, for her sake—and I didn't give a damn if Shane Ward's grammar ever improved.

Would I see her again, a one-night dinner date I thought about much too often? Would I see my children? If my boys got married, would my grandchildren know me, or would I be just a name and photograph they'd forget about? Would I be missed by my friends? For that matter, were there any genuine friends left?

I believed Shane Ward was going to kill me; he'd killed before. So on this bumpy, uncomfortable ride, I was forced to come to terms with dying.

I wasn't afraid of death—but it was my second choice. If I didn't get to say goodbye to my sons, that would be a big regret— but I knew they'd care, and I knew that in their own way, they'd miss me. Cisne would probably feel bad, but the truth was we hadn't gotten to know each other well enough yet, and whatever grief she'd suffer would soon fade away.

What bothered me was that I still had many important things I should do. Unfortunately, I had no idea what they were.

"You won't get away with this," I said, just because the silence was getting to me. "A hotshot high school athlete won't mean a damn thing when cops get you on their radar and start asking questions like I did."

"Cops won't do that."

"You think all your dad does is write a few checks and you skate clean?"

His cackle was hard and empty. "Checks? Cops smile if you buy 'em Dunkin' Donuts."

"Doughnuts don't buy off murder."

"They do when you're rich," he snickered. "But you wouldn't know about that. Listen, pal," he said—strange calling somebody "pal" when you're about to kill him—"I got a great father, money, any pussy I want just for the taking, and every college on the East

Coast is yapping after my ass. Football scholarships, baseball scholarships—it's all there with my name written all over it. But when somebody takes something away from me, I don't sit on my ass and let 'em! I do something about it."

I watched the road signs as Shane curved off I-90 and onto the Ohio highway heading for Conneaut. I don't think I'd been in the lakeside town of Conneaut before except once, years earlier, when someone dragged me all the way out there for what was supposed to be the best pizza in Ohio. "That's why you killed Earl Dacey?"

Shane had begun breathing more heavily, getting angry all over again. "The little shit taking pictures of my girlfriend's cunt up her skirt, right when I'm standing there? You think I'd let him get away with that?"

"You chased him out to the parking lot. Why didn't you kill him then?"

"He got into his car before I caught up with him. Besides, it was too crowded."

"But you wrote down his license plate number. How did you find out where he lived?"

"I got ways."

"What ways?"

He looked over his shoulder at me. Contempt dripped off him like poison, but no answer was forthcoming.

"So," I said, "you went to his house."

"Near his house."

"And you beat him to death?"

Shane sniffed. "I didn't start out to kill him. I just wanted to mess up his shit in the worst way. But—" He shook his head and pushed his hair off his forehead. "Sometimes you get carried away."

"Then why take him to Summit County to get rid of him?"

"Why you wanna know?" Shane said.

"Idle curiosity, I guess."

"I took him to Summit County the same reason I'm taking you to Conneaut. Neither place is close to where I live. Nobody'll connect me with you."

I had to bite the inside of my cheek. Cisne Kelly knew I'd gone to see him, and if I disappeared she'd be the first one to call the police. That would serve Shane Ward right—but it'd be too late for me. I didn't mention that to Shane, fearful he'd go after her, too. He was transmogrifying from superstar athlete/rich kid to domestic abuser to psychopathic serial murderer.

"You dumped Earl Dacey in Tinker's Creek in Macedonia. Planning on leaving me in Conneaut Creek?"

"Conneaut Creek has the best steelhead fishing in Ohio," he said. "I won't foul the water with you."

"I don't like steelhead, anyway," I said. "It tastes too fishy."

It took us another ten minutes to get to the beach. I'd been try-ing to twist my wrists discreetly and somehow get loose from all the duct tape, but it was too tight—so I was stuck, trying to figure out what to do to save myself.

In July, people come to the beach almost every day to cool off from the relentless heat, but at midnight there were no cars in the parking lot and none within sight of Lake Erie when Shane turned off his headlights and barreled onto the sand. When he cut the ignition, he breathed heavily for a while, a nervous hum-ming at the back of his throat like the soft, menacing growl of a wolverine moments before it went for your neck. Maybe he was working up his nerve—but he'd done this before. More likely, he savored the anticipation. Meantime, I'd rubbed my wrists raw; the duct tape hadn't ripped, but it loosened a little bit.

"Does this make you a hero, Shane? Icing someone all tied up? You don't have the balls to do that, do you?"

"I'll show you what kinda balls I have," he threatened.

"We don't have to make it even, because you don't have the guts. Cut me loose, and I'll fight you—me empty-handed and you with your baseball bat. That'll be a big advantage for you."

"Are you shitting me, you old fart? Christ, you're old enough to be my grandfather. I'd give *you* the baseball bat, and let you take the first swing, and I'd still beat you to death."

He was absolutely correct, and I knew it. Still, it'd give me an outside chance. "Beat me to death with a bat? That's your M.O., you dumb little boy—it'll announce to the world, and to the po-lice, that the same one who killed me killed Earl Dacey. They'll have you behind bars before the sun comes up."

He breathed even harder. Then he got out of the Hummer, came around to my side, and dragged me out. I went to my knees on the sand, but he roughly raised me to my feet. "Thanks for the tip," he said, his mouth close to my ear. "I won't use the bat on you. How's that for lucking out?" And he punched me in the middle of my back.

I could only grunt. Lake Erie was about seventy-five yards away, its minuscule waves lapping gently on the sand. The quarter moon was out, but it didn't cast much light. A strong wind blew, whistling across the water. Shane brought his face even closer to me, almost nose to nose so I wouldn't miss his sneer. His breath made me gag; he probably hadn't brushed his teeth for a good sixteen hours. "I'll just wring your fucking neck instead."

I took a deep breath and stomped hard on his instep with my heel. I think I heard bones crack, but I wasn't sure. Then I butted him hard in the nose with my forehead. He screamed an obscenity and staggered back a few steps, his hands up around his nose, blood squirting through his fingers.

I turned and foolishly tried to run. My balance was compromised with my hands taped behind me—and no one can run in the sand in dress shoes. After only a few yards I tripped and went to my knees. No harm; there was no place I could run *to*.

I couldn't make out what Shane was screaming and growling, but he limped quickly over to the Hummer, opened the door, and took hold of his baseball bat, pushing the rottweiler back with his other hand. The poor dog wanted to get out and run around in the worst way but wasn't having any luck. Neither was I.

The whole world tilted, rotated around me, colored lights flashing and blinking, and I was barely able to see the bat hurtling toward the top of my head. If it had hit me squarely it would have probably killed me, but I had enough inner strength to move at the last minute so it struck my neck instead. My teeth clamped down on the side of my tongue, which was excruciating. I could actually track this new pain, running down through my shoulder and into my fingers, rendering them numb.

I collapsed onto one side. It seemed too much trouble keeping my eyes open. I was tired; I just wanted to sleep. Moments blazed across my memory—faces. My sons, Milan Junior and Stephen.

My friends Ed Stahl and the late Marko Meglich. Lieutenant Florence McHargue. Other women—women I'd loved, women I'd simply banged. All those faces, those moments—and I sensed rather than saw Shane Ward readying himself to hit me again with his bat, ironically aware that what I was seeing behind my eyes was my life flashing before me.

I never before believed that actually happened. I'd always thought it was writer's bullshit. I mean, who knows for sure, anyway? Well, I do—now.

Because of the wind howling across the water, and because I was within seconds of losing consciousness permanently, I didn't hear the other car drive up in the darkness, wasn't aware of it until its headlights flashed on, bright, blinding Shane Ward for a few seconds. By the time he raised his bat against whatever had just arrived on the beach, a slight figure dashed into the light, and with one well-placed kick with (I found out later) a heavy work boot, relocated Shane's kneecap from the front of his knee all the way to the side, and I knew he'd never play serious football again. Not on that knee.

It was K.O., of course. His surprise arrival jerked me awake, and I watched him with awe. He moved incredibly fast, kicking the bat from Shane's hands and then tucking his head down and going in under Shane's flailing arms, delivering crippling punches to the midsection. I hadn't heard K.O.'s car drive up in the sand, but there was no mistaking the staccato cracking sound of one of Shane's ribs.

The dog was going crazy in the front seat, snarling and howling and throwing himself against the window, trying to get out. He had more fight in him than his master, because Shane didn't have much left. He turned away from K.O., stumbling back to his Hummer, possibly to free his enraged dog, but K.O. reached him first. The crushing blow to the kidneys dropped him, his bladder surrendering control as he pissed all over the front of his pants. When he got to his hands and knees, K.O. pulled him up the rest of the way, or far enough to send one more punch to Shane's jaw, putting all his weight behind it.

When Shane was stretched out, immobile at his feet, K.O. looked at me for the first time. "I'm done," he said.

He went to the Hummer, opened the front passenger door, and brought the rottweiler out, a firm grip on his collar. When the dog got onto the sand, K.O. knelt beside him, petting his head, stroking and scratching his neck. "Shhh," he said in almost a whisper. "It's okay, boy. Calm down. It's all over. Shhh, quiet."

It took less than a minute for the dog to go from hysterical fury to sitting quietly, allowing K.O. to hug and stroke him. Kevin O'Bannion had just beaten senseless a much larger man wielding a baseball bat, and then turned an enraged dog twice his size into an overgrown lap sitter—without becoming breathless or breaking a sweat.

Now I *was* impressed.

"It didn't take me long," K.O. said, "to find out what a piece of rat shit Shane Ward really is."

We were comfortably ensconced in my living room three days later, and I use "comfortably" in its broadest sense, because I was *not* comfortable. Every part of my body hurt. My wrists were still raw and sore, my shoulders and back ached, and my head felt cleaved open with a rusty hatchet. I was sipping tea, but not enjoying it.

"I got Sergeant Foote to poke around in those juvenile files," K.O. continued. He was wearing khakis and a dark blue polo shirt. "Shane was busted five different times for assault before he turned eighteen, three times on other boys—and I really mean boys, like twelve or thirteen—and twice on girls."

"Busted but never went to court?"

K.O. shook his head. "Daddy wrote checks and it all went away."

"Shane actually thought that money—and his good looks and athletic abilities—gave him a 'Get Out of Jail Free' pass to do anything he wanted."

"Not this time. They got him for one murder and one attempted murder." K.O. grinned. "That's you."

"I think Carolyn Alexander will press charges for battering, too. Cisne talked to her."

"She sounds nice on the phone, Milan. Cisne, I mean."

"She *is* nice."

"In a roundabout way she saved your bacon. After Jake Foote fed me that background stuff, I tried to let you know but couldn't reach you—so I phoned her instead. She said you'd gone to see Shane. I was driving over to the baseball field when I saw what was left of your car smoking in a ditch, with cops and firemen all over it. They said there was no sign of the driver anywhere, so I put two and two together."

"You came over to the Ward house?"

He nodded. "When I got there, two cars were in the driveway— a yellow Hummer and a black Lincoln Town Car—and I peeked in the garage and saw a brand-new Corvette. Bright red. Anyway, I figured lots of people were home, and I wasn't going to crash in there without weapons. So I hung out across the road behind some trees where no one could see me—for nearly four hours. Finally I saw them march you out of there—them and the dog— with your hands tied behind you."

"Duct-taped," I said, gently caressing the raw welts on my wrists.

He looked at me with patent contempt. "I wasn't exactly close enough to see what tied your hands, Milan. It was dark. But I saw them shove you in the Hummer, then Shane and the dog got into the front seat and you all took off." He sighed. "Clear out to Conneaut I trailed you."

"Afterwards you took Shane to the police station?"

"Yeah. I called Jake Foote when I was on my way. I didn't want to have to drag a beaten-down kid slopping around in his own piss pants to jail without an explanation. Foote got to Painesville before I did. He cuffed him on the spot and slapped him into a cell. Not even his father waving a checkbook got him out this time."

"And Daddy?" I said. "Sending me to get killed makes him as guilty as Shane."

"Yep—he's in the slammer, too. They'll both be up for arraignment in Lake County tomorrow. I'm sure they'll set Daddy's bail amount pretty high, but whatever it is, he can pay it. As for Shane—well, Jake Foote says they won't set bail for him at all. He's in there until he goes to trial."

"His trial?" I wanted a cigarette in the worst way. "Well, I'm the main witness. You're a witness, too. And I guess Carolyn will be there with photographs of her bruises. As far as Shane killing Earl Dacey—well, he and his father confessed it to me, but I doubt he can cop a plea on that one."

"It's frustrating."

"It happens. We can't be the catcher of bad guys and also judge and jury."

"And executioner." K.O. rubbed his bruised knuckles without thinking. "Even if Shane gets out of it, he won't play football on that knee again."

"He won't get out of it."

"Lake County is my territory. Ward'll hire the best lawyers in the county—or find better ones in Cuyahoga."

"Still tough. Tough for the father, too."

"I hope so," he said. "Hey. You want a dog?"

"I can't keep pets here, K.O."

"Why don't you move somewhere else, then? If both the Wards get time in prison, who'll take that rottweiler? He's a good old guy, even if he is big and scary looking."

"You and your animals," I said. "You're like St. Francis."

He made the sign of the cross. "Bless you," he said.

"I'm really thankful you showed up just in time or I'd be floating in Lake Erie. I can't tell you how grateful I am to you."

"You've said that—about fifty times. You're welcome, all right? Let it go."

"Well, here's the thing, though."

Immediately, he looked suspicious and on guard.

I took a moment to think how to put it to him. "K.O., I've never had an assistant before. It worked out great between us—"

"Yes, it did."

"And you did a hell of a job. Not just riding over the hill at the last minute like the cavalry, but all the research and the interviewing."

"Don't forget," he said, "my beating the snot out of two different people."

"That, too."

He seemed to be giving up. "Here comes the big word now, right?"

"What word is that?"

He cleared his throat. "But."

I agonized over it, that big three-letter word—and in my physical condition, squirming hurt like hell. I tried not to grimace. "I always work alone, K.O. Most of the time it turns out fine. I'm just not—well, not comfortable putting you on full time."

"Uh-huh."

"If I need someone to fill in somewhere, do research, you'll be the first one I call. And I'm sure Suzanne will have work for you, too—just like now."

He nodded. "Part time."

"I know you'll understand."

"Suzanne said you need full-time help; you've been hurt too often, and you need someone—well, younger—out in the field."

"Younger? Christ!" I swore softly.

"Royce could've killed you. You're lucky I was there instead. To say nothing about what I did with Shane."

"I've been in plenty of fights. I can handle myself."

"At sixty?"

"Not yet!" I snapped.

"Let me enlighten you," K.O. said. "All my teen years were spent behind bars for beating up two guys bigger than I was—and that time was no walk on the beach. I had to fight guys once a week so they wouldn't steal my shirt or my shoes—or to keep from being anybody's candy-ass. Then I got out and went to war for the good old United States—so many tours that when I got back from Afghanistan I couldn't find my way around Cleveland anymore. What the hell happened to the Flats, anyway? And yeah, I killed people over there. Don't ask how many—I lost count, but I took out more than one with my bare hands. So let's not compare whose dick is bigger." Embarrassed by his own monologue, he flushed red—and smiled anyway. Well, it was sort of a smile. "Keep me around. I won't cost much—until I earn my wings. You need me, Milan."

Nobody listened to me except me, which was a damn good thing—but I couldn't seem to say it, even to myself, to admit I *did* need someone like Kevin O'Bannion to run around doing the rough stuff I'd done myself all my life. The pain in my head, which had diminished slightly but hadn't gone away since Shane Ward brained me with a bat, was still there to remind me—when I moved my neck or my eyes—that I've had more than enough concussions and should stop stepping into situations where I'll get punched in the head again.

But that's lousy. It made me feel *old*—too damn old—and I didn't think I could handle that. So I shook my head and smiled back at Kevin O'Bannion as best I could.

"I can't. But I do want us to be friends, K.O.," I said.

"With thirty-five years between us?"

"Maybe we can learn things from each other."

"Like what?"

I had to think about that for a while. "Well—you can teach me how to program my damn cell phone."

He laughed. "That'll take too many years."

The buzzer rang; someone downstairs wanted to get in. K.O. rose and walked to the door. "I'll get it," he said. "You just sit and heal—and think about your cell phone." When K.O. pushed the button and said "Yeah?" the voice from downstairs was unmistakable—crisp, brusque, to the point, and not very friendly.

"It's McHargue."

K.O.'s buzz opened the downstairs door. "Should I quiver in my boots?"

"We both should," I said, settling into a better sitting position. "I have more experience quivering."

When McHargue came through the door, there was no greeting—just her regular frown, this one deeper than usual. Her brow glistened with perspiration, and I'd never seen that before. Maybe it was climbing all my stairs. "You two," she said, looming over me like a teacher who'd caught me cheating, "have stirred up a shit storm."

Even though my neck was stiff, I looked up at her. "Forgive me for not rising to greet you. What have I done now?"

"I didn't make a list, so I won't remember all of it—starting with not one, not two, not three, but *four* district attorneys, from Cuyahoga, Lake, Ashtabula, and Summit counties."

"I don't know the names of three of them," I said.

"Me neither," K.O. put in. "What's their problem?"

McHargue looked around for someplace to sit, and lowered herself into a chair. "Like county commissioners, they all want a piece—of the Ward family." She looked straight at me first—but she always did that. "Earl Dacey was a Cleveland resident—killed in Cleveland. Naturally the D.A. wants Shane Ward's trial right here, so he can score voter points."

"Sounds right," I said.

"Dacey's body wound up in Twinsburg—Summit County. They threw it in our lap, as you recall, because Dacey lived here—but now *they* want the trial because Shane Ward dumped Dacey on their doorstep."

"Another D.A. running for office?"

"None of them ever stop," McHargue said, "and that's going to be a mudslinging festival before it's over. All righty, then—even though O'Bannion here called Sergeant Foote from Lake County to come make the arrest in Conneaut, now the Ashtabula D.A. wants to try Shane Ward for attempted murder—even if he gets convicted of killing Earl Dacey in one of the other two counties who want his ass."

"If he gets life without parole," K.O. said, "what's the point of trying him again?"

McHargue and I spoke the same word together—the first time that ever happened between us. "Politics," we chorused.

"We're missing Lake County," I said. "But I have a sneaking suspicion what that's all about."

She crossed her arms in front of her. "Let's see how smart you are, then."

"The Lake County D.A. wants this case in his bailiwick because he's *dying* to get both Shane and his father off the hook; Daddy writes big checks wherever he goes, and that includes checks to local politicians. I'd bet every city and county official in the area has cashed Scott Ward's campaign contributions, and they'll do *anything* to make sure the money doesn't stop."

McHargue almost beamed. "Very good. Right on the button."

"Wow," K.O. said, looking at me with new appreciation.

"There's not much of anything you can do, Lieutenant."

"No," she said, "it's out of my hands. It's not my job." She glowered at me. "It's not your job, either. If it wasn't for you, I wouldn't be hip deep in crap."

"And if it wasn't for him," K.O. put in, "Shane Ward would be walking around out there, beating up girls and killing people he doesn't like."

"Well, well, well," McHargue said. "You have a fan, Milan."

"A friend," K.O. corrected her.

"You think, Mr. O'Bannion, that your friend here will keep his mouth shut?"

"I don't know as how I can," I said. "No matter how many trials there are, in how many counties, I'll be called as a witness. Did Shane kill Earl Dacey in Cleveland? He more or less confessed to me that he did. Did he and his father conspire to have me killed in Lake County? Sure did. And did he try to bash my brains out in Ashtabula County?" I gently massaged my right temple. "My memory's not what it used to be, but I remember that perfectly. As for Twinsburg—Summit County—I don't know what I could testify about, but if they ask me to, I'll think of something."

"And here I am—right in the middle," McHargue groused, "holding the shit end of the stick. Because of you, Milan—and you, too, O'Bannion. You went where you weren't supposed to go."

"And a killer's in jail," I offered.

"Thanks for nothing. I'll have to stay awake for a week figuring how to explain it to the district attorney. If I could pull your license out from under you, I'd do it before I go home. Since I can't—here's your last warning. You're done. Finished. *Kaput.* Stick to your corporate security shit and let cops be cops, or I'll crucify you, and pound the nails in with my own two hands."

She rose and turned toward the door, then whirled around again, this time leveling that purple-tipped finger at K.O. "And you," she said. "Find yourself another line of work."

It was silent after she left. My body ached, my head throbbed, and my tea was too cold to drink. I studied my shoes—white canvas walking shoes—because I had nowhere else to look. There was a black smudge on the inside of my right shoe, probably from my right foot brushing against the brake pedal when I stepped on the gas in my car. I'd have to do something about that, I thought.

"Well," K.O. said. That's all he said.

My chest was heavy. "Wait a second, K.O. I want to write you a check."

"Added up my hours?"

"Yeah," I said, taking my checkbook from a side table drawer, "but this is a bonus."

He laughed—dry, staccato, and not amused. "A bonus for saving your life? Forget it, you don't have enough money for that. It came with the job—the part-time job." He got up slowly. "I guess I should head north," he said. "Take care of yourself, okay, Milan?" He came over and shook my hand; we hadn't done that since the first moment I met him—and that seemed eons ago. He was much more gentle this time, even though my hand was one of the only parts of my body that *didn't* ache.

I started to get up.

"That's okay," he said. "Gimme a call sometime when you're not busy. I'll be around."

"K.O.," I said.

"Forget about it, Milan. Like you said, we're still friends. That's a good thing. Right?"

His small wave before he closed the door felt like the curtain dropping at the end of the third act.

only took three more days off work, until I was well enough to function, and then headed back to where I did my job every day. I had much to do.

My office smelled musty and unused; the windows hadn't been opened for several days, the air conditioner had been off, and nobody even bothered sweeping or dusting. A large pile of mail on the floor cried out for my attention. I sifted through it quickly, throwing most of it away unopened. I had already typed up my final report to the warehouse regarding their employee trying to collect money by faking a bad back. Now they owed me a final check, which hadn't been in that pile.

There were seven voice-mail messages awaiting me. I'd fielded enough calls at home for the past week to hold me for a while. Several times I'd heard from Lieutenant McHargue or Bob Matusen, and twice from Ed Stahl, who was in the process of writing a juicy column about Earl Dacey's killing, and he was fishing for tidbits more than inquiring as to my welfare. Suzanne Davis's message told me I was a damn fool for letting Kevin O'Bannion slip through my fingers without hiring him full time. My son Stephen rang me up from Kent; somehow the word that I'd been banged up drifted down to Summit County, and he wanted to make sure I was recuperating. I heard nothing from Milan Junior—I guess the news hadn't spread to Chicago.

I'd taken a call at home from Special Agent Jeffrey Kitzberger of the FBI. You'll not be surprised to learn that he didn't give a damn one way or the other about Earl Dacey or the Wards *père et fils*, but he was delighted to inform me that due to my diligence, the FBI had served federal arrest warrants on Carol Shepard and Riona Dennehy for producing pornographic films involving minors. He kvelled in his victory—that's a Yiddish word, *kvell*, meaning rejoicing good happenings. However, in his short, happy phone call I hadn't detected the words "thank you," not in any language I knew. Every kid in the civilized world is taught "please" and "thank you," but I guess that page fell out of Kitzberger's FBI training manual.

I'd rented a car—this one a Mitsubishi Galant—until I could talk my insurance company into paying for a new one to replace the old one Shane Ward had rammed and burned. I knew McHargue had contacted Savannah Dacey to tell her about Shane's arrest for the murder of her son. However, I owed her a visit in spite of it. We'd been through a lot; I solved the case for her, and though she hadn't called me, I felt it incumbent on me to go talk to her one last time, face to face. The weather had cooled off, finally. Clouds obscured the heat of the sun, and temperatures were topping off in the low eighties—tolerable in the throes of summer—so I opened the windows before I left, and hoped it didn't rain in on my floor while I was gone. Operating the Mitsubishi still felt strange, but I'd adapt to it. After all, a car is just a car.

When I drove up to the curb and parked, the Dacey household looked as if it were midwinter; all the doors and windows were closed, shades drawn, and there was no music or TV playing inside. I'd told Savannah I was coming, but still had a flutter of nerves when I rang the doorbell.

She answered it wearing very tight short shorts in a bilious shade of lime green, and a skimpy orange top with spaghetti straps. She hadn't donned her usual over-the-top makeup, but she still looked as if she were about to stroll on the beach looking for a man.

She studied me as never before, her examination critical and obvious. "You look like crap."

"I'll get better. Savannah, it's over now—the search. The young man is in custody. Well, it's up to the courts what will become of him, not me. I'll testify against him—but that's all I can do."

She didn't look at me. "Whatever you've done," she said, acerbic and resentful, "you didn't do it soon enough. My son is dead."

"Your son was dead before you ever contacted me. I'm sorry." I tried my most sympathetic look. "I know what it must be like to lose a child."

"You don't know shit about what it's like," she snapped. Her lips were in the shape of an upside-down U. "You've never been there."

I hadn't—thank God—so I didn't reply.

"Now every time I walk into this house, Earl is here waiting for me—my memories of him, haunting me, making me feel so terrible." She sniffled and wiped her nose with the back of her hand. "I was a goddamn good mother—you know I was. Now that he's—gone—I can hardly stand to be here." She fumbled on the coffee table for a cigarette. "I think I'll sell this place—move away somewhere. Not out of town, just out of the neighborhood."

"That's probably a good idea."

The amount of smoke she sucked into her lungs made her cigarette shorter by three-quarters of an inch. She held it inside for too long and then blew it out—right at my face. "You don't give a damn, do you?"

"I want what you want—what's best for you. If you want to get rid of the house, you should."

"You're such a rude son of a bitch. You rejected me, Milan."

It took me far too long to hear that, process it, and react. It almost knocked me off my feet; all I could say was: "*What?*"

"You slammed the door in my face, right from the start. I flirted my ass off at you, and you never gave me a second look."

"I was working for you, Savannah—trying to find your son. I wasn't thinking about flirting back."

She looked away. "Ah, what the hell—it doesn't matter. It wouldn't have—under the circumstances."

I reached desperately for a lifeline. "There's somebody that didn't reject you—and he's still interested, I think."

"Everybody rejects me!"

"Not Stan Majkrzak. He speaks very warmly about you. Why don't you give him a call?"

She turned up her nose. "Are you crazy? I'm not running around with Stanley. My God, Milan! He's—he's *old.*"

That word was beginning to haunt me. "Savannah," I said as gently as I could, "we *all* are."

"I've got good news and bad news," Ed Stahl said as he slid onto the bar stool next to me. We met at five o'clock that afternoon at Flannery's, an Irish chop house on Prospect Avenue downtown, about a block from where the Indians play baseball. The team was out of town this week, though, so Flannery's was relatively quiet. Lots of younger people who live downtown drink here when they can't afford the more elegant bars and restaurants right around the corner on West Fourth Street, but on this particular afternoon a few of the older imbibers at the bar looked as if they'd been sitting there since the Clinton administration.

"Bad news first," I said. My Stroh's was already in front of me. "If the other news is good, I just might walk out of here smiling."

Ed waved at the bartender and ordered his usual. He stuck his battered pipe in the corner of his mouth, but because he wasn't as well known in Flannery's as in some other bars he frequented, he didn't light up. "Scott Ward," he intoned like someone announcing the guillotine was ready to fall. "Unlike his son, Scott's only crime—that we know about, which is conspiring to commit murder—took place in Lake County, where he lives. So at his arraignment the judge set him loose under his own recognizance. That's pretty light-handed, don't you think?"

I shook my head. "Doesn't surprise me in the least. I'll guarantee Ward was a generous donor to the judge's last election campaign."

"He's a very generous guy. I didn't look it up," Ed said, "but he's rich and powerful and he gets what he wants, and that means he makes campaign contributions to just about everybody. When he goes to trial—and Christ only knows when that will be—he'll have the best lawyer in his corner that money can buy. My guess is they'll cut a slap-on-the-wrist out-of-court deal that won't even make the newspapers. He'll get some sort of silly-ass probation,

X number of hours of community service—which he won't do and no one in his right mind will expect him to—and before you know it, his so-called criminal record will be sealed for the next hundred years, and nobody will know it. That's what happens when you're a big shot in your own county."

"There really are two levels of criminals, aren't there, Ed?" I said. "Those who are convicted and go straight to prison, and others rich enough to buy their way out of it—with whatever they have jingling in their pockets."

"Ever since the world began. Read the Bible—that's where it starts."

I laughed. "I haven't read the Bible since I was a kid."

"You should pick it up again," Ed said. "Murder, theft, adultery, betrayal, and almost all the kings and authority figures get away with it, scot-free."

"Does that sound like the inspiration for a column of yours?"

"Everything you do might be an inspiration for my column, Milan. Usually I'm kinder to you—but this one will play out to the hilt."

"My luck! Okay then, Ed—what's the good news?"

"The good news is that young Shane Ward's in much worse trouble than his Daddy—in too many counties to mention. Cuyahoga gets him first and hangs him up there for Murder One—and since he's eighteen, and was eighteen when he killed your porno kid, they'll go for the death penalty but eventually settle for life without possibility of parole. Naturally Shane has the same Cadillac lawyers as his old man, but if they nail him with either of those two penalties, probably Summit, Lake, and Ashtabula counties won't even bother with him."

"If they don't? If somehow his jury finds Shane Ward innocent? Then what?"

"Then," Ed said, throwing his Jim Beam down his throat as if he were swallowing a handful of pills, "if I were you I'd stay the hell off the road in Lake County." He stopped for a moment to catch his breath, then took a sip of water—just to mollify his complaining ulcer. "Don't you think you should start taking things a little bit easier? How many more punches to the head will you be able to stand before you start seeing flocks of geese flying over you that aren't really there?" He waved his empty liquor glass at the bartender, signaling for a refill; I could tell this was going to be one of his serious drinking evenings. Then his eyes warmed behind his Clark Kent spectacles. "You know, Milan—you're not as young as you used to be,"

I nodded in offended agreement. Then I said, "Neither are you."

It wasn't until I got home and rummaged around in the woefully empty refrigerator to discover my only possible evening meal without going out to the store was a grilled cheese sandwich— and I wound up not grilling it, anyway—that I realized I hadn't called Cisne Kelly for several days. I picked up the phone and started tapping out her number, guilt crushing my chest. It was Cisne who got me to go out and talk to Shane Ward in the first place. And then I was so busy talking to police forces and district attorneys from four different counties—so busy healing, trying to make my headache go away and my stressed muscles feel better—that I didn't have the courtesy to call and tell her what happened.

"I read all about it in the newspapers," she said when I began telling her. "That was horrible. It must have been horrible for you, too. I'm sorry, Milan."

"Don't apologize," I said, gently stroking the back of my head with my fingers. "I solved a case by accident. I should have called right away to thank you. I apologize—and for not calling just to talk to you. It's been a hell of a week."

"Well," Cisne said, "as long as you're all right." A pause. "Carolyn's parents said she'd be a witness if necessary. She hasn't been back to school; I'm not sure she's ever coming back. Poor, sad little girl."

"We got Shane away from her—and that's a good thing."

More of a pause. Then: "Cisne, I want to take you out again."

"Milan," she said slowly.

It's my name, all right—and the solemn way she spoke it was, I suppose, meant to prepare me for what came next.

I would *never* be prepared for it.

"I really like you. You're a great guy—what you did for Caro-lyn—what you did for a lot of teenage girls who are in abusive relationships. And by the way, you're a very good kisser."

"Thanks—but I sense a goodbye coming,"

"Well," she said, accompanied by a sigh. I felt I was falling into a deep, dark, bottomless well. "I didn't want to do this over the phone, because it's—impersonal. But you shouldn't be wasting another evening. I'd like to be your friend—but I don't think we should take it any further."

"Is it our age difference?"

"Partly. It's our—lifestyles, I guess. You've been hurt badly. You almost got killed—because of me."

"*Not* because of you," I said, adding lamely, "just—indirectly."

"And you waited four days before calling me. If I didn't read the paper, I wouldn't know if you were dead or alive."

"It was thoughtless of me—"

"That's the least of it," Cisne said. "You're dangerous, in a dan-gerous business. Sure, that's exciting and romantic—in my twen-ties, I suppose I *was* attracted to bad boys. I even married one, which was a disastrous mistake. But I'm pushing forty now, Mi-lan, and I can't go through it again."

"I'm slowing down, Cisne."

"You can't. You wouldn't know how."

I got defensive. "You don't know me well enough to make that judgment."

"I don't have to. You've been a private investigator since I was in middle school. It's your life. I understand it and I respect it. I have a huge amount of respect for you."

"I respected Mother Teresa, but I never fantasized about dat-ing her."

She ignored that. "But it's not my life, Milan—and I'm at that juncture where I can't adjust. I'm—sorry. I'm *really* sorry."

Her words rang true—her regret was genuine.

Why did it not make me feel better?

Because everyone I knew who was close to me had either died off or turned their back on me and walked away. I had no lover now. My almost-healed relationship with Lieutenant McHargue had dried up and blown away, as had my longtime acquaintanceship with Victor Gaimari—and I was fast running out of friends. My movements even seemed to echo in my apartment, like when someone shouts hello into the Grand Canyon—a hollow, distant, all-alone sound.

I didn't turn on the TV, or open a book. I opened quite a few Stroh's, however—not as many as I used to, but enough—and stared out the window at the passersby, the lovers, the friends, the lounge drinkers at the Mad Greek, and the busy traffic zipping up and down Cedar Hill. I don't remember what time I went to bed, but I awakened with a hangover to go with all my other hurts and pains and headaches. I couldn't even think about breakfast, and drinking green tea sounded terrible. I brewed a half pot of coffee—and the hell with what it was supposed to do to me.

When I got down to my office I read in the newspaper what the Indians had done the night before—not much—and what the Browns *intended* to do when the football season began in six weeks. It wasn't until ten thirty-four A.M., after I'd finished the comic pages and was starting with the obituaries, that the phone rang.

"Milan Jacovich?" He pronounced both my names correctly. "It's Bert Loftus. City Councilman Loftus."

The receiver seemed to get extremely hot in my hand. Bert Loftus, who's been a Cleveland city councilman for over twenty years, was widely believed to be the illegal-bribe champion of the world, and the FBI—ah, them again!—was in the process of examining *everything* in his life, right down to the tissues in which he blew his nose. If I hung around more often with gamblers, I'd bet even money that he'd be indicted before the first autumn leaf hit the ground. I wondered what he wanted with me.

"We've met before a time or two, haven't we, Milan?"

"We have indeed," I said, although I couldn't remember where.

"And I just read about you in the paper. Good job with that punk from Lake County—I imagine if and when they ever let him out of prison, he'll be bald and toothless."

"Thanks for the support, Councilman."

"Bert—please call me Bert. Listen, I've called you a few times in the last couple of days. Did you get my messages?"

"I've been out of the office—and I haven't played my messages yet."

"I understand that perfectly. Milan, here's why I'm calling. I want to hire you."

I was glad we were speaking over the phone so Bert Loftus couldn't see me covering my eyes with my hand. If he was half as guilty as the media said he was, as soon as I signed on I'd once again have Special Agent Jeffrey Kitzberger in my face. I didn't think I could stand it.

"Councilman—"

"Bert," he corrected.

"Bert," I said. "You're in big trouble—and frankly, I don't want any part of it."

"This has nothing to do with a federal investigation. You know what a tough town Cleveland is, you were born and raised here just like me. That's why I desperately need your help." He stopped, coughed, sniffled, and then said, "Somebody's trying to kill me."

"What? Who?"

"I can't talk about it on the phone, Milan."

We made an appointment for eleven o'clock the next morning—and he promised he'd come alone, not with his staff and his assistants and his hangers-on that all of us pay for on the bloated city payroll. And as I scrawled it onto my calendar, it got me to thinking.

I'd been right: I couldn't keep getting hit in the head—and as Loftus pointed out, unnecessarily, Cleveland *is* a tough town. I guess that's why I love it so much.

I thought about it for almost an hour. Then, lifting the phone again, I made up my mind.

"K.O.? Hey, it's Milan. Listen—I've rethought this a little, and I think I *do* want to hire you, if that's all right. It is? Great. Uh— can you come in to the office at nine o'clock tomorrow morning? We'll talk about some stuff—and then we'll have a meeting with a new client at eleven. Sound good?"

I grinned when he responded to me. He'd like everyone to believe he's the coolest guy in the world since Steve McQueen died—but he was more than excited, sounding like an eleven-year-old kid who gets to sit on the sidelines with the team during an NFL football game. It was a huge career step for him—getting even closer to scoring a license just like mine.

Will he deserve it? I'd weighed it in my mind before I called. I'd known him barely a week before he'd badly beaten up three men. He was sullen. He was easily smitten—one look at the very pretty Carli Wysocki was all it took. He didn't negotiate with me, not for money and not for silly unenforceable rules. And while he followed them perfectly, he made rules of his own as he went along. He was—difficult.

Then again, I didn't have to think twice about his coming to work for me full time. He'd saved my life.

So I couldn't do anymore what I did when I was thirty—or forty. I had to live with that reality, or one morning I wouldn't wake up at all. I'd have to remodel the office a little, giving him a room of his own. Put up movable wall boards, buy another desk and chair and get him pens and a calendar and scratch pads—and oh yes, a telephone of his own. That was more work than I wanted to handle—but all that remodeling just might save me from another disastrous concussion.

Probably.

Cisne Kelly was right about one thing, though. I *can't* quit. It's my job. It's what I do. It's who I *am*.

God help me.

ACKNOWLEDGMENTS

To Lakeland Community College Chief of Police Jim McBride (retired), Cleveland P.D. Lt. Ron Timm, Cleveland P.D. Sergeant Tom Shoulders, Cleveland P.D. Officer Valerie White—for their help, encouragement, and for making sure I don't commit *too many* errors.

To Milan Yakovich—the real one—and to Diana Yakovich Montagino.

And to Holly Albin—first reader, first red-pencil editor, and best critic who's almost always right. She's my best friend, my best caregiver, best caretaker—and the love of my life.